The Flickers

RACHEL FLETCHER

ISBN: 1499204787
ISBN-13: 978-1499204780

DEDICATION

For my dad, who pestered me until I finally finished my book.

ACKNOWLEDGMENTS

I'd like to thank my parents, Glenn and Cindy for encouraging me to realize that following my dreams was, and always will be the right thing to do. No matter how stubborn I was. As well as for teaching me to love reading, because one thing leads to another; One of my best friends, Kimberly, for drowning me in her pool and inspiring me to write the death of Levie, as well as the rest of the trilogy; not to mention, for getting me started on writing to begin with; My lovely, and extremely talented editors, my other best friend Lenette, and my aunt Fran for making this pile of sentences form a coherent story, and not a second language; My online family—Alley and Hannah—for being there during those late nights when I just couldn't figure out how to write what I needed to. As well as my real family, for not abandoning me because I wanted to write stories to make a living; Thanks to Obsidian Dawn Resources for the beautiful graphics on the cover; Thanks to Sito Alvina, for allowing me to use the beautiful image of Susan Coffey on the cover; And of course, thanks to anyone who ever read this measly little story in the beginning, because you are the ones who got me where I am today. As always- Thanks for reading, and Godbless, Rachel.

CHAPTER ONE

Focus. This is what you're best at. You lead. You were chosen to lead. Don't screw it up.

I glanced to my right, flashing a smile at Arthur, chuckling when he winked back. He was practically my father, and I knew he wouldn't let me make a fool out of myself. Despite my knowledge of that, I had to play my role. There were others watching . . . people more important than he or I.

He couldn't show me any favoritism. I was in this alone.

"Miss Levie?"

"Yes, sir?"

"Are you well enough to run the course?"

"What makes you think I'm unfit to run this course, sir?" I could see the frustration in his eyes. Pissing Arthur off was a daily routine.

"Your arm is still in the stages of healing. I'm merely wondering if you're capable of using your arm, or if you would like to wait until a later date to do this?"

"Am I capable of doing this?" I asked, pulling an arrow out of the quiver on my back. Then, notching it on the bowstring I took aim and shot it through the bulls-eye four hundred yards away where the target field stood.

The higher-ranking leaders behind us chuckled at Arthur's misfortune.

I raised a perfectly shaped eyebrow and lowered my bow.

"Your arm is bleeding. You've popped out the stitches, Levie."

"I don't care, Arthur!" I muttered defiantly.

My seeming disrespect caused the others behind us to start whispering. I was growing tired of the charade Arthur and I were trying to put on—they all knew how we were, anyway.

"Then proceed." Arthur muttered back, exhausted with me already. I stepped up to the red line painted across the grass and allowed one of Arthur's commanders to stab me in the neck… literally.

Somewhere within the cloudy liquid there was a tiny chip that I had actually grown to love, unlike the others here on base. The tiny chip prevented me from using my psychic abilities—a quality that was stronger in me than in others. A quality I detested.

The shadows I saw weren't faint, like the others. They were obvious silhouettes that remained visible hours after those who had made them were gone. The amount of focus it took to get rid of them drained all of my energy.

The visions I saw were very clear, and never vague. I had practiced enough prevention over the years to keep them from randomly coming—now they only came when I wanted them to, or in my dreams.

My heightened abilities were part of the reason why I was in the position I was in now, but that didn't matter to the other commanders watching me. They wanted to see my *natural skills.*

As the commander slowly pushed down the plunger in the syringe, I tried not to flinch, and instead chose to focus on Arthur's face. He was much older than me, even though appearance-wise he looked no older than a man in his mid-twenties. As a Flicker, once we hit a certain age, we aged much slower than our normal human ancestors. Our mutated genes were a product of magic rather than evolution—as were our psychic abilities.

"So you're not going to drag me out before I'm done this time, right Arthur?"

"As long as you don't slice your arm open on a *tree branch*, I'll leave you in," he snickered. I rolled my eyes and stepped away from the red line; I shoved Arthur playfully and earned myself a few more whispers from the commanders behind us.

The oldest looking commander—a man who appeared to be in his forties, though was probably much older—stepped forward to stand to my right.

"You'll have a half hour to find and kill the wolf inside."

"That's it? A half hour?"

He nodded and tapped his watch with a harsh smile. "You're on the clock."

I bit my lip in order to refrain from saying anything I would regret, and ran in to the woods.

Since I only had a half hour to complete the test, I lacked our normal survival supplies. Other than my clothes, I had four things to my name: my bow, my quiver of arrows, and the tiny pill in the front pocket of my jacket.

If we were captured for information or torture, dying a painfully slow death, or going through a change from Flicker to Monster, we were to use our last resort... a pill about the size of a tooth that held the ability to shut down the production of energy in cells, which resulted, of course, in rapid death. I shuddered at the thought of using the pill as I continued to wander through the course watching for signs I knew could indicate possible danger.

Paw prints and claw marks were the easiest to distinguish. If a Flicker was *really* good, they knew to watch for things like broken branches and freshly moved dirt. These things all told me I was going in the right direction.

I had no idea how much time had passed. I was beginning to wonder if the time limit I had supposedly been given was a hoax.

The darker it grew the harder it was to see the signs the wolf had left behind, so I decided to climb the next climbable tree and watch for signs of the wolf from above. With every tree I passed, though, none of them were climbable. All of them were either too high for me, or low enough for the wolf to climb.

When the sun disappeared I walked to the closest tree, since I no longer had the option to do something different.

Thanks for all the decent trees, you bastards, I thought as I stared up at the behemoth of a tree and tried to come up with a way to get to the nearest sturdy branch. I knew there was no possible way I could climb it on my own. There was no traction on the bark and a severe lack of branches made hoisting myself up impossible.

I dropped my bag of arrows to the ground and removed two to clench in my mouth. I pulled the strap from the quiver to use to help climb the tree trunk. I would have had no problem making it up the tree if only I had a few seconds more.

The key word here being *if*.

Somewhere off in the distance, I could hear the sound of footsteps as they crashed through the foliage. From close behind me, I heard the unmistakable snarl of a wolf… guttural and menacing. Before I could completely spin around the creature lunged. It grabbed me by the leg and threw me down, causing a wave of dark, wet dirt to fly as I hit the ground. The impact had stunned me enough that, even when the wolf stood over me, I had problems moving.

I reached up with my left hand, and yanked at the wolf's fur as hard as I could—causing it to growl loudly and snap in the direction of my fist full of fur. I took the momentary distraction to plant a solid kick to its side. As it stumbled off of me, tripping over its own paws, I lunged for my arrows.

Even dazed, though, four feet were faster than two, and the wolf beat me to the bag by a long shot. It began to snap at me, its teeth coming together only inches away from my face. Its claws continued to dig into my sides as I fumbled around in an attempt to get at least *one* of my arrows from the bag.

When my fingers finally made contact with the sleek, carbon metal shaft of one of the arrows, I took my chance and swung it around—praying that the correct end would be where it needed to be. The sickening sound of flesh being torn open followed the swing of my arrow, and the crushing weight of the wolf landed completely on me when it's heart was pierced by the arrowhead.

It's head crushed mine as it collapsed, and caused the world around me to grow dark and silent.

"Levie, you need to wake up. If you don't wake up for me, Arthur is going to step in. Come on, get up."

I growled under my breath and allowed my eyes to flutter open.

Scotty's face was close enough to mine that his blonde hair tickled my nose; he had been letting it get too long for my taste. I reached up and playfully pushed his face away from mine.

"What, don't you want to wake up to your best friend?"

"No," I said stubbornly. When his face fell, I smiled to reassure him. "You have no respect for personal space. And you need to cut your hair." He rolled his eyes at me and flopped down on an empty space on the small recovery bed.

The recovery room itself was bleak, as was the entire recovery wing of the base. The recovery wing was a small, all white building with black tiled floors and dim, comfortable lighting that could be considered 'romantic' lighting. But there's something very un-romantic about a hospital.

Its cold and sterile rooms could be smelled from miles away. The only thing that brought them any life at all were the patients in need of care. And none of us ever stayed for very long. What with the increase in technology our elders provided for us, the average down time for anyone was a matter of hours—rather than days or weeks.

"So what's the deal?"

"Temperature is supposed to get down pretty low tonight. It will send all of the leeches running for cover. The wolves are planning on following—and so are we," he smirked as he spoke. His excitement for the night to come leaked into his words and seemed to fill the room with invisible electricity that had me charged and ready for the fight along with him.

"Awesome," I grinned back at him, reaching my hand out for him to give me a high five.

"The commanders were coming to get you out of the arena whether you had finished the test or not. They're not willing to admit it, but they actually need you for this mission."

"Did I kill it?"

"You wouldn't be here if you hadn't, Levie," He grinned and pulled a claw out of his pocket. "We can make it into a necklace or something."

"Where did you get the claw?"

He frowned and glanced down at my arm, where it laid limp beside me.

"They pulled it out of your arm. Don't ask me how the

hell you managed to get it stuck in there, because I don't know. All I know is that you're a badass, and that's all I have to say on the subject."

I giggled and held out my hand for the claw. I wanted to really see the only thing left of the monster I killed.

It was decent in size—close to the size of my thumb. The light brown tip was stained red from the blood of my arm, and the darker end was smooth and glossy.

"I'm glad I didn't feel that happen. I'll bet that hurt like a bitch," I handed the claw back to Scotty. "Keep that safe for me, Lord knows I'd lose it." He shoved it back down into his pocket and flopped down beside me again, wobbling the bed with exaggerated movement.

He stared at me for a moment before leaning down and kissing me lightly on the lips. I didn't even flinch; kissing was common between . . . well, *everyone*. I was well over the shock of being kissed by my friends, especially given that most of them were guys.

"What was that for?"

"I'm just glad you're okay."

I smirked and stared him down. "Are you sure you're not just trying to get into my pants?"

"Dammit, you caught me. It wouldn't be hard, either. Considering you're not wearing any pants right now," he winked at me, throwing me into a fit of laughter.

"You're such an ass, ya know that?"

He nodded while he laughed, unable to say anything through his gasps for air.

We had barely managed to calm down by the time Arthur stepped into the room with a nurse in tow.

"Just stick her wherever it will work the quickest," he said quickly.

"How much time does it have to do its job?"

"*None*," he snapped. The nurse's lip pulled up in a snarl as she rolled her eyes and walked my way.

"Sit up, Levie." I did as she asked, and was rewarded with a stab to the jugular. With one hand, she shoved the syringe down, and with the other the opened a tube and squeezed some of the contents onto her finger. When it was empty, she jerked the syringe out of my neck and slathered on the mint-colored gel.

The gel on my neck healed the tiny wound before it could bleed, and the medicine coursing through my body already had me feeling somewhat high.

"You've got about 3 hours of no pain, and we're leaving. Now," Arthur's husky voice rang out through the small recovery room.

"What about my things? armor, clothes, weapons?"

Arthur held up a duffle bag with the number nine on the side; a tag that contained the same information as the leather strap around my wrist, hung from the strap on the bag.

A new bag, a new tag… I had passed the course today. I was one level higher in rank.

"So I take it I satisfied you and your goons with my skills today?"

"Just get ready, please," Arthur muttered, letting the bag fall to the floor.

I ripped off the stiff hospital sheets and stood up, stretching my limbs and assessing the damage. I didn't feel any pain—no aching, ripping, burning… nothing.

"Other than the arm, what am I even in here for?"

"Your leg," Arthur and Scotty mumbled at the same time.

I frowned and bunched up the long hospital gown to reveal a jagged line of stitches from my mid-calf to my thigh.

"What the fu-"

"You landed on one of your arrows. If it had been the

wolf, you wouldn't be here right now," Arthur stated harshly. As in, they wouldn't have saved me. I would have been infected, therefore, not worth saving.

I grabbed the bag and stomped into the small bathroom to change.

With every article of clothing I pulled out of the bag, I went over the dressing process in my head out of habit.

Tights: pull them down over your heels, so the boots will hold them in place and keep them from bunching up.

Tunic: pull the belt as tight as possible to avoid loose clothes, loose clothes meant more room for getting something caught or making a mistake. Tighten the wristbands on the sleeves until they're almost cutting off your circulation. Those were Arthur's words, not mine.

Boots: tie them tight and tuck the strings in. Strings tapping against the sides of your shoes make noise. Noise is bad when you're trying to be stealthy.

The armor was a little trickier than our normal mission clothes, but years of practice had taught me the quickest way to get everything on.

The chest armor looked like a poncho. A metal plated poncho with an equally thick metal collar that clung to our necks turtleneck style.

The chest armor sleeves were the same style as the tunic sleeves, complete with ties proven to cut off circulation.

I looked in the poorly lit mirror and grimaced as I tugged at my hair, weaving it into a braid. I always preferred to have my hair down, but Arthur didn't allow it on missions. It made sense, but it still pissed me off.

There were a total of two redheads in the entire compound, and I was one of them. When I was younger, Arthur used to tell me I couldn't leave my hair down because he couldn't bare the idea of it getting snagged on something and getting cut off. That after all, the base couldn't afford to lose one of its few redheads.

Now he just told me it was too long, that I needed to keep it out of the way.

I walked out of the bathroom and threw the duffel bag back on the bed in the corner of the depressing room. The recovery staff would have it sent back to my room, and it would be there when I got back.

"Am I Arthur approved?" I asked, grinning sarcastically at Arthur, who rolled his eyes.

"You're fine, can we please just go now?" Arthur held out my bow and a quiver full of arrows. I smiled and took them both. The familiar feeling of my hand wrapping around the bow was comforting; it made me feel safe.

I could kill with this bow. Nothing can hurt me while I have my bow in my hand.

As we left the recovery wing of the hospital and walked outside, the temperature began to drop. It was going to be a cold and miserable night.

We only had to walk a few yards for the helicopter to come into view.

So dark that it blended into the night sky, the helicopter was big enough to transport four teams of higher-ranking comrades. That was four teams of six, twenty-four of us, plus a team of commanders; one for every group. And finally, the two pilots to fly the damn behemoth.

There were thirty people total in each helicopter.

Long story short: they were all monstrous in size.

"Levie! You're Team Leader now! Pick your team, I'll be your commander!" Arthur shouted over the spinning blades of the helicopters. There wasn't only one, but three copters out on the flight deck. The others had already taken off.

I spun around and grabbed Scotty's arm and tugged him along with me.

One down, four to go.

I darted through the crowds in search of my old team. As of now, I refused to work with anyone else. I knew my team best.

They stood off to the side, all packing their bags full of their usual weapons. Tiny, little Bridget stood off to the side, sweeping her head back and forth in panic.

"Bridget!" her head spun in my direction and she heaved a sigh of relief.

"Levie!" Everyone looked in my direction and grinned.

"Levie! You made it!" Keegan shouted, as I got closer.

"Hell yeah, I made it! What'd you think I was going to do, die?"

"Well you did end up in the recovery unit," Alan grinned as he zipped up his bag and threw it over his shoulder.

"Just a flesh wound!"

"Yeah, I'll bet," Luther muttered as he braided his hair back. We always teased him about his hair because it was longer than Bridget's and mine combined.

The receiver in my ear crackled as the line on the other end connected, then Arthur's loud, bossy voice assaulted my eardrum.

"Where the hell are you Levie, we need you in this copter *now*!"

"Which one?" I asked looking back at the three helicopters that still sat on the deck, loading in more teams and equipment.

"Far right!" he shouted, and then the line went dead.

"Come on guys, you're with me!"

"So I take it you're leading now?" Alan shouted over the noise of the helicopter's engines. I nodded rather than waste my voice, and took off sprinting back toward the helicopters.

The pilots didn't waste any time once we made it on board. We barely had time to sit down before the helicopter launched into the sky.

It took less than ten minutes for the mission scene to come into view.

The crawlers had started fires to keep themselves warm; with so many fires, things had quickly gotten out of hand.

There was fire everywhere; burning anything and everything it touched. Even from the sky, and through the smoke I could see the large figures of the wolves running wild through the burning ferns and trees beneath us.

We'd all been in situations like this before; we were trained for this. This could even be considered normal.

Something about tonight was off, though.

I closed my eyes and waited for the lights that danced in front of my eyelids to piece together and form a vision.

Darkness, smoke, shadows, and fire all danced across my eyes.

I tightened my grip on my bow and repeated my earlier pep talk.

I could kill with this bow. Nothing can hurt me while I have my bow in my hand.

We landed then and the doors opened flooding the cabin of the helicopter with orange light and smoke.

Arthur's voice sounded in my ear again.

"Get out there, get somewhere dark and under cover. Give me a chance to get your location coordinates and then I'll tell you where to go. You got it?"

"Got it."

I could kill with this bow. Nothing can hurt me while I have my bow in my hand.

CHAPTER TWO

Exhaust fans hummed above our heads, sucking the smoke out of the area. As soon as I could see I made my way through the nearest exit only allotting enough time to confirm the rest of my team was with me before moving again.

There wasn't much shelter left to hide in. The leeches who were fed enough to be in their right minds had started fires to keep warm. When the wolves beat us to the sight, the fires were abandoned and left to wreak havoc in the forest around us.

I shoved my face into the crook of my arm to avoid inhaling the smoke that hung in the air. Then, as a team, we dashed the few yards to where fallen trees would give us a little bit of cover away from the flames and chaos that had taken over the landing sight.

Everyone huddled around me, kneeling on the ground in an attempt to remain inconspicuous. Alan stood in front of us all, crossbow drawn and eyes focused. He watched the surrounding area while listening to me whisper our plans.

"Arthur, we're good to go. What's the deal?"

"Stay hunkered down and give me a second." The line crackled with static. "Jesus, I told you to stay still!" he shouted through the headpiece.

"I didn't move, Arthur! There are too many goddamn people out here! Too many connections going at the same time!"

"Okay, okay! Then we'll make this quick! Two teams arrived here about 15 minutes ago. They headed east and started to clear the way through the surrounding woods in that direction. They haven't been heard from for a few minutes, and they didn't call in a mayday."

"*Wow*, Arthur. You're sending us on a babysitting mission?"

"No, I'm sending you somewhere where you'll get some action! Do you *want* to do something productive tonight?"

"Yes..."

"Then get over it."

"So you want us to just catch up to them?"

"That's a start."

"*Fine.*"

"Good girl. Don't die." And the line went dead.

"Go to hell, Arthur!" I shouted, knowing he couldn't hear me. I turned to face the rest of my team. "Why does everyone always assume I'm going to die?"

"Because you're a girl." Keegan snickered.

"Bridget's a girl too, you know?"

"We don't know for sure with her. We know for a fact that *you* are." Luther threw me an evil grin and winked.

"You guys are all sick. You know that? If I didn't actually need your help tonight, I'd stab you and leave you here for the wolves. You're all just a bunch of pigs."

"I'd help her!" Bridget spat, flicking wisps of her brown

hair away from her eyes.

I smiled at Bridget; the realization of how young she really was hit me, and I had to hold back a grimace.

She was barely fourteen now. It had been only four short years ago that she had joined our team, and how she had managed to keep herself alive within a group like ours. I had no idea.

She had managed to hold her own since the day she stepped in as the sixth member of the team I was now leading.

Alan had laughed at the idea of a ten year old joining us in our missions—a few hours later he had found himself on the ground underneath little Bridget. She fancily sliced at the clothes he had on and then stood up as if nothing had happened.

When Alan stood up, his clothes fell off. I high-fived her, giggling the way I had used to when I was younger. We were level 6 comrades then. Later that night I had saved her life, and she hadn't left since. Not that I minded.

Bridget was something else, though. She had been trained from a young age to be somewhat of an assassin. She had flourished in that area, and therefore, ended up on my team for her skill level. At the time, we were on a fast track to grow higher in the ranks; the only way we would be able to do that was with a sixth member to complete the team.

"Are you guys ready?"

"Are we ever *really* ready?" Luther muttered, standing up and throwing his bag over his shoulder.

"Never," Alan grinned. "Lets go!"

We crouched low to the ground and darted out from the cover the fallen trees had provided us. Eerie darkness and silence enveloped us as we made our way through the already cleared woods.

Translucent shadows of things that had once stood near

where I was standing now skipped across my line of sight—changing position with every sweep I made with my eyes. I had to let them be for now, though. I didn't have the energy to spare in order to make the shadows disappear.

"Okay guys," I whispered. "Stay close."

"If a shadow moves, *shoot it.* It's not a shadow," Luther muttered.

They all whispered "Got it's" and "Okay's." I felt someone's hand touch my forearm and then a pair of lips at my ear.

"Something doesn't feel right…" Scotty whispered, tightening his grip on my arm. "Something bad is going to happen, I can feel it."

I could feel it, too. It was like a palpable, heavy fog that hung in the air. The world seemed to be pushing down on us, warning us to stay put and not go any further.

As a group, we seemed to simultaneously slow our breathing—all of our hands itched toward the weapons we carried into every mission.

"There aren't any shadows left," Bridget hissed so quietly that I almost couldn't hear her.

"The only one left that I can see is over there." Alan pointed up ahead to where a body lay in the middle of the path.

"That's not a shadow." I whispered. "Stick close, no one lag behind."

Slowly and carefully, I made my way towards the body that lay on the path.

I didn't recognize the girl; she lay sprawled out in the dirt. Her blonde hair was caked with blood. Her face was splotched with sweat and dirt. Her mouth hung open mid scream.

She had fought until she couldn't fight anymore, I thought.

At a loss for words I checked the leather bracelets on her

wrist. We wore them as a sign of what position we held and what rank we were.

Comrade 6 was inscribed on her bracelet, with the word *Arrows* underneath it.

She could have been a spitting image of me at that age. She couldn't be any older than Bridget.

"Does anyone know who she is?" I asked quietly, tucking the girl's bracelet back inside her jacket sleeve.

"Her name is Elisabeth. She went by Ellie most of the time though," Bridget murmured, biting her lip.

"Was she your friend, Bridget?"

"No… I just knew her name, that's all. They were deciding between she and I for who would be on your team back when we were all Comrade 4's. That could have been me…" she whispered.

"You wouldn't have made the mistake that she did, so no, it couldn't have been you." Keegan blurted out without thinking.

"Levie…" Luther whispered. "Look around us."

I knew what his words meant before I began to look, but I looked nevertheless.

Bodies. Twelve of them. Two teams… every member brutally maimed. Blood stained the dirt and grass and turned everything the same brownish color of rotting flesh.

The scene of a horror movie, and we had put ourselves in the middle of it all.

I quickly switched the earpiece I had in my ear on, and tried to keep it together while I waited for Arthur to respond. When he didn't respond I switched stations to the public one so anyone with an open signal could hear my call.

"*Mayday*—this is Levie from comrade 9; two teams dispersed east of landing sight are all terminated." No one called back, and I felt my breathing hitch. "*Mayday, mayday, mayday.* We need back-up and another god damn way out of here!"

Growls began to erupt from all sides of our team.

"*Mayday, mayday, mayday*!"

"Levie, is anyone calling back?" Scotty growled from behind me.

"*Mayday, mayday, mayday*! We're out here all alone! We're being surrounded! *Mayday, May-*"

"*Levie*!" Scotty screamed again, digging his hands into my shoulders and jerking me around to get my attention.

"*No!* No one's answering! The lines are too busy!"

"Looks like we're fighting tonight, boys." Luther spat. Everyone drew their weapons as the wolves began to emerge from behind the surrounding trees and bushes.

"Final mayday, final mayday. We are preparing to engage. Final mayday. We need help!" I clicked the earpiece over to the coordinates setting, so it would broadcast our coordinates and hopefully lead help to us. When the switch clicked into place, a high squealing screeched through the tiny speaker. I wrenched the piece out of my ear and shoved it into my pocket. "We're in this alone, guys. I tried."

"We can take 'em." Alan growled.

The area grew eerily silent for a few moments before the world seemed to explode with sound.

The wolves leaped into the air at what seemed like the exact same time. We moved immediately, shooting, stabbing, and wrestling our way through round after round of wolves that came our way.

We went through the weak ones quickly, ending their lives with barely a hint of effort. The longer we lasted, the longer it took to kill a single wolf.

Fights were growing harder to win; with every fight we won, we grew weaker. But still, we continued to win; until there were only six left.

One for each of us, they seemed to be the most experienced of them all.

I immediately feared for Bridget's life, but my focus was turned away from her when the Alpha--the strongest of the pack that had come at us--stepped into my line of vision.

His eyes were oddly human-like; they were furious and sad. The sadness in them almost made me regret what I was about to do. *Almost.*

I raised my bow and put the creature in my sights.

I released the arrow at the same time he lunged, and I hit the target I had aimed for. The wolf that would have been Bridget's dropped to the floor in pain as the arrow sliced underneath its shoulder blade.

I felt pain similar to what the wolf must have felt when a rock dug into my shoulder once I hit the ground. The pack alpha was on top of me immediately; vicious, snarling teeth snapping mere inches away from my face.

As the wolf had tackled me, my arrows fell and scattered.

The rocks underneath me ripped through my tunic and cut my skin; the arrows in the quiver on my back stuck out at weird angles, and one was stabbing my left arm.

The smell of blood fueled the wolf further, pushing him over the edge.

The inches between his face and mine became centimeters.

It was now or never.

I threw my left arm out to protect my face while I reached for the dagger that hung from my belt.

I let my right arm fly out as soon as I had a grip on the dagger. The silver flashed in the light from the moon as it sliced through the chest of the wolf above me.

But I was too late…

Even as I stabbed him, his teeth remained firmly lodged in

my left arm; biting through the armor, and through my tunic.

One last good thrust of my dagger had him off and running through the woods. Without any followers, though.

The rest of my team was finishing off the rest of his.

My arm began to shake uncontrollably as everyone finished up and walked over to me.

"All good everyone?" I asked in a shaky voice.

"We're definitely going to be in recovery tonight, that's for sure." Scotty laughed, wiping blood off of his forehead only for it to be replaced by more seconds later. There was a two-inch slice over his right eye.

Everyone else had similar injuries, though Bridget had wounds more similar to mine in amount, anyway.

"No terminations tonight, right? No one got bit?" Alan laughed as if the idea was funny. I resisted the urge to break down and cry.

There was a chorus of "No's" and a few chuckles of relief; then everyone looked at me.

"Levie? No bites, right?"

I hesitated before answering.

"Right, no bites. No one's getting terminated."

Everyone sat on the path, not caring about the dirt or the blood that clung to their clothes. All they could do was laugh; laugh with relief at the fact that they were all alive.

"I'm going to try and get a signal so I can call out and try to let everyone at base know we're alive." They nodded without much acknowledgment, so I left them to talk and walked back down the path a little ways.

Once I was out of sight, I yanked my armor and the sleeve of my tunic out of the way . . . revealing the bite underneath.

It was already festering; fighting off an infection as though it had been inflicted weeks ago rather than minutes. I knew from seeing other wolf inflicted wounds that it would heal fast; at the same rate their own injuries would heal. It would be nothing but a scratch by the time we made it back to the helicopter; and nothing but a scar by the time we got ourselves cleaned up.

It would disappear altogether before we even made it to the recovery wing to have our wounds stitched up.

Rumor had it, that it took four days for the venom of the bite to make its way through your system. All I had to do was make it four days without dying.

When your heart stops the venom takes over completely and turns you into one of them… a monster… a werewolf.

You only have to make it four days.

The rumors also said the venom --- the burning; stinging, aching, rotting pain --- was enough to make death a relief.

CHAPTER THREE

"Levie, it's your turn," Keegan said coming through the white doors looking as good as new. "You've procrastinated long enough."

I had ushered everyone ahead of me so the bite on my arm would heal in time for it to be unnoticeable. As of now, I was pretty confident I could pass it off as an old scar or scratch. It wouldn't be so hard to pretend… except the burning hadn't gotten any easier to handle. It had only grown stronger.

"What's the damage report?" I asked him, putting the recovery check-up off even longer.

"Some slices, some cuts, a broken rib, a broken thumb, a sprained ankle and neck, and a concussion. Not the worst fight I've been in, but sure as hell not the best," he laughed. "Have fun, Levie. I'd love to wait for you… but I'm just too tired to care."

"Thanks Keeg, you're a doll."

"Hey, Levie, I'll wait here for you. But I'll probably be

asleep when you come out. So if you could just carry me to my room…" Scotty muttered sleepily.

"It's so nice to know how concerned you are, Scotty."

"Mmhmm," he mumbled, laying his head on the plastic armrest of the seat next to his. "Go get your check-up."

I forced myself up out of the plastic chair in the waiting room and walked slowly into my least favorite place on the planet.

I hated recovery with a passion. It was the worst part of the day, worse even than the fight itself.

Nurses watching me shower, and writing stuff down on a clipboard just wasn't my idea of a good time. Some people would beg to differ though.

"You missed a spot, Levie." One of the nurses said, pointing to the back of my arm with her pen.

"I'm saving that for last because it *burns*," I said. She was referring to the gash on my shoulder blade that the fall had caused. It seemed like I could still feel the rocks in my back, although I knew they weren't really there.

The disinfecting soap made my skin itch all over. When it got in my scrapes and cuts it made me wish I could pull my arms and legs off to stop the pain.

"Levie, you're going to have to get your shoulder blade clean so we can stitch it up. Either you do it, or *we will*."

I looked at my sponge while the nurses jabbered on about how important it was to stay clean. The nurses brought out the worst in me; so I attempted to stay calm by taking in all of the sponge's tiny details.

It was that sterile blue color that should belong in a hospital. Covered in tiny, rock like exfoliating pieces, it had the ability to work the disinfecting soap down into your pores. Rather than the rocky little pieces allowing soap to soak into my skin, it tended to rip open the wounds that had started to heal all over my body. Every time the sponge tore into my skin I wanted to scream.

The nurses didn't appreciate screaming.

"Fine," I shouted, throwing the sponge at the nurses' feet. My voice echoed off the walls of the eerily white and clean shower. "Do it! Just get it over with." I squeezed my eyes shut and clenched my hands into fists; my nails dug into my palms and began to draw blood.

"Levie, I think we're just going to give you some time to rest. That way we can get you fixed up without you being in pain."

Normally I would have refused additional pain meds and told them to just get it over with, that I'd be fine. This time around, however, I couldn't wait to not *feel* anything. Something was off, wrong. My body seemed like it was both going into overdrive and trying to shut down. Part of me was trying to have a panic attack, while the other half was trying to pass out.

"Please… do whatever you want. I don't care right now."

The nurses looked at one another, and exchanged looks of shock and surprise. Apparently, they weren't expecting me to be this cooperative.

I barely had time to blink before I felt the slight stab of a needle in my upper arm.

The nurses were way *too quick with that,* I thought. *They had to have had that in their pockets… Sneaky bitches.*

I had to give them credit though, whatever it was they used to knock out their patients *worked.* The stuff was strong… I was out in seconds.

Flashes of light danced across my eyes; flickered, then pieced together to form a picture.

The man was tall; brown hair, chiseled face, dark eyes. He was yelling at me…

Why?

"Do you even know how much trouble you've put me through?" He shouted, throwing his arms up in the air. The feeling of the vision told me I hated him, but I didn't know why…

Rolling over hurt. It always did when I woke up from recovery; but it didn't stop me from doing it every time. I'd roll over, groan, bury my face in a pillow, and come back to reality just in time to feel the consequences of my movement.

"Sonova-bitch," I groaned. My back gave up on me as I tried to sit up. I collapsed back onto my pillows.

"Careful. We need you in good condition. Don't hurt yourself more than you already have," A familiar voice murmured from the chair next to my bed.

"What the hell are you doing here, Arthur?"

"The nurses are making me play the parent game again, since you're injured to the point that you need supervision."

"Sorry…"

"You're fine, it doesn't bother me. And since when do you say sorry?" he handed me a glass of water and two greyish pills.

"Since it became a form of respect." I muttered, popping the pills into my mouth and swallowing them quickly to try and avoid the nasty, chalky taste they left behind.

"Since when do you respect me?"

"That's a logical point…" I smiled and he rolled his eyes.

The truth was, while I may not have *shown* Arthur my respect, it was always there; ever since I was little. Sometimes I wondered if I would have respected my own parents more than Arthur—probably not. There was no way of knowing either way.

The story I had been told since I was little was one of

valor; my parents had died on a mission similar in many ways to the one I had just been on. There were rumors, though—always told by someone cruel—that said my parents hadn't died, they had just deserted me. This is why I haven't ever liked *people.*

For some reason unknown to me, someone decided that Arthur should take care of me when my parents passed. From six years old, to fourteen I lived with him as my guardian. At fourteen I was finally old enough to get a dorm room of my own with the other teenagers.

Arthur's name was still on all my papers as my guardian.

A lot of people asked me if it was weird to live with Arthur, and to have him as a guardian. I told them no, because I got special treatment. It wasn't actually true, however that reply usually got them to go away. In reality, I just didn't want to talk about it.

"How bad is the damage? Not just me, the whole team." I mumbled before taking another swig of water.

"Not so bad; you and Bridget took the most damage. All the guys have taken worse, but then again they don't fight as hard as the two of you do."

"That doesn't tell me how bad it all was."

"The guys are fine. They were given a sedative that will knock them out and heal the worst of their wounds. You and Bridget will probably have to work a little harder at defending yourselves for the future. You guys focus too much on getting in a hit."

"How bad is Bridget?"

"Wow, disregard *everything* I just said why don't you?"

"Arthur!" he rolled his eyes and sighed.

"She's got a broken collarbone, a concussion, a nice, pretty little gash on the back of her neck and another pretty gash on her waist."

"That's it?"

"She has a busted rib too… a couple, actually. Then again, so do you."

"I'm worse than her?"

"Oh, yeah. You're lucky you're not completely bedridden… which brings me back to the fact that your defense skills *suck*."

"You're the one who's trained me this whole time. So if you're going to blame anyone, blame yourself." I mumbled, trying to get up.

"No, no, no… don't you dare try to get up. You need to rest."

I grumbled, but decided it would be easier to listen to him rather than to argue.

It didn't make much of a difference, though. The comfortable silence between the two of us had Arthur out in a matter of minutes.

I giggled at his sleeping form—he seemed so much younger asleep than he did when he was awake.

No one knew Arthur as well as I did. And *I* didn't even know him that well. He was different from the other commanders, though. *That* I knew for sure. He wasn't a robot—programmed to think and act a certain way, like the others were. I hadn't once heard of him sleeping around like the others, either. He broke the rules, and encouraged us to break the rules as well.

The majority of his students had grown up to become commanders, or members of high-ranking teams.

He was a good man, and a good trainer—that was more than most could say. He had trained my mother before me. When I was younger, there hadn't been a day where he wouldn't tell me how much like my mother I was.

The only problem was that I didn't care for my mother much—she had died and left me here alone. I didn't want to be like her.

He finally figured this out as I grew up; now, he didn't speak of her ever.

Sometimes I wondered how Arthur managed to live with us all – *all* being the rest of the Flickers here on base including myself. He was understanding. He was kind. And he could live a much better life elsewhere.

Then again, this loveless, dangerous, war-filled life was all he knew. It was all we *all* knew. This was life, though. And there wasn't anything anyone could do to change it.

A day in bed was a day too long. I couldn't stand being bedridden, even if it was very leniently controlled. It wasn't so much that I had to stay in bed; if that had been the case I would have gone insane. No, I just wasn't allowed to leave my room.

Every time I tried, and believe me I tried *a lot*, I was caught and lectured to about how important it was for me to *stay* in bed so I could get better. After close to fifteen tries, possibly more, I gave up. The effort just wasn't worth it.

Slowly but surely though, the doses of healing sedatives grew weaker and weaker. Eventually, the nurses just came in and took off the bandages covering various areas of my body. They removed the stitches from my less serious cuts, and rubbed some gel across the areas where the cuts had been so there wouldn't be any serious scars.

When they finally left, all that was left was the bandage wrapped around my waist for my cracked ribs, and the stitches for the gash on my shoulder.

Oh, and the bandage they had wrapped around my forearm, where a seemingly healed cut had opened back up. The nurses blamed themselves for not getting it clean enough, but I knew the real reason why it hadn't gotten any better.

Damn werewolves.

I was scared. The rumors I had heard from everyone said that the pain from a werewolf bite was unbearable—since I had woken up from the sedative the day before, I hadn't felt *anything.* It wasn't just a lack of pain either; it was a lack of *feeling.* My entire body was numb; I had pinched myself countless times, pinching so hard that bruises formed . . .yet I couldn't feel it.

I had to admit, it was nice to not feel the pain from my ribs every time I breathed. If there was anything I hated more than anything else, it was the pain that broken ribs caused.

Through all my worrying, I finally remembered that Arthur had let me know the funeral for the teams we had found the other night was later today.

I was receiving a medal for my "courageous acts" and for finding the teams.

There was no way I could skip the funeral, even if I *did* want to.

Arthur would ring my neck.

I hated funerals with a passion. I didn't fit into any of the niches that presented themselves throughout the day. There were the leaders who had always tried to lead the teams through the mess they were in, the families of the team members, the friends, the living members of the teams, the comrades who had gone through training with them.

This time around though, I would at least have my own niche to fit into. I made up part of the team that had found those who the funeral honored. My team had made it through the shit the others hadn't. We'd get some nasty glares today, no doubt.

A knock on my door brought me out of the trance I had been in for who knows how long…

"Come in!" I shouted.

"Levie, what are you doing still in bed? The funeral is in an hour…" Scotty muttered, draping a garment bag over the back of my desk chair.

"Sorry, it's just been one of those days." I mumbled, forcing myself up into an upright position. "I thought Arthur said *he'd* be bringing my clothes…"

"What? Am I not good enough for you?" He chuckled and rolled his eyes. "Arthur said if he had to see the inside of your room one more time today he'd kill himself."

"Heaven forbid that Arthur have a little compassion."

Scotty threw the garment bag at me and I groaned.

Zipping open the bag revealed the exact thing I had been fearing.

My uniform consisted of a leader's tunic and a petticoat, complete with my emblems and recognition medals. There was a note from Arthur with strict instructions on it . . . I was to roll my hair up into a tight French roll.

I managed to get into my uniform, even though it took me twenty minutes to get my petticoat buttoned up. The damn thing buttoned all the way up, from bottom to top; there had to be at least a dozen buttons.

The only thing I was really having trouble with was getting my hair to stay up in the goddamn French roll . . . as required by Arthur.

"Scotty, do you know how to do this?"

"Do I *look* like I'd know how to do that?" he answered from my bed where he had been sitting for a good forty minutes now.

"I was just asking."

I tried again, and failed miserably.

"You really need to work on your hairstyling skills."

"Just go get Arthur, please!" I screamed, throwing my hairbrush across the room.

Scotty rushed out of the room before I could throw something his way, and hurried back a few minutes later with Arthur hesitantly following behind him.

"Arthur, I can't get this to work! I can't do my hair like this!"

"Levie, Levie, Levie… what are we going to do with you?"

"Help me put my hair up?"

Arthur chuckled and came up behind me.

He began twisting his fingers through my hair. I watched in the mirror as my hair seemed to magically go from hanging down my back to being tightly rolled and pinned to the back of my head.

"Thank you." I mumbled, slightly awed and embarrassed.

"Where did you learn that skill, Arthur?" Scotty asked teasingly.

"I had to teach Levie's mom how to do her hair that way."

"Oh…"

"Levie, you *do* look a lot like your mother right now."

"Thanks… I guess," I mumbled. "Let's get this over with."

We had been trained not to show intense emotions; something we all practiced now, as the coffins were placed and opened.

My team stood on the platform near the coffins; paying our respects by nodding to those who walked by. We'd get the chance to pay personal respects later, after we were rewarded for finding them and for fighting off the pack of wolves that had attacked us shortly after we had found them.

The bodies had been dressed in clean tunics and armor; the uniforms they had been wearing during their fight would be placed on a manikin---blood and all---and put in the hall of remembrance. Though their faces still showed the cuts and pre-mortem bruises, their expressions were forced, made into the way it looked now rather than the scary, rigor mortis state. Their eyes were sewn shut to mask the fear they had held during the last seconds of life.

I will never understand why they show the bodies during the funerals. I suppose it just provided the families with one last look. The bodies would be burned later, and ashes added to a very large urn in the middle of the garden in the compound.

This was where all of our fallen comrades went after their funerals. The giant urn represented what we did; how we all fought for the same thing… how we died for the same thing.

Personally, I didn't want to die for the same thing they did. I didn't want to die at all. I wanted to live through the revolution; I wanted to see the final result of why we were fighting.

Half the time I couldn't even remember what we were fighting for in the first place. It wasn't over the wolves like it always seemed to be, though. We were supposed to be allies—not enemies. The rivalry had started long before even Arthur was born. What we were taught as children was a petty game of he-said-she-said—accidents were involved, and fingers were pointed… *deaths occurred…* but in the end, our alliance disintegrated under the crushing force of hatred.

Accidents were involved, and fingers were pointed… *deaths occurred…* and the cycle continued.

I thought this through, and through again while the names of my team were called one by one to receive their honors.

"Comrade Level 9 Leader—Levie Russ."

I stepped forward and accepted my medals. I would add them to the growing box of junk in my closet later tonight, when I was alone and could think for myself once again.

CHAPTER FOUR

"Levie, block dammit! *Block*!" Arthur screamed as I took another hit to the side. I gasped for air and stumbled back, clutching my ribs with my bad arm, while clutching my bad arm with my good arm.

"Shut the hell up, Arthur!" I sucked in air as best I could, and tried to dodge another blow. I ended up taking a wooden staff to the shoulder. "*Shit*, that hurts!"

My legs seemed to decide they were finished being strong, and collapsed beneath me.

"Arthur, I'm not going to hit her while she's on the ground." Landers mumbled through the mask he wore to protect his face.

Landers was a sorry excuse for a commander… he didn't have an ounce of the skill Arthur or the rest of the commanders had, so they stuck him with defensive training. He was a pasty, freckly, rude man with a lot of upper arm strength and good aim when it came to waving around a stick.

"Levie, get up *now*!" Arthur shouted, waving his arms in the air like a maniac.

"You know what? No, Arthur, screw you! I'm *done*!"

"Levie, if you say you're done… you're *really* done! I'll take you off of the leading position and send you all the way back down to comrade three, so you'll be *forced* to learn defense!"

"What the *hell*?" I screamed forcing myself up off the ground, only to have Landers crack me in the back of the legs with the staff. I collapsed to the ground again, twisting around and wrenching him down to my level. In one fluid motion, I used him as leverage to pull myself up and sent my knee straight for his "area", before throwing him back to the ground.

"That wasn't a fair hit, Levie." He winced.

"Oh, because hitting me in the back of the legs when I had *just* gotten up *was* a fair hit? You're such a scrawny little *prick*." I spat before I limped over to where Arthur stood with Bridget.

Bridget wasn't doing too well either. She was sprawled out on the ground, breathing heavily still, even though her defensive session had ended close to forty-five minutes ago. I knew the pained look on her face, and was sure a similar one masked my face as well.

Her ribs were killing her. I wasn't in any better shape than her, though. It would have been nice if that were the only thing causing me pain, though…

Last night, my arm had been numb—*dead* numb. Today it felt as though someone was repeatedly sticking knives in it and twisting them.

And this was only day two…

"Thank you for saying something I've always wanted to say to him," Arthur whispered as we watched Landers stand up and waddle his way in the direction of the dorm buildings to change.

"It was my pleasure. *Trust me*."

"I wasn't joking about the threat, Levie."

"*Why*, though? I don't understand…"

"Because, Levie… every time you get hurt, you get weaker. You're team is going to start to get hurt; *really* injured, if you don't start developing your strength--physical as well as your mental strength. It's important, Levie. You know that. You need to learn to defend yourself so you don't get hurt anymore. Do you understand?"

I sighed with frustration. As much as I wanted to deny the fact that he was right, I couldn't. His logic was as solid as steel.

"Arthur…" Bridget winced. She clutched at her sides and tried to gulp in more air. "I'm pretty sure I re-broke my rib…"

"Yeah, you don't look so good…" he muttered.

"I think I might have punctured a lung." She gasped again as if to prove her point.

Arthur whistled and motioned for the medical team that had been watching from nearby to come and get her.

"I can't believe you let her out here so soon after getting hurt! She coul-" he motioned for me to be quiet when the medics got closer. I bit my tongue in frustration and resisted the urge to slap Arthur.

"Pump her full of healers, I don't care if you have to knock her out to do it. I need her better than new as soon as possible, got it?"

They nodded, hoisted her up into a wheelchair, and wheeled her away. Arthur waited until the medics and Bridget were out of hearing range, before turning on me.

"You're getting *way* too cocky, Levie. No more telling me what I can and can't do."

"You deserve to know when you're *wrong*!" I said, disregarding what he had said.

He grumbled to himself and started to walk away.

"*Hey*! I'm not done talking to you yet!" he threw his arms up in frustration and spun around to face me again.

"*What*, Levie?"

"Do you have anything planned for the team tonight?"

"Not much, do whatever you want. Just get some rest. All of you," he grumbled. With that he left; walking through the damp and misty courtyard before disappearing into the nearest hallway.

Bridget's recovery room was set up the way it always was.

When you finally hit the age at which they actually let you go on missions, the administrators at the medical building also required you to fill out a mountain of forms. Most of the forms had to do with your medical history; which at that time was a very short list.

Tucked inside the many packets of forms to fill out, had been a form for preferences. As in, what you wanted in your room when you were "recovering". Whereas I had barely glanced at that particular form when filling everything out, Bridget had milked it for all she could.

Even at a young age, she knew *exactly* what she wanted… Lots of pillows, classical music… she even went so far as to request candles.

At ten years old, we were practically babies in the medical wing of Sicura. Within the next few years of our lives, the nurses in the hospitals would remember our faces, full names, dorm addresses, and ranks. It was ironic, though, that in the beginning we thought we'd never see the inside of the medical wing. And now we all almost expected it.

Hell, we all practically lived there.

"Damn, every time I come in here to visit you, I think about having them pull my file so I can change my room requests!" I spoke in a hushed voice, both to keep Bridget relaxed and to keep the nurses from knowing I was here.

It was well past visiting hours, and they hated me enough as it was…

"I have high standards, what can I say?" she murmured, smiling sleepily.

I sat down next to her and smiled.

"How're you feeling?"

"I feel like I'm floating on a cloud; they've got me full of healers, just like Arthur told them to do. But I can breathe again, so I guess that's a good thing."

"Yeah, that's a good thing." She smiled again, and yawned. "They're trying to keep you asleep, huh?"

"Mmhmm," she yawned again. "But I woke up right before you got here and they gave me another shot of whatever-the-hell they call that stuff…"

"Morphine?"

"Oh." She mumbled, and rubbed her eyes. "Can you hand me that glass of water?" she pointed to the bedside table near the headboard of her bed.

I nodded, and reached over to grab the glass.

The amount of pain that shot up my arm at the slight movement didn't seem possible. It felt as though someone had taken a knife, shoved it completely through my arm, and then forced me to bend it. The worst part about it, though, was that I couldn't scream. I couldn't let anyone – not a single soul – know how badly it hurt.

I winced as I handed her the glass; watching my hand shake through slits for eyes.

"What's the matter, Levie?"

For the first time tonight, Bridget's voice sounded like her own; there was no haziness, or sleepiness to it. Looking her in the eyes, there was no sleepiness there either. She was one hundred percent alert… and I wanted to tell her, *badly*. To have just one person know; one person who wouldn't turn me in. The relief would be amazing. Someone to cover for me… someone to make sure I got through the last two days of this torturous pain…

"I…"

No. She'll tell. No matter how much you want to believe that she'll keep this for you, you know she won't. She's a good girl; you taught her to be. She'll turn you in with tears in her eyes; it'll devastate her…

No.

"I'm *fine.*" I murmured, putting a cool hand to her clammy forehead. "Get some rest, you'll need it for tomorrow."

Before she could say anything more, I left the room.

I walked as slowly as I possibly could; praying that the cool, damp air outside would soothe the pain ripping its way through my arm.

Of course, it didn't.

I made it about half way across the main courtyard before my legs decided they were going to give out on me. I managed to make it to one of the few stone benches before I completely collapsed to the ground.

I had been exhausted all day; even before defensive training.

Now I was just… there were no words to describe how I felt.

I was tired beyond repair; and in more pain than I had ever been in, in my entire life. Eighteen years of combat, and I had never once been hurt so bad that I wanted to just die.

But that was exactly what I felt like doing now.

Dying.

That was a bad thought to have running through your head at a time like this… if I killed myself, I would be jumping right into what I was trying to avoid.

Calm down, I told myself. *The last thing you need right now is a nervous breakdown.*

I took the time to try and clear my mind; I surveyed the courtyard.

It was a misty, foggy night. It would rain later, the way it always did during late fall.

This is the time of year you love, I reminded myself. *Take advantage of it.*

Everything stayed damp during the fall and winter months. As of now, though it was only November, everything was just beginning.

It was nights like this that were my favorites, though. A slight hint of fog was beginning to roll in, clouds above were threatening to let loose a misting of rain.

Oddly enough, my favorite part was that the moss was just beginning to grow back onto the stone walls and the statues throughout the compound. Fog and clouds constantly hung over the area, casting a dark, yet comfortable, feeling over everything.

Of course, I could only really appreciate nights like this when I *wasn't* in pain. That's what made tonight *suck*.

"Levie, are you alright?"

"I've been feeling a little dizzy." I murmured to Arthur. I opened my eyes and tried to focus on his face; but it remained distorted. "I'm pretty sure I need to sleep."

"You're *pretty* sure?"

"Take me to my bed." I commanded, throwing my arms up in demand and wincing when the movement threw my arm into another pain-ripping frenzy.

"You're still in pain?" he asked as he hoisted me up into his arms.

"My ribs are still healing; I have one more dose of healers left, then I'll be okay…" *Not.*

By the time Arthur had set me down on my bed, things that *should not* be spinning, *were.*

He kneeled down and began unlacing my shoes for me; pulling them off along with my socks.

"Well, you'll have plenty of time tomorrow to get back to being yourself again."

"Mmhmm…"

"So get some rest…"

"*Mmhmm…*"

He tucked the blankets in around me, and patted one of my pillows before turning to leave for the night.

I was out almost immediately. I didn't even hear the door click shut behind him.

The smell was cold, damp, and musty. The floor was damp also; or was it just my clothes? Damp with sweat, probably… I couldn't tell.

Chains cut into my arms and legs; not slicing them, but hurting me nonetheless. I pulled and yanked them in every direction with as much force as I could.

There was an odd, pulling ache that seemed to emanate from every limb on my body. Everything was shifting or moving in some way, and no matter how hard I tried, I couldn't stop it.

A voice whispered from behind me; but the pain prevented me from opening my eyes enough to see who was talking.

"I promise that you'll make it through this. Everything is going to be okay, I promise…"

With that, my spine wrenched in opposite directions; twisting and stretching to compensate for something a lot bigger than a mere human.

I wrenched myself up in bed; screaming loud enough to wake up the entire compound.

Dear God, please let that just be a dream…

CHAPTER FIVE

I woke up in the morning to the warm sun shining in through my bedroom window, and the sound of four young men running around my room raiding my underwear drawer.

"Hey, Alan! Why don't you keep this pair? You can hang 'em up on the wall alongside all of the pictures of the girls you'll *never* get." Keegan sniggered.

"You mean the *blank* wall in my room?" Alan countered … a chorus of snide remarks followed.

"*Really*, you guys? What time is it?" I sat up in bed and did my best to push the runaway strands of hair out of my face.

"It's like seven already," Scotty shouted as he sauntered out of the bathroom.

"You better have put that seat down," I grumbled. Scotty waved my empty threat off like a gnat. The guys continued to run around my room and dig through everything. I tried to do my best to get back to sleep, but there was no use with all the noise around me.

"*What are you doing here in the first place?*" I snapped at them gruffly. Their heads flew to face me like deer caught in headlights.

"Arthur told us to come and get you and make your day worthwhile. He said we could have the day off as long as we hung out with you…" Keegan admitted. Alan and Luther were sitting side by side with a pair of my underwear on each of their heads.

"What is that supposed to mean?"

"He thinks you need a break…"

"If I need a break from anything, it's from *you guys*." I flung the covers away from me and slumped out of bed.

"How could you get tired of *this*?" Luther said, motioning to himself and the rest of the guys.

I shook my head and plucked the pair of underwear off the top of his head, "I'll take these if you don't mind. I'm going to take a shower. I'd appreciate it if you would leave my underwear *alone* while I'm in there, too."

I started toward the bathroom, but Scotty yanked me back by my arm, causing me to wince.

"What's the matter with your arm?"

Shit.

I looked down to see my arm; unnaturally bruised to the point where it was almost entirely purple and grey in color from my elbow down.

"Arthur had me in defensive training yesterday, that's all," I blurted quickly, hoping my poor excuse would be enough to satisfy the guys' curiosity.

"Damn, Landers is such a dick," Luther said angrily. "Do you want me to take care of him for you?"

"*No.* The only thing I want you to do is leave me alone so I can take a shower!" I wrenched my arm out of Scotty's light grasp and stomped towards the bathroom. Right as I closed the door, I heard them whispering amongst each other.

"*Something's not right with her…*"

Today was going to be a long day.

"**Is this all** we're going to do all day?"

We had been sitting in the middle of the courtyard doing absolutely nothing for almost half an hour now.

My hair was hanging uncomfortably around my neck and sticking to my back. It hadn't dried completely since my shower, and now it remained damp from the misty air outside.

It was *cold*, too.

"My nose is running faster than *I* run on missions." They all stared at me and shrugged.

"We thought you would know what to do," Alan muttered. "Aren't girls supposed to know this shit?"

"*Really*? Funny, I thought Arthur told you to entertain *me* for the day. I guess I misunderstood that."

"Oh, we can *entertain* you all right." Alan sniggered along with the rest of the guys. I forced myself up off the ground and started to walk away.

"Oh, come on, Levie! We were only kidding with you." Scotty jumped up and jogged the short distance to where I stood. "What's the matter with you, Levie? Huh? You're not acting normal."

"I don't want to talk about it," I replied. My good hand automatically went to my other arm, cradling it while it throbbed.

"Are you sure? Is it about what happened the other night? Things *did* get pretty tense…"

"Why would that change anything? I've come close to dying plenty of times before, this isn't any different."

Scotty growled quietly under his breath and grabbed my arm, applying pressure until I whelped. "Does this *hurt*?"

"*Yes*!

"Then there *is* something *wrong*, isn't there?" He squeezed my arm harder. I whimpered… keeping my eyes tightly shut and trying as hard as I could not to cry.

I *didn't* cry… *Ever.*

"You can't lie to your best friend. I'll let go when you tell me the truth."

"I'm *hurt*! *There*! I said it! Are you happy?"

"What *happened*?" He hissed.

"I can't tell you!" I screeched. The others heads shot up and watched as I attempted to wrench my arm out of Scotty's grasp. "*Why can't you understand that*?"

"Stop being a *liar* and *tell me*!" he grabbed both of my arms and shook me fiercely once before I tripped and stumbled to the ground. We stared back at each other, our eyes angry and full of shock.

"Who do *you think you are?"* I demanded, pushing myself up off the ground. I put both hands on his chest and shoved him back harder than he had shoved me. When he didn't fall, I got angrier.

"I *think* I'm someone who deserves more *credit* than what he's getting!" I knew Scotty and I were speaking loudly to begin with—but the angrier I grew, the louder I became.

"You don't deserve anything… you *earn* it! Right now, you're not doing so great at earning *anything*!"

He let out his own version of a snarl and turned to walk away muttering under his breath about how unreliable I am. Before I could even think to stop myself, I attacked him.

His body hit the ground with a heavy thud, and immediately his training kicked in. He fought back without any consideration for the fact that I was hurt, or that I was a *girl*.

Scotty was so familiar, though. That's what made me so angry. I knew him inside and out—I was closer to him than I was to anyone else on base—and yet here we were, fighting over a secret.

He used his forearm to pin me down against the concrete, his fingers twisted through my damp hair and yanked in the opposite direction. I cried out and planted a solid kick to his stomach.

By then the others had swarmed around us, failing miserably to break us apart with their best efforts.

I was having no problems holding my own until Scotty landed a vengeful hit to my arm. The pain that exploded at the contact would have been enough to knock me out had it not been for the adrenaline high I was riding. I pushed myself away from him and curled up on the ground, pressing my arm against the cold cement in an attempt to get the pain the stop.

When the pain finally started to fade, I forced myself up off the ground and looked around at the guys who stood in front of me. I didn't have any idea how long I had been down, but somewhere between when the fight ended to now, Arthur had shown up.

"Have you ever considered that I didn't tell you because I didn't want *you* to get hurt?" I spoke while, brushing the dust off of my clothes to the best of my ability. "If *any* of you show up at my door tonight, you will be shot."

I didn't have enough energy to figure out how long I had soaked in the tub. It had relieved a lot of my stress. The second I got out though, tension tightened up my limbs and had me longing to wreak havoc on anything that moved.

Arthur checked up on me eventually. He had ducked just in time to miss my arrow when he opened the door. Then we couldn't get it out of the wall.

The arrow was the last thing on my mind. Especially after Arthur chalked me full of healers, with the demand that I take them every hour, on the hour, until I went to bed. Something important would be happening tomorrow, and I needed to be prepared for it. He finally left after I threatened him for the thousandth time that if he didn't leave me alone, I would ruin his plans for me and cut my own arm off.

I wanted to be alone… and I finally got my wish. I curled up under the covers of my bed and allowed myself to think about everything that I had avoided in my mind for the last few days.

Technically speaking, I had two days to live through. There were two ways that could go, one way being that I would make it through the next two days and be off – free to do as I please.

The other way – ending in me becoming a monster.

Would I ever meet the monster that did this to me in the first place? Had it been punished for biting me? Was it even still alive?

What would happen to me once I turned?

That last thought had me scared. I wasn't sure how well I would handle being tortured. I could take more pain than the average girl, but I wasn't sure for how *long*; and that was *without* regard to the fact that they could end up wanting information from me. Information that I would refuse to give under *any* circumstance.

I was a few thoughts away from getting up and marching with what was left of my pride down to Arthur's room to tell him the truth, when I heard my door click open.

"I thought I told you guys that I don't want you up here," I growled from under my covers. When silence followed, I threw back the covers and sat up dramatically. I knew exactly who it was the second I saw the blonde hair on his head.

"*Especially you.*"

"Levie, I'm so *sorry*," Scotty whispered. "I didn't mean to hurt you."

"Too bad you can't take back the pain."

"I wish I could."

"Well you *can't*," I said feeling my anger rise. "As a friend, what you did was wrong. As a part of *my* team, it was unacceptable."

"I know." Scotty murmured, studying the floor.

"Look at me, Scotty. I will only say this once… I might be new to the Rank of Lead position, but as far as I'm concerned, I've been *leading* this group for a long time now. You have no choice but to respect the Rank. Everything I say should be regarded as *true*, whether it is or not—because everything I do will be for the well being of you *and* the entire team. Do you understand?"

"*Yes*," Scotty nodded.

"And Scotty?"

"Hmm?"

"Next time I won't hesitate to take you out."

"I'm surprised you hesitated this time," Scotty mumbled quietly.

For the first time today, I smiled.

"If you hadn't pulled a low-blow on me and hit my arm, I would have."

"Speaking of which, are you alright?"

"I've been better." Almost as if on queue, my arm began to throb.

"Is there anything I can do to make it feel better?"

*Chop my arm off? Kill me? Send me to the elders so **they** can kill me?*

There was no getting out of this… I was completely and

utterly in this battle alone. One on one combat had never been my strongpoint…

"There is nothing you can do, Scotty."

CHAPTER SIX

My night had sucked… *bad.* **I** hadn't been able to distinguish the difference between my dreams and my actual visions. I guess it didn't matter much which one was which; I had woken up after every one of them, anyway. Eventually, I woke up for the last time; it was finally light outside, so I took it as a sign to get up.

No more sleeping, I told myself. *You'll only have another dream.*

My quest to find the bathroom in the morning was always hard; slipping on a piece of paper, and nearly falling on my ass didn't make it any easier this morning. Even with the paper being on the ground, it was hard to mistake Arthur's sloppy handwriting.

And he thinks I don't respect him, I grumbled while I bent down to pick up the letter. *If this had been from anyone else, I would have just ignored it until after my shower.*

Levie,

No defensive training today, I'm having the nurses bring you another round of healers… just to make sure…

I need you strong for your team, Levie.

If I see so much as a scratch on you when I come to check up on you, you're dead.

You have all day to pack; there's a packing list taped to your door, as well as the doors of everyone else who's going (in case you'd like to know who you'll be in charge of).

I'll be here at 6:00 pm to pick you up. From there we'll head out to the tarmac. I'll brief you on what's going to go down before the teams get there, and you can brief them.

This is big, Levie.

Arthur.

I looked at the clock on my wall and sighed. It was only five. I had thirteen hours to get ready.

Showers are magical. Just plain magical…

One of the best things about having a room to yourself was that there was no one around to tell you to get out of the shower. I had spent a good three hours in the shower this morning, knowing full well that it may be the last time I get to shower for a while…

I had also fallen asleep while I was shaving… but that was beside the point.

I finally stumbled out of the shower and wrapped my prune-like body in a towel at 8:00.

From there, I got started on packing.

I chuckled at the few looks I received when I walked outside to grab the packing list off of my door. I couldn't blame them; I *was* wrapped in a towel, after all.

This would be my first big mission of the "Hunting"

season, as we called it. The weather was just starting to level off. These days there was only one temperature—*freezing.* And the colder it got, the more uncomfortable the Night Crawlers were. They enjoyed the heat. Being cold-blooded creatures they relied on heat to keep them warm. As long as the blood kept warm in their stomachs, they were semi-quiet. But once the cool weather came, they went psychotic—running around, ravaging streets and entire towns in an attempt to warm up their bodies.

Filthy, cold-blooded creeps.

I was definitely looking forward to catching some of the little nasties, and torturing them to death.

Please let us be catching them. I told myself.

I ripped the list off of my door and flipped the bird to a guy down the hall who seemed to be looking *through* my towel.

In the few seconds I had been out in the hall, I had clearly seen the amount of doors with blue packing lists taped to them—there were a lot. The thought of leading so many people at once made me shudder… I barely had been able to get my own team out of an ambush alive the other night. What was I going to do with four times the amount of people?

I shoved that thought back into the furthest corner of my mind and focused on packing everything I would need and then some.

This list was two pages, stapled together; printed on both the front and back. It listed everything we would need, down to how many pairs of underwear we were supposed to bring. We were to pack no more, and no less.

I started with the first page, crossing stuff off as I found it and threw it on my bed, and circling the items that I'd need to retrieve from the storage house on the far side of the base.

By the time I finished throwing everything I needed onto

my bed, it was close to two o'clock and I couldn't see my bedspread.

I sighed and got up off my ass; making my way toward my closet so I wouldn't have to go outside in a pair of sweats and an old t-shirt.

Apparently, being comfortable was frowned upon in this establishment.

The storage house was extremely busy by the time I got there. Apparently, everyone had the same idea that I did... and there were *way* more people going than I had originally estimated.

There were a good 35 people mulling around in front of the large warehouse door that was the only way to get inside the building.

I immediately picked Keegan's red hair out of the crowd, and jogged towards him.

"What's going on?"

"As far as I know, we're all waiting to get our stuff out of storage." He muttered, clearly a little annoyed.

"*All* of us are going?"

"Mmhmm, this is everyone. All six teams."

"Thirty-six of us..." I mumbled, doing the math quickly in my head. "That's a lot of people to be in charge of."

"Lucky *you*."

"Oh yeah, lucky *me*." I said sarcastically. "How come no one's going inside?"

"The doors are locked. There was a note on the door letting us know that Arthur would be here at 2:30 to let us in."

I looked at my watch—it read 2:28.

"He'll be here pretty soon."

I said this in time to look up and watch Arthur stroll to the doors and scan his key card through the reader at the bottom of the huge doors, before punching in a three-digit code to roll the doors open.

He murmured apologies to us all while we filed inside to retrieve our belongings.

Our rooms were small; therefore we didn't have much room to store the things we needed on missions, such as tents, cooking supplies, etc. In reality, while we were on missions, our camps were fairly similar to military camps. And there was *no* way you could store that much equipment in a tiny, 10x12 room.
Not only that, but the highest ranking leaders on the base are required to keep an inventory of all the weapons and supplies by the Elders. It was a long line of historical failures that led to the government-like rules and regulations; but it was for the best.

The Elders… I shuddered. You had to screw up pretty badly to have to pay them a visit. Usually it was those who were accused of conspiring with the wolves or, in the worst case, the vampires. *That* didn't happen very often…

The infected Flickers were sent there to be executed, and even though it had never happened in my lifetime, I still shuddered at the thought.

"Are you cold or something?" Keegan asked, bringing me back down to Earth. I realized that our other teammates were tagging along behind us, quietly talking amongst themselves about tonight's missions.

"Yeah." I lied.

We all made our way to the different areas of the warehouse, grabbing what we needed. With every grab I made, my body ached in protest. It reminded me that I only had one day left to make it through.

Only one more day, and I'd never have to worry about the fear of becoming a monster again. Though, I'd be spending that last day out on a mission… with no one around to keep me from dying. I was sure my team would try—though it wouldn't make a difference.

Karma wasn't on my side; and while it was easy to defend myself against other opponents, I couldn't fight off nature no matter how hard I tried. I had heard many whispered stories growing up, ones told around bonfires by other elementary level kids. Stories that said when you make it to the last day in the transformation period, nature seems to try it's hardest to get rid of you. When nature conspires to kill you, a few friends will *never* be able to keep you alive.

Arthur was right where he said he'd be. Pounding on my door at exactly 6:00 pm; from there he made me lug all of my stuff out to the tarmac and throw it down, motioning for me to leave it behind.

"Now," Arthur muttered, bringing his hands together with a *clap*. "Come have a drink with me."

"What?" I chuckled. "Arthur, the government outside of our compound frowns upon giving alcohol to minors."

"Yes, but *our* government is careless, and they drink wine all the time."

"I can't stand the taste of wine…" I mumbled.

"Well, then pretend you're drinking it—for my sake. If I don't drink something, I'm going to explode." I followed him to the inside of the helicopter and sat down in the co-pilot's seat; watching him pour me a skimpy glass of wine, and pour himself a hefty one.

"Stressed much?" I asked, taking a whiff of the wine in my glass, and making a funny face at it.

"This is a suicide mission, Levie. If I could, I'd hold you and your team back… but they're making me send you as the head of the mission."

"What are you talking about, Arthur?" I muttered, setting down my glass as my hands began to shake.

"They're sending you out in the heat of it all, or rather—the cold. It'll be freezing while you're out. The crawlers will be everywhere."

"We've all been in that situation before, Arthur."

"This one's different, I can just *feel* it."

I wanted to run and hide. To hide my team, my friends… I had been so excited about running this mission, and now the last thing I wanted to do was get on that helicopter. But instead, I told Arthur what he needed to hear.

"Just tell me what I need to do, and I'll get out of there with as many people as I possibly can." He nodded.

"There'll be six teams going out. We'll have you guy's set up a semi-permanent camp. You'll be out for four weeks, on the lookout for anything pertinent to those nasty *leeches*. All you're doing is scouting through the woods and trying to find them… *any* of them. All we're doing is looking for some way to get information from them."

"Sounds easy enough." I mumbled. Despite my fears, it *did* seem like a pretty easy mission.

"I know… but I just have the feeling that something's going to go wrong." He sighed, and took another decent sized gulp of his wine; and poured himself another glass. "We're sending you out with this," he reached around behind him and pulled out a metal box the size of a shoebox.

"Portable perimeter…"

"Mmhmm… it'll be big enough to cover your camp, you'll just have to program it to reach that far." I nodded in understanding.

They only sent you out with perimeters if they *knew* you'd be attacked without one.

The sounds of footsteps brought Arthur and I out of our trance-like state.

Now I had to break the news to the others.

"Don't tell them if you don't want to—about the suicide

part, I mean." He muttered, downing the contents of the glass, before throwing it underneath the pilot's seat.

Once again, the entire group was here at the same time. *Creepy.*

Are you guys sheep, or what?

"Okay guys… *hey*! Come take a knee, so I can let you all know what's goin' down, then we can get the hell out of here!" I earned a few *whoops* and some laughs, and everyone huddled around me and took a knee.

"Things are pretty simple this time around. We've got one month to catch a crawler and bring it back here. They're sending us out with a perimeter, because they think we can't handle things *ourselves*." I smiled and winked, and everyone laughed.

Damn, I am good at this leading thing.

"My team leads, you guy's just have to listen to me and we won't have any problems. And I'm not hard to please—hopefully we won't have any conflicts." I glanced around the circle of people, and they laughed. I grinned again. "What do you say we get the hell out of here?" I shouted, earning more *whoops* and some whistles this time around.

Once we began the long trek to our campsite, the realization that I had just lied to 35 people—5 of them being my teammates—hit me square in the chest and knocked the air out of my lungs.

They could die, and they didn't even know it yet…

We had walked in a comfortable, quiet manner for hours to get to the camp. By the time we got there, everyone had fallen into the familiar routine of setting up camp.

"I'm letting you all know now; if any of you plan on having sex with the person in your tent, I'm sticking your ass outside of the perimeter so you get eaten by crawlers, you got that?"

People chuckled, and continued to put up their tents; completely ignoring my comment.

"So, Levie… Is our tent going to be outside the perimeter?" Alan murmured from behind me.

"Thanks for the offer, but I'm sleeping with Bridget." I turned around and winked.

"Ouch, you're refusal hurts, Levie."

"Sorry. You'll get over it, I'm sure."

It took everyone a little while to calm down after setting everything up. Once they were, the camp became almost peaceful. The perimeter made a soft, humming noise that had already lulled half of the teams to sleep. It was getting to me, too. Bridget had gone to sleep a little more than an hour ago; and I now sat alone near one of the few fires that had been lit for warmth.

Alone with my thoughts; alone with my pain.

Only one more day…

I could make it through one more day—no problem.

I sighed, and hoisted myself off the log I had been sitting on for hours, unable to ignore the pain that shot through my body when I stood up.

I methodically went through the process of getting my tunic off—tugging the belt out of the loops, peeling off the leggings that went underneath, undoing the leather strap I used to tie my hair up. Leaving myself in only a thin pair of under-armor tights and an undershirt.

I lay down on the roll out mat I had designated as 'mine', and tugged on the covers that Bridget was hogging. She let them go hesitantly, grunting in her sleep as she tried to keep a hold on them.

I smiled sleepily; reveling in the relief that came with going to bed. I gave one last look around the tent, imagining it was my room back home before finally giving in and closing my eyes.

I had sleepovers with Bridget all the time… it was just something we had always done. I would have never thought that this would be the last one…

CHAPTER SEVEN

CHRISTIAN

This was *not* how I wanted to spend my morning—being called in to discuss arrangements with the Elders concerning someone I didn't even *like*.

I prayed that it would simply turn out to be a trip to learn about my next group of kids to train, but the likelihood of that was slim to none. It was the fourth day of the changing process… the last day for her to make it through the change; that goddamn girl that had to be at the wrong place at the absolute wrong time.

The fact that she was a Flicker didn't help the situation any more, especially *my* situation.

If Jace wasn't as scared of the Elders as I was, I would be screwed already.

"Remember, what they don't know won't kill them. As long as they have no clue about her 'origins' you'll be fine; and more importantly, so will *I*."

Jace was a scheming, weasel of a man with mostly good

intentions. I wasn't going to let him down; and I sure as hell wasn't going to let myself down.

"Good morning, Christian." Adelaide cooed as I walked through the door---the same way she did when any fresh meat trailed in front of her.

Both Adelaide and her twin brother, Byron, were ancient beyond belief. Though, when it came to looks they could easily pass as being in their early twenties.

"Mornin' Adelaide, Byron." I nodded towards them both and forced down a grimace.

"We heard you've made a mistake… accidentally changed someone." Adelaide spoke in a shrill, almost unbearable voice.

I nodded.

"And this is the fourth day of the change, correct?" Byron murmured in a collected tone.

I nodded again. "Yes, sir."

"Don't you think you should be following her around, then? We wouldn't want her to run off after she changes." Adelaide stated dramatically.

"I realize that. But she's very strong-"

"Even the strongest fall at the hands of nature, Christian. You must make sure she's here by the time she wakes up from the change. If she isn't, there could be consequences we wouldn't want to deal with." Adelaide began to shriek something again, but Byron held up a hand to stop her.

"You *will* track her down, and you *will* follow her until she either makes the change, or the time strikes midnight. Do *not* come home until then."

With the clap of his hands, and the point of Adelaide's skinny finger, I found myself turning around and following the orders that had been given to me. Pack mentality had been driven into our heads from a young age; when an Alpha gives you orders, you *follow* them.

Until the time strikes midnight! Why don't you just call me Cinderella? I thought as I walked out of the room.

"How'd it go?" Jace asked as I kept on walking. As I turned a corner he continued to follow me…

"They want me to go out and find her!" I said. "I'm never going to be able to do it! She's a Flicker for God sakes! What am I supposed to do, bust through the giant-ass brick wall that *completely surrounds* their base and ask the nearest guard where she is, *before* they rip me to shreds? *I don't think so*!"

"Hey, Kid. Calm down. The patrol guys have spotted Flickers out near the Crawler's territory line—they're looking for captives to take in and interrogate. You said the girl you bit was high rank, right?"

"Yeah, but-"

"No buts, kid. You go out to where they're at, and sniff her out. It shouldn't be that hard. You'll be drawn to her anyway because *you* bit her. Now go! If they know you didn't leave immediately, there's no telling what they'll do! Especially Adelaide…"

While Jace explained to me where the Flickers' camp was located, I focused on forcing myself through the change—deep breathing, mentally pushing out my limbs, and imagining my joints and bones forming into those of a wolf. Years of practice had made the change nearly effortless, so as soon as he finished explaining, I was off; running as fast as I could while still concentrating on making the change.

By the time I had ran through the gates, I was running on four legs rather than two. The woods swallowed me up immediately; the world around me transformed from a comfortable and familiar settlement to a world that was damp, cold, and green… but still familiar.

I ran through the woods with caution, knowing full well that the Flickers could begin their job at any minute. Running into a group of them wouldn't do me any good at all… especially while I was completely alone. I went the longest way around possible.

I got there just in time to watch as everyone woke up; making their way out of their tents and stumbling toward the center of the camp, where the smell of food seemed to be overwhelming to all of them.

She sat off to the side of the camp's open center… sharpening her already deadly sharp arrows.

Sweet Jesus, I thought. *Don't kill yourself with one of those here, in front of everyone! That would only make it harder for me to get you out of here…*

She held the arrow she had just sharpened up to the light, inspecting the tip before placing it back inside the quiver that held the rest of the arrows.

Why did it have to be me? Why did I do this to myself?

Being an alpha by bite is like teenage pregnancy. You can't help but feel bad for bringing the person into this world, but you can't get rid of them… and in the meantime, you've got someone following you around for the next few years until they decide they can do things on their own.

I watched from the bushes as she lifted her bag of arrows up onto her shoulder; the look on her face was one that went along with a wince. She rubbed her arm, and looked around as if to make sure no one had seen her.

With an almost visible jolt of surprise, I realized that she was keeping her injury a secret.

You're keeping it a secret? How the hell did you do that? I wondered to myself.

It didn't seem entirely possible. Considering all the pain she had to be going through—how could you hide *that*?

She walked to the middle of the camp, setting her stuff down and motioning for the rest of the Flickers in the clearing to circle around her.

While I waited to hear what she would say, I picked up on

a gentle, humming sound.

Perimeter… They must have had quite a night to have to put up the perimeter. While the perimeter could prevent vampires from both seeing and getting through to the camp—werewolves had no problems at least when it came to *seeing* through it. No one had ever really attempted to get *through* a perimeter of theirs though, considering it would be a suicide mission to even try.

"We all know where the camp is. We can all see it, which means there's no reason for anyone to have any issues. You all have your own teams, I expect you all to work together and search. We can all go off in a different direction."

Someone in the circle snickered. "Yeah, yeah, I know… I'm no good at this at all! I'm sorry. Any way, you guy's get it right?"

Some people chuckled at her, while others just rolled their eyes. She was in charge… and trying *very* hard to gain the trust of her comrades.

They had always seemed so harsh… so stoic. It didn't make sense for this girl to care so much about what the others thought of her. *Shouldn't she be indifferent?*

"I expect you all to know how to track, too. You should probably know how to get back here." She grinned and rolled her eyes when the others began to laugh again. "If you don't know how to do either of those things… you should probably just kill yourself now."

"Eat as much as you can possibly eat… until you feel like you'll explode. We won't be back here to eat for the rest of the day." Said the man who stood next to her. He had dark hair and scary, wild eyes. His muscles showed through his tunic without much effort on his part.

The others started to drift back into the activities they were doing before the group meeting… And the dark haired man was giving the girl a serious look-over. His eyes drifted from her shoulders, down to her feet, and then slowly back up.

I snickered when she caught him looking and gave him a solid slap across the face.

"You're not getting anywhere, Alan. So stop trying."

"Damn, someone's in a bad mood." The man grumbled, giving another free-basher.

"Just shut up, Alan. I'm getting really tired of your shit."

The guy was a pig—a total jerk.

Rumor had it they liked to sleep around with each other, and that the adults didn't really care. Some people said the adults even slept with the younger one's there…

I used to think it was a load of crap… but not so much anymore…

They argued some more, before the girl turned around and stomped away; at the same time the man—Alan—was cursing her name.

Levie.

The two of them continued to argue with each other until a handful of flickers showed up at their side. It was the same group she had by her side the night of the fight.

I was so caught up in my own thoughts about that night that I didn't even realize they had left. I raced around the camp—hiding within the ferns and bushes—and followed them deep into the woods surrounding their camp in all directions.

The stupid group of flickers had been trekking through the woods for *hours*. *I* had been *following* the stupid no good flickers through the woods for *hours*. Occasionally they'd talk about seeing signs that hinted at one thing or the other—I never did *see* what the hell they were talking about in the first place.

They talked about 'shadows'—one girl, the smallest one—called them echoes. I found myself confusing them for two different things half of the time, the other half, I was too busy trying to figure out what it was they were referring to.

It hadn't been so bad until one of them decided it would be a good idea to cross the river that divided the woods into territories. Then the colder it became, the more downhill my day went. They had crossed it at one of the many man-made land bridges through the water—where the soil and sand under the water was built up so that a person could walk across quickly without getting swept into the current.

I, on the other hand, had to make a wide sweep around and swim across…

"I stopped seeing echoes of them like, three hours ago." The smaller girl stated quietly—I could barely hear her. Levie on the other hand, I could hear loud and clear.

"I told you guys that going over the river would be a *huge* waste of time! *Hello*, the river is *freezing*. What crawler in their right mind would go through freezing water?" she was beyond frustrated with her team; and tired, no doubt.

"Levie, don't be so negative." One of the blondes—the one without long hair—said. He kept a firm grip on Levie's shoulder as he stepped off of a fallen tree trunk; giving it a visible squeeze of reassurance along with his words.

"It's hard not to be negative right now. Especially because it's only getting colder, and we'll have to cross back through the river again…"

I had to admit, I was on her side. The last thing I wanted was for them to cross the river again.

If only they could wait until the sun came up tomorrow morning to move again, then my job would be over, I thought hopelessly as they began to move again.

"We'll be okay, Levie. The water isn't too cold. We've been in colder." She nodded stubbornly at the blonde's words.

"Let's just get back to camp then, I'm freezing."

I resisted the urge to run headfirst into a tree, and chose to growl instead—turning with them and following from within the trees as they made their way back in the direction of the river.

Even as the wind died down to less than a breeze, the temperature around us was dropping. This was obvious to Levie; she shivered violently as she walked.

Somehow they managed to cut their travel time in half on the way back to the river. It had grown dark within the hour and a half it took them to get back to the river, and that made me nervous.

Even as they made it to the river's edge, the temperature still seemed to drop. Levie started to play with the watch on her wrist; it lit up, illuminating her face.

"Guys, it's *literally* getting colder with every minute that passes. Let's just hurry up and get through the river and get back home." Everyone agreed.

They pushed through the weeds that lined the river and stood at the edge, hesitating, not wanting to make themselves any colder than they already were. I didn't like them, but I knew *exactly* how they felt.

The river had risen visibly since they had crossed it almost four hours ago. Before the water had only gone up to their knees, now they would be halfway submerged.

"Maybe we should try to find another spot to cross at..." the man with the long blonde hair shouted over the river's roaring sound.

"You and I both know this is the shallowest spot for miles, Luther! We can't afford to be out here that long—we'll risk the chance of becoming crawler bait."

If chuckling in the form of a wolf were possible, I would have. It had been a long time since I had heard anyone refer to those nasty leeches as *crawlers.* But the situation itself didn't allow for any humor. If these guys made it through the river, I could laugh later.

Levie entered the river last, following behind her teammates and taking the longest to cross.

There was something on her mind that caused her to worry—I could see it clearly on her face. Whether her worry was caused from the bite or from other things, I wasn't sure.

God, I hate this stupid girl for getting me into all of this, I thought.

Her worry was the last thing on my mind, and my hatred for her grew stronger as I watched her hit the water with a splash that was inaudible compared to the roaring river.

If it hadn't been for the girl who had gone into the water before her, they wouldn't have even known she had gone down. It was the girl's deafening screech that alerted the others.

"*Levie*!"

The others scrambled to get across the river and took off at a run along the banks in an attempt to catch up to the fast moving current.

I raced ahead of them, knowing by the feeling in my chest that no matter how fast they ran they would be too late. She was already gone.

Their jobs of serving under her were over.

My job had just begun.

CHAPTER EIGHT

I woke up a lot warmer than I had been when I went to bed the night before. It wasn't hard to figure out why. Bridget's skinny little arms were wrapped tightly around my waist; her head buried in between my shoulder blades.

"Bridget…" I murmured; elbowing her lightly in the stomach to get her to move.

"Mmmm…" she groaned.

"Bridget, you have to let me get up. I need to be up before the others." She mumbled something incoherent and rolled away from me.

I pulled on the leaders tunic that I had been required to bring, tugging at the underarmor sleeves that bunched up at my forearm because they were too long.

I slowly unzipped the tent, hesitating before stepping outside into the cold. I put my boots on as quickly as I could.

The last thing I wanted was frost bite.

The camp was utterly *deserted.* I checked my watch, and

saw that it was barely four in the morning. I could just see the sun beginning to rise in the east. It cast a greyish hue over the motionless tents.

Other than the humming of the perimeter, and the singing of the birds in the trees above us, the camp was as silent as the dead.

I walked silently on the balls of my feet, towards the center of the camp where we had started our bonfire last night. I tossed a dozen or so logs onto the top of the smoldering ashes; topping the logs off with a few handfuls of dried up leaves.

I grabbed a book of matches that had been left outside from the previous night—lit a few—and tossed them into the now growing fire.

I sat near the fire by myself for quite a while; contemplating the night ahead.

During the last few nights, the pain that came with a werewolf bite had been teasing my body; coming and going as it pleased. Today, my body didn't hurt at all. It was simply *alive* with feeling. Everything in my body seemed to be moving at hyper speed. Even as I sat comfortably by the fire, my leg bounced uncontrollably.

I tried to reason out what chance I had of living through tonight. The statistics were bad. In reality, though, I wasn't dying. I was simply changing forms. I was changing into the form of a dirty, mangy, obnoxious monster—regardless of whether or not I really wanted to.

And I really *didn't* want to…

I sighed and hoisted my jittery body off of the log I had been sitting on for a good hour. I knew where the supply of oatmeal was that we were supposed to be eating for breakfast. I knew if I didn't fix the food, no one else would… and then none of us would be happy.

I searched around until I found the huge pot we had

brought along for cooking; filling it about half way with water, and taking it back to hang it over the fire.

I hung it just high enough so that the oatmeal wouldn't burn while I left it unattended.

If all anyone got for breakfast was oatmeal they'd be grumpy, regardless of the fact that they weren't the ones who had to cook.

Tracking down some eggs, and possibly some birds would ensure that no one was grumpy; not to mention it gave me the opportunity to get up and move my unstable body.

As soon as I stepped outside of the camp, I could tell Arthur had made the right decision by sending us with a perimeter.

The woods surrounding us were covered with shadows, left by the crawlers that had passed by our camp the night before.

The way the perimeter worked: it prevented the crawlers from coming too close by radiating a semi-freezing temperature, as well as a deadly shock to any crawler that tried to pass through it. It also made it impossible for them to see our camp from the outside, which was something that came in handy.

The hungrier a particular clan of crawlers was, the worse they smelled. When they were full of blood, and content—they looked like normal people… pretty even. That was where the 'beautiful' vampire stereotype came into play. But the more hungry they grew, the more they resembled the living dead; nasty, ugly, rotting flesh, crazy red eyes… the works. They not only looked half dead, they *smelled* that way as well.

The smell that hung in the air would send any unsuspecting person into a gagging frenzy; it smelled like someone had just dumped a half-rotted body into a garbage can and let it sit there for a few days.

Which meant not only were the crawlers hungry…they were *ravenous.*

Luckily none of them had been ravenous enough to try and pass through the perimeter. The only thing worse than the smell of one of the crawlers was the smell of one up close as the leftovers of a dead one were being cleaned up.

No bodies to clean up today.

It seemed like the birds had taken the day off. After walking around the woods immediately surrounding the camp for about an hour, I came up empty handed. Much to my surprise though, the others didn't mind too much.

I figured it was because they were too tired to care—as long as they got *something*, they were willing to be cooperative.

I chose to sit off to the side and sharpen my arrows rather than fighting for my share of the oatmeal. It wasn't the most important thing on my mind now, anyway.

My arm ached continuously as I moved; sharpening the ends of my arrows, putting them back in the bag, grabbing an unsharpened one… my arm ached with every movement. I was able to contain the pain until I lifted the quiver of arrows up and threw it over my shoulder. I couldn't help but wince, and pray that no one had noticed.

Taking a rough count of the people around the camp, I figured most of them were up and awake enough for me to give orders. I walked to the middle of the camp, dropping my bag in the dirt and propping one of my legs up on one of the logs.

"Hey guys, let's circle up really quick and get this over with. We all know where the camp is. We can all see it… which means there's no reason for anyone to have any issues. You all have your own teams, I expect you all to work together and search. We can all go off in a different direction…" Someone in the circle snickered. "Yeah, yeah, I know… I'm no good at this at all! I'm sorry. Any way, you guys 'get it' right?"

Again someone snickered and I resisted the urge to curl up into a ball and hide.

God, I'm so terrible at this.

"I expect you all to know how to track, too. You should probably know how to get back here." She grinned and rolled her eyes when the others began to laugh again. "If you don't know how to do either of those things… you should probably just kill yourself now."

"Eat as much as you can possibly eat… until you feel like you'll explode. We won't be back here to eat for the rest of the day." Alan boomed, walking until he stood within inches of me. He crossed his arms and puffed out his chest.

"Knock it off, Alan," I hissed.

"Knock *what* off?" he hissed back mockingly; with a wink, he freebashed me without even attempting to cover it up. I felt my lip curl up immediately as I planted a solid slap across his left cheek.

"You're not getting anywhere, Alan. So stop trying."

"Damn, someone's in a bad mood." He grumbled.

"Just shut up, Alan. I'm getting really tired of your shit." He scooted closer to me and leaned down to whisper in my ear.

"Can you blame me for trying?"

"Mmhmm," I mumbled as the others began to appear at our side; dressed and ready for whatever lie ahead.

We had been roaming through the woods for hours now, searching for something that seemed almost impossible to find.

"I stopped seeing echoes of them like, three hours ago." Bridget mumbled.

"I told you guys that going over the river would be a *huge* waste of time! *Hello*, the river is *freezing*. What crawler in their right mind would go through freezing water?" I shouted. The truth was—I was tired, I was cold, and I *had* told them we shouldn't cross the river when they had suggested it.

That had been four hours ago.

"Levie, don't be so negative." Scotty murmured. He kept a firm grip on my shoulder as he stepped off of a fallen tree trunk; giving it a squeeze of reassurance along with his words.

"It's hard not to be negative right now. Especially because it's only getting colder, and we'll have to cross back through the river again…" The idea of having to cross back through the river, with the temperature rapidly dropping, left me wanting to sob.

"We'll be okay, Levie. The water isn't too cold. We've been in colder."

He was right… we had been in frozen waters before; accidentally breaking through the ice that had covered one of the rivers we had attempted to cross had left me with my first case of frostbite.

It was a good thing our doctors and surgeons had created *very* advanced medical techniques and tricks over the years… otherwise I wouldn't be on this mission—I'd be in a wheel chair, missing both of my legs.

This time felt different… off. It was cold—this was true. But when it had been this cold before, the wind had been blowing. Now, there was absolutely no wind. Nothing; not even a small breeze.

"Let's just get back to camp then, I'm freezing.

The temperature continued to drop… feeling colder

and colder with every second that passed. It couldn't be possible for the weather to change that fast, I knew that for a fact; but knowing and feeling were two totally different things.

I shook and shivered as we made our way back to the river; using our own echoes as 'bread crumbs,' so to speak. Being able to literally *see* where we had been made things very simple in finding our way back to camp.

It also cut our travel time in half. It had taken us three hours to get to where we had been, and only an hour and a half to get back.

It didn't seem like it took that long to find our way back to the river… but when we did, it seemed as though the temperature was still dropping.

I pressed the small button on my watch, illuminating the watch's screen. It displayed the temperature in the upper left corner; I watched as it dropped one or two degrees with every minute that passed.

"Guys, it's getting colder with every minute that passes. Let's just hurry up and get through the river and get back home." Everyone agreed.

We stepped through the bushes and high, sticky grass and came within inches of the river's edge.

When we had crossed the river hours before, it had only been up to our knees—hard to walk through, but not impossible. Now, it seemed as though the water would be up to our waists in the spot we had crossed before.

"Maybe we should try to find another spot to cross at…" Luther shouted over the river's roaring sound.

"You and I both know this is the shallowest spot for miles, Luther! We can't afford to be out here that long—we'll risk the chance of becoming crawler bait."

He nodded, and proceeded to tip toe into the water. I followed behind everyone else—it seemed to be a customary thing; everyone knows it's always the last one in the group that gets picked off first in dangerous situations. It only made sense for the strongest to be the last one.

Even though I wasn't really the strongest, I was just in charge.

It didn't really make sense… me being the leader of our team. I wasn't the strongest. I wasn't the quickest thinker. I wasn't the smartest, by any means… so why was it me?

Leaders should be strong, they should be smart, they should be able to come up with amazing plans… they should be everything I'm not. People should look up to their leaders, with awe and wonder; leaders should be able to give advice when it's needed, and be a role model.

I wasn't *any* of these things.

More than anything… leaders shouldn't trip in dangerous places…

I did.

I was focusing too much on why I *shouldn't* be a leader, to realize that the current had picked up, and that I was in the exact middle of the river.

At the same time I realized this, and took another step forward, a rock rolled straight underneath my foot.

Before I had a chance to even *try* and catch my footing, I was down in the water.

It was cold… *so cold.* It soaked into every bit of clothing I had on; and filled up my bag of arrows weighing it down, and pulling me with it down to the deeper part of the river.

I gasped for air before the quiver dragged me beneath the surface, and tried with all of my might to get the strap for the bag untied from around my waist. With every second it took me to untie the knot, my chest screamed in protest.

Breathe! My instincts shouted in my head. *BREATHE!*

I finally got the knot undone, and pushed myself back up to the surface of the water. I was up long enough to see that my team was still making their way across the river—totally oblivious to the fact that I was no longer behind them.

I tried to scream out for help, but instead water filled my mouth and lungs; choking my words before they could be said.

My eyes felt prickly, as if I was crying—there was no way to tell if I actually was.

I got up to the surface of the water again, and took another breath—only to have it stolen away by another wave of the river's current that sent me back down underneath the water again.

This time, I couldn't get back up.

The pain in my chest was unbearable, piercing straight through my lungs. It forced me to gasp for air, air that didn't exist. As of now, the only thing I could see, smell, feel, breathe… was water.

Only water.

The others had been right ahead of me, no more than a few feet away. Sure, it was dark; the night around us was almost as dark as the water we were treading.

I heard thrashing now; was it them coming for me, coming to save me? Or was it just the sound of my own arms and legs, trying to make contact with anything that would pull me up over the surface of the water.

One minute passes. I've screamed and thrashed around enough that I had been able to reach the surface. One gasp of air entered, and then left my lungs too soon. I was half way through another breath when I was thrown back down deeper than I had been before.

Two minutes. I hold my breath for as long as I possibly can. My mouth clenched shut tight while the ice-cold water throws me around, hitting rocks and sunken logs as I go.

Three minutes. The force of hitting a particularly large boulder finally forces the air out. I tried as hard as I could to keep my mouth shut, but the instinct to breathe was too strong. My thoughts blurred together while I focused on trying to get back up to the surface for another breath.

Four minutes. I close my eyes and focus on the dots dancing across my eyelids. *Tell me I'm going to live!* I screamed in my head. No pictures formed, no glimmer of hope was given. Just more dots dancing across my vision.

Five minutes. It was over. I screamed letting the last bit of air I had left float up around me. Closing my eyes, this time I couldn't see anything. No visions, no colored dots or blobs. Just the same dark shade of the water around me.

Six minutes. The water finally stopped moving. So did my mind. I could feel myself shutting down. It was becoming harder and harder to think, to move, to do anything. How ironic, that the water would stop throwing me around at the same time I stopped wanting to move. I could easily swim up to the surface now, I just didn't want to anymore.

The moon shone through the trees surrounding this part of the river, illuminating the water. I could clearly see the halo my hair formed as it wrapped and twisted its way around my face.

I closed my eyes once more; saw a flash of grey across my eyelids…

And then saw nothing.

***I had almost** made it… It was the fourth day… why? Why me?*

I opened my eyes, and tried to focus on anything, *anything* at all, that would let me know it was all a dream.

I was in a room I had never seen before. Dark, wood ceilings, monotone beige walls.

I was laying on a couch I had never laid on before; it was a brownish-leather couch that had been covered in an old blanket, rather than a normal slip cover.

And there was an unfamiliar pair of eyes the shade of the sky during a storm…

They held so much hatred in them, I instantly felt like I had done something wrong… and yet, I wished I could see those eyes with something other than hatred filling them.

CHAPTER NINE

Tears instantly filled my eyes.

"No… no, no, no, *no*!" I screamed, covering my face with my hands and sobbing. I had never cried like this before… not even when my parents had died. This was too much. It was *overwhelming*. I hadn't made it. I wasn't a Flicker anymore. I wasn't *myself* anymore… "What-how… w-why? Why me?"

"I don't have the answer to that…" the man murmured.

I started to sit up; covering my face with my hands. I was on the verge of a breakdown.

"You really need to stay covered up until your temperature stabilizes…" he put his hand against my shoulder in an attempt to push me back down. With a move faster than he could comprehend, I had both hands on either side of his arm; popping his elbow out of place. He growled under his breath—a sound that sounded *very* animalistic—and winced, holding onto his now oddly-angled arm.

"Don't. Touch. Me. *Ever*."

"*God*, I was just trying to help you out!" I grimaced; an expression that pulled my upper-lip up to show my teeth.

Why am I doing that?

"Nice to see you've already got *that* particular face down…"

"What are you talking about?" I demanded.

"Your *snarl*."

"Asshole…"

"You're just going to be *loads* of fun to take care of, aren't you?"

I stood up slowly; and quickly understood what he—I still didn't know his name—had been talking about earlier. As soon as more than half of my body was uncovered I was *freezing*. I immediately started to shiver.

"See… I told you," he muttered, grabbing an over-sized sweatshirt that had been laying over the back of a chair and throwing it at me. I caught it and put it on without hesitation.

"W-why am I s-so c-cold?" I managed to slur without biting my tongue off.

"Because you died in the water… and the water was cold."

"What are you talking about?" I spat I wasn't a fan of cryptic messages.

"When you make the change, you have to die in order to *become* an actual werewolf. I'm sure you knew that already…"

I nodded.

"Well, when you die, your body remains at the temperature it was when you took your last breath."

"How long does it stay like this?" I asked, forgetting for a second how much I hated him. It was his eyes—they still held hatred for me, but they were so *mesmerizing*…

It was the color of them, I was sure of it.

"Until you go through your first phase… Even after then, your body temperature will be really susceptible to your mood." He murmured; he started to pace back and forth, clearly uncomfortable. "Why are you staring at me?"

I forced my eyes away from his face; instead I stared at my hands and avoided his question by asking one of my own.

"How long until then? I hate being cold…"

"It'll be about a month." Tears started to roll down my cheeks again. "Are you going to fix my arm? I *know* you know how to do it. You know how to do *everything*."

"Nope." I mumbled, wiping at the tears that wouldn't seem to go away. "Not until you answer more of my questions."

"What more is there to ask?" he shouted throwing his arms up in the air, and whining when the movement jerked his arm in an un-jerkable direction. I watched his eyes grow pained and angry; filling with tears that he refused to let fall. "What more is there to ask…" he whispered again in a pained tone.

"Why me?"

"You already asked that! And I already told you—I don't have an answer to that question!"

"You don't have an answer you're willing to tell me? Or you just don't know what the answer is?" I screamed; my temper flaring up—getting the best of me.

"I don't have an answer at all!"

"So, what? You just bit me out of boredom!"

"*No*! I just…"

"You just *what*?"

"I don't know, okay? I don't know why I did it! Is that what you'd like to hear, Levie?"

"H-how do you know my name?"

"I'm your creator… your alpha… I knew your name the

second I bit you."

"*I hate you.*" I whispered. He knew my name. He didn't have a reason for biting me. He was heartless, careless, *evil.* "You *ruined* my life. I didn't have much going for me! I didn't have many friends… and you took everything away from me! Now, I have *nothing*! And it's *all your fault*!" I had gone one step above screaming;]… I was screeching.

"I'm sorry. I can honestly say I'm sorry… especially because I'm not your biggest fan either."

He spun around, and walked out of the only visible door in the general area—shutting it behind him.

I heard the scratching noise that came with the dragging of a chair; but by the time I had reached for the door knob it was too late. The door was already blocked; preventing me from turning the knob to get out.

"What are you doing?" I yelled through the door.

"Giving you time to cool off before you hurt yourself!" He shouted back through the door. Then he was gone.

I kicked and threw myself against the door countless times, screeching some more and screaming for him to let me out. When he didn't return, I quickly grew tired. My exhaustion seemed to fuel my anger—which in turn caused my body to shudder even more. I crawled back to the couch I had thrown my fit on earlier and curled up in a ball; pulling the unfamiliar blankets up around me and trying my hardest to stay still so that I would warm up.

Sleep refused to come easily, but eventually, it came.

I could hear them talking outside my door… talking about *me*. *Him* and some girl… clueless, by the sound of it.

She was probably his girlfriend.

The door creaked open, and I stood up—ready to lunge at him.

He walked in with his arms up; closing the door behind him.

The girl was still out there… I could hear her breathing—her heart beat.

"I can tell she's still out there. I can hear her breathing."

"It's because you're angry. Your senses are heightened." He murmured. I realized that he was still being careful not to move his arm too much.

"Why is she still there?"

"I couldn't talk her out of wanting to meet you…"

"Tell her to go away-"

"I can't, Levie. It'll hurt her feelings; you *have* to be nice to her. She's sensitive."

"Awe, how cute! You think your girlfriend's *sensitive*."

"She's not my girlfriend. She's practically my little sister." He said quietly, keeping his cool. He looked toward the door before moving closer to me. "She's *different*," he whispered; tickling my ear with his breath.

"What the hell does that mean?" I whispered back sarcastically.

"You don't know what—Oh, never mind. You'll see in a moment. She was just born different from other people. She's really sweet… just… be nice, *okay*?"

Before I had a chance to say anything else, the door creaked open once more, and a petite, blonde head appeared in the crack. Her eyes were blue… not like *his;* her eyes were very clear and innocent.

"Christian? Can I see her yet?"

"Yeah, Matelyn… you can come in."

Matelyn's hair was almost white… her petite form couldn't be any smaller without her looking like a child. While she didn't look like a child, her personality was definitely *childish*. She walked with a gracefulness that reminded me of a dancer—one hand held out as if for balance, the other tugging at her hair nervously. She wore a pair of sweats and a tank top; one of her bra straps had fallen down and was now resting on her arm rather than her shoulder. Her hair was slightly wavy, and had a single braid down the right side.

Her eyes were bright, and her smile was genuine.

She was the perfect description of innocence as she stood in front of me, chewing on her lip and batting her eyelashes.

"I'm Matelyn." She murmured almost too quietly to hear. I realized that I could no longer hear her heart beat… she had calmed me down…

"I'm Levie." I murmured back.

"You're pretty." I was unable to smile. *Who was this girl?*

"You're pretty, too." I blinked, and suddenly her tiny arms were wrapped around my shoulders; her hair tickling my face.

"You'll be my friend, right?" she smiled encouragingly.

"Uh, *sure*?" She smiled again. And skipped away, out of the room… without saying another word. "I think I'm confused…" I mumbled. It was as if the girl was stuck in the toddler stage of life.

"I told you she was different," he mumbled closing the door behind Matelyn's long disappeared figure.

"Is she *sick*?"

"We don't know… maybe. Some days she'll be like this, other days she'll be not necessarily normal, but not as *crazy*— "

"She's *not* crazy. You said she was different."

"It's just a figure of speech, Levie."

"She's *kind*. She's the only one who's been kind to me *here* so far, so you can't expect me to have any problems with her."

"She's still a wolf."

"Yeah? Well so am I now, apparently. And if you think

I'm *idiotic* enough to *attack* a wolf on *your* territory, you're out of your mind."

"That's *not* what I was *saying*."

"Whatever you're saying is irrelevant to me. I don't *care*."

"All I ask is that you protect her in any way you can. Even if you don't like the rest of us," he grumbled quickly so I wouldn't have a chance to interrupt again. "We protect her, so I'd hope you would too."

"*We*?"

"The others and I… and hopefully you…"

"You're asking an awful lot of someone who doesn't like wolves and was just turned in to one. I think you should know that," I muttered. "And I'll protect anyone who *deserves* it. I'll protect her."

"Whatever you say." He sat down on the couch where I had been laying for an hour or so.

"So have you figured out why you did it?" I asked him quietly. I sat next to him and sighed; leaning back and making myself comfortable.

"Nope, Levie, I haven't. I don't know if I ever *will* have an answer for you…"

I let out another sigh, and closed my eyes—I could have jumped for joy when little lights began to dance across my eyes.

"I can still see!" I whispered excitedly, more to myself than to him.

"Being a werewolf doesn't make you blind, Levie."

"No, you idiot. I can still use my visions!"

"Really?" He murmured, sounding somewhat interested in my latest discovery.

"Yes!" I smiled excitedly, once again forgetting the situation I was in. I caught him staring at my lips; pulled into a smile as they were. "What?"

"Nothing, really… You just look a lot different when you're happy."

"Don't get used to that…" I muttered. "That doesn't happen often."

"I figured." He mumbled, rubbing his eyes and hoisting himself up off the couch.

"Where are you going?" I asked without opening my eyes; I was watching the little lights dance around, without making them form a picture of my future.

"To get you more blankets so you don't freeze, then I'm going to bed."

A dozen blankets or so later, I didn't think I'd be able to move at all in my sleep. And of course, he was walking out of the room and leaving me alone, *again.*

"Goodnight, Levie." He muttered, uncaringly.

"Thanks," I spat. "For ruining my life."

He shook his head, and flicked off the lights. Leaving me in complete darkness.

I froze for the entire night. I wrapped myself up in a cocoon of blankets, and still shuddered uncontrollably.

I drifted in and out of sleep without gaining any relief or rest.

The only thing I was able to gain, were visions of the future… my new future.

I woke up once again—freezing, as was to be expected. I half expected to wake up in a tent with Bridget and the rest of my team; the entire thing having been a dream…

My team, I thought. They had to be looking for me. I wasn't even sure how long it had been since I… *drowned.* How long had they been looking for me?

You have to get out of here! You need to get back to them! They could get hurt without you!

I started to unfold myself from the blankets; panicking

when it seemed I would never get out of them—which only resulted in me growing colder.

I felt something warm and hard underneath my foot the second I stepped off of the couch. It whined when I moved…

I looked down to see a heap of blankets, and an old, beat up pillow. The blankets stirred again, this time to reveal a tuft of white-blonde hair…

Matelyn…

It didn't matter that I had only known her for a few hours…

How could I leave my poor, innocent, clueless little friend behind?

What would she do if Christian told her I had left? I was her *friend…*

I couldn't leave her alone.

Since when do you have a conscience, Levie? Especially when it comes to people you don't even know! I cursed myself for telling the girl I would be her friend; but she was just so *kind*—kinder than even the majority of my comrades.

I sighed. Instead of climbing back underneath the thousands of covers that lay in a heap on the couch, I grabbed a few blankets and a pillow and threw them down next to Matelyn. I plopped down beside her; using some of her blankets as a makeshift mattress.

It took only seconds for her to roll over and wrap her skinny arms around my waist.

It then only took me seconds to fall asleep again.

CHAPTER TEN

"Matelyn," I murmured, prying at her arms that were wrapped in a death grip around my waist, as they had been for the entire night.

"Mmmm…" She grumbled and tightened her grip.

"Matelyn, come on. I need to get up." Her head was pressed against my shoulder; her body couldn't get any closer to mine without her being on top of me.

"Here, let me help." Christian mumbled. He had appeared out of nowhere, without me realizing it.

I'm losing it… completely losing it. He scratched at his head before wrapping his burly arms around Matelyn's sleeping form and tossing her on the couch.

"You didn't have to do that. You could have just unhooked her arms."

"Too late now. And who cares? She didn't wake up…"

"Man, you're a *dick* in the morning."

"Only when someone I don't like is *sleeping on my couch*."

He retorted.

"I wasn't on the couch, I was on the floor." I spoke sarcastically and unwound myself from the blankets wrapped around me.

"And where do you think you're going?" Christian spat in return, grabbing my arm tightly as I got up.

"*I'm* going to the bathroom. Unless you want me to use your *floor*?" I smirked the second he let go of me.

"Put the toilet seat back up when you're finished."

His bathroom wasn't too small, like I had been expecting. The amenities were as basic as was to be expected in the middle of nowhere. The walls were unpainted; the floor, a boring continuation of the linoleum flooring found in the kitchen. The tile around the sink was a clean yellow-ish color that stuck out sorely next to the white shower. The wolves weren't sticklers for uniformity. They got their hands on whatever they could, and made it work.

The toilet wasn't anything special, either. When I used my foot to put the lid down, it clacked loudly – the way plastic almost always does when it hits something.

My hands smelled like chemicals after I washed them. There would be no more girlish amenities for me; my life of pretty soaps and shower gels was over.

I left the toilet seat down purposely and left the bathroom, dodging out of the way in time to avoid getting shoved by him as he made his way – clothes and towel in hand – into the bathroom to shower. With out looking, I heard the door shut, and the lock click in to place.

What did he think I was going to do, peek in on him?

I sighed and waited quietly until I heard the water come on, before standing up to stretch.

I had been too upset and preoccupied to look around the room the day before; so I decided to take advantage of my situation, and look around.

The walls were all the same uniform, beige color. The light fixtures were plain—nothing special. I guessed that I was in what would normally be the living room—though the room itself hardly seemed "lived" in.

The couch was hard, and not broken in—something I had learned from attempting to sleep on it the night before. A dusty coffee table sat on the left side of the couch. Across the room from the couch were two chairs and another small table in-between them. The chairs were chocolate brown, and looked just as uncomfortable as the couch was.

Off of the small living room, was an even smaller kitchen. The cabinets were made of some unidentifiable wood, and the counters were covered in the same dingy looking yellow tile that could be found in the bathroom. There was a miniscule refrigerator. No stove.

I crept to the refrigerator and glanced inside. To my surprise, it was fully stocked with no rotting food in it at all. I made a mental note to remember the food was there, and moved on to the rest of the place.

I crept up to the bathroom door, making sure the water was still running, before I made my way to the last room of the house.

I wasn't sure why I felt like I needed to see his room, but boredom fueled my curiosity. Unlike the rest of the house, it *wasn't* beige, or yellow, for that matter. It was a creamy, off-white color. Some areas of his room were almost grey, where others reminded me of the color of buttermilk frosting. His floor was covered with the same white linoleum as the kitchen and bathroom, but there were so many rugs – not a single one matching – on the floor that the linoleum was almost invisible. There was a chair in the corner near the door that had a few blankets draped over it; I assumed they were left overs from when he had brought me blankets the night before. In the opposite corner, there was both a dresser and a closet.

The dresser was cluttered with pictures and handwritten notes from people I didn't know… people I would probably *never* know.

His giant window was covered with frothy curtains that were so long they spilled onto his floor and reminded me of soft, white waves.

In the middle of his room, was what had to be the biggest bed I had ever seen.

White, and covered in blankets and pillows; it seemed like a bed someone would never want to move from. I hesitantly touched the blankets, feeling how soft they were –how warm and comforting they could be. I felt a pang of jealousy at the thought of him sleeping here --on this bed fit for the gods-- while I was sleeping on the sorry excuse for a couch in the other room.

His nightstand was cluttered with empty glasses and books ranging from dusty and untouched to recently read. I picked up the one that appeared to be the least dusty and skimmed through the pages towards the middle of the book.

I heard the bathroom door click open in the other room and immediately threw the book down and darted for the door, arriving just in time to nearly collide with him.

"What are you doing in here?" Christian spat the second he saw me. "Get the hell out of my room!"

He shoved me out of his way.

"I hate you."

"If you hate me so much, why haven't you tried to kill me yet?" he grumbled while he changed. I had barely heard him from the couch I had apparently been relegated to.

"Because I'm not stupid."

"Some would think otherwise."

"*Try me*," I hissed. "I could take your ass down in a *second*."

"Levie, being smart isn't the same as being skilled-"

"Don't call me *Levie*."

"What the hell am I supposed to call you then?" he shouted, stepping out of his room to stare at me incredulously. When I didn't answer, he shook his head and continued to slam me with more insults. "And besides, would you be able to take me down if I phased first? Hmm?"

"Get away from me."

"I'm sorry? You're in *my* house."

"*Get. Away. From. Me.*"

"Fine, have it your way. You can't run away from this, *Levie.* You don't have any other choice but to accept it. You're one of us now, whether I want you here or not."

With that he walked out the same door he had the night before—the one that led to lord knows where—slamming it behind him. I heard the familiar sound of the chair being slid under the doorknob before hearing the sound of his footsteps stomping away.

I was trapped again. I backed up to the nearest wall and slid down it.

I finally let myself cry—I was well overdue that luxury.

Matelyn came eventually. I heard her throw the chair that was in the way of the door down what I assumed to be another hallway. She stepped through the door carefully, closing the door behind her with her hip while balancing two plates in her hands.

"I brought lunch," she smiled. She set the plates on the coffee table and motioned for me to come eat. I rolled off the couch and tried to keep my excitement over the food from showing.

I never thought I would get so excited over a turkey sandwich—but considering how much had changed in my life over the past two days, I was allowed to find joy in at least one simple pleasure. I wolfed down the sandwich she had brought for me, and even ate half of hers once she was full.

"Is he not feeding you?" she asked bluntly as she tossed the paper plates I had all but licked clean into the small garbage can in the corner.

"Is he supposed to be feeding me?"

"Don't be ridiculous, Levie. Just because he doesn't like you it doesn't mean he can *starve* you to death. You're his responsibility." Christian had been right about Matelyn; she seemed to be having one of her normal days today. "Are you still hungry?" she asked me, cocking one of her pale blonde eyebrows.

"Yeah, but-"

"But *nothing*. If you're hungry, you'll eat." She grabbed my hand and dragged me to what I considered to be the front door.

"I can't go out there! He'll see me!" I hissed, wrenching my hand out of hers.

"No one's home. Not even Christian. It's just me…"

"Why are you all alone?"

"No one needed my help with anything today, so I just stayed home. Now come on!" she opened the door and darted down the hall with a girlish, excited squeal. I followed her slowly. She had already disappeared before I started to move, though. Having rounded the corner at the end of the hall and gone out of sight.

"Matelyn?"

"I'm in the den!" she shouted back. I followed the sound of her voice down the hall and picked up my pace.

The walls were paneled in oak. The floor, covered in very light, cream colored carpet. The lighting stayed dim through the entire hall, until I reached what I assumed to be the den.

It was much more obvious that this room was actually *lived* in. The room was large—to accommodate a lot of people.

Three love seat couches, and three chairs were scattered somewhat haphazardly around the room—all of them faintly orbiting within reach of the decently sized coffee table in the middle. The chairs were leaning toward tan in color, and had seen a lot of use. They didn't really match the couches very well; two of which were greyish-blue in color, they other one was olive-ish. The only thing that made them all match were the identical dark brown throw pillows that were scattered throughout the room… most of them were currently on the floor.

There were a few blankets that matched the pillows color wise thrown over the backs of the couches or wadded up in heaps. Of course, some were on the floor as well.

There was a plush looking grey blanket on one of the couches, and I immediately knew it was Matelyn's. On the other end of the same couch, was a similar blanket in pink.

An abandoned card game was spread out on the coffee table, along with some leftover bowls of cereal and glasses of water.

All of this had been just outside my personal, *monotone* prison cell.

How many of the people who usually inhabited this room knew I was here? The same amount that had chosen not to come to my rescue…

"You can sit wherever, Levie. Just don't mess up the card game on the table."

I nodded and sat on one of the couches, ignoring the overwhelming feeling that I was encroaching on someone's privacy.

"Matelyn, how many people live here?"

"Seven, counting you."

"Oh, but you don't really count me, do you?"

"*I* do. Who cares if Christian doesn't?" she wrenched the metallic door of the refrigerator open and stared at the contents inside.

The kitchen in here—the *common* kitchen, I supposed it could be called—was similar to the one in Christian's room, only on a bigger scale.

"There's not much to eat, really," Matelyn murmured, closing the refrigerator doors. "We can make something if you want, though."

"Like what?" Matelyn hesitated before darting over to the pantry across the room and peering inside. She popped her head back out with a smile. "We've got stuff to make spaghetti!"

"*Deal.*"

I helped Matelyn make what was probably the biggest pot of spaghetti I had ever seen. She explained that she might just as well make it for dinner, and that there were a lot of people to feed.

After chopping our way through most of the kitchen's supply of tomatoes and onions, the den smelled amazing, and I was starving again.

"Once it's heated up altogether, you can have some."

"I don't know if I can wait that long," I grumbled. She laughed at me.

"You'll be alright." She grabbed a spoon out of one of the many drawers in the kitchen and sampled some of the sauce from the pot. "It's pretty warm now, if you're ready for some."

I practically dived for the bowl she handed to me. I filled it to the brim with spaghetti and went back to my place on the couch to eat. Matelyn followed me and sat on the opposite end.

"Do you like Christian?" I asked Matelyn between bites.

"Christian is like my brother, I've known him for as long as I can remember, so of course I like him."

"He doesn't seem like such a nice guy," I grumbled, avoiding saying what I *really* thought about him.

"One of these days you'll see how he really is. The way he's acting now—this isn't the real him."

"Then why is he acting this way?"

"Because of *you*. Can you really blame him? He hates himself just as much as he hates you. Not only because he has to take care of you for the rest of *his* life; he knows he's ruined *your* life."

"Yeah, he especially doesn't seem like the selfless guy that would care about ruining *my* life."

"You'll see, one of these days, Levie. You'll understand who he really is."

CHAPTER ELEVEN

The doorknob rattled. Matelyn and I had been chatting quietly for a while, both of us being careful about what we said to each other because in all honesty, neither of us truly knew what was safe to say. The food had been placed in the oven to keep it warm while we talked. Things were calm, up until now.

The sound of that door opening made me drop everything. I slammed the cleaned plate onto the coffee table and bolted for the nearest hallway, hoping it was the one out of several that actually led to Christian's room.

"Levie! Where are you going?" I heard Matelyn shout after me. I said nothing. I was already rounding the corner into the hallway. I was out of sight already, and so close to my safe haven that I didn't realize the chair in the hallway, the one Matelyn had thrown down when she came to rescue me. Before I could stop running, my legs had already gotten tangled in the chair. I threw my arms out to brace myself; I fell *hard* and prayed that no one would come running to figure out what had happened.

Who am I kidding? No one cares enough to waste their energy.

I scrambled up; ignoring the ache in my legs and throwing the door open ahead of me. I closed it quickly, locking the inside lock behind me and finally allowing myself to breathe.

I slid down the door until I was sitting on the floor and listened to the voices coming from the other room. Only two people were speaking, and I recognized both of their voices. Christian and Matelyn were arguing, *quite* loudly. I listened as Christian screamed about how I didn't deserve to leave that room; Matelyn screeching back that I was still a person who needed the basics of life. That I had to be fed, regardless of the fact that Christian had "screwed up".

I bit my lip, knowing that would piss him off. It was too low of a blow to go unnoticed. Moments later I heard the plate I had left on the coffee table shatter against the wall. I flinched at the sound that seemed to echo through the halls.

"Christian, you need to calm down *now.*" I heard someone new say in a loud, yet calm manner. It was a girl; her voice held a tone that was almost as commanding as Christian's had been. Like an alpha's, only with more malice. I could imagine the way her face must have looked as she said that—her eyes narrowed, her eyebrows pulled together in frustration, her lips in somewhat of a grimace as she spoke calmly enough to scare someone.

"Watch your place, Elena." He snapped back. I heard the sound of chairs scooting against the wooden floor.

"*Make me.*"

"You're not her *alpha*, Christian."

There was the girl again, and then someone new—another man's voice. They were standing up, their voices escalating. Would they really fight over me? People were taking my side, having no clue who I was.

They knew who Christian was, though. They were siding

against him regardless of that—what did that say about *him*? Matelyn had said he was a good man. But was he really? Maybe they were enforcing tough love. I couldn't tell from behind my prison cell door.

I knew I had to stop this before it tore up a family, though. If he were going to fight anyone it would be me. Without a lot of thought behind my actions, I unbolted the door and ran down the hallway straight into the semi-circle of arguing friends. I had never felt like such an outsider.

"*You*," Christian hissed. "Get *out*."

"If you're going to fight someone because of *me*, it should be *me* you fight. Don't you think? There's no reason to tear up a family—so tear me up instead."

"*Get out*!"

"*No*!"

"You are overstepping your place, *Levie*."

"Then teach me a lesson. *Come on*. Or are you *scared* I'll kick your ass?"

Internally, I was terrified. He was angry now; angrier than I had ever seen him. Angrier than he had been the night he had bitten me. I could see the others in the room consciously take a step back, away from Christian and I.

I was shivering like I always did when I was worked up. That much was obvious. But regardless of what I felt on the inside, I was still angry. And *that's* what showed on the outside. I took a step forward as everyone else took another step back.

"What, are you afraid to hit a *girl*? You've hit me before, it's not going to make a difference now."

Christian's face looked different; the difference between anger and rage could be made clear on his face. His skin shined with a layer of sweat; his face grew red as his breath came faster. He was *beyond* mad.

His blue eyes were burning; smoldering with hatred.

"Levie, you're pushing it," Matelyn whispered. "Let him calm down."

I ignored her and took another step towards him. I could see it in his eyes how badly he wanted to hit me; how much he wished he could lash out. He was struggling to hold his rage back. I was slowly knocking down the wall he had built up. He did a pretty good job of holding himself together until his back hit the couch and there was nowhere else to run.

All it would take was one more step. One step closer, and he would snap. It all came down to the fact that you can't trap a wild animal. And as of now, Christian was wild to the core.

"I ruined your life, right? So get rid of me!" I took that step and instantly regretted it. He took me down to the floor before I even had a chance to protect myself. Christian didn't seem like the kind of person to hit a girl, no matter how mad he got. But he didn't see me as a girl, especially not now.

I was a nuisance, a plague that made him *sick*. I wasn't identifiable, in his eyes, as anything other than something to hit. So when he hit me; I had already been expecting it. I hadn't been expecting it to hurt as much as it did, though. He went straight for my jaw, hitting me hard enough that I bit through my cheek. I could taste the blood pooling in my mouth as I made attempt after attempt to hit him back. I let him think he would win for a while. Though the truth was that neither of us would win this fight. We each held our own as the others stood by, horrified, but not making a move to stop anything. I saw my opportunity to end this all, and took it.

He was on top of me for a moment, sitting on my stomach and breathing heavily as we fought off each other's blows. I hit him as hard as I could in the stomach, causing him to wheeze and loose focus for a moment. That moment was all I needed.

I slid my leg up and used it as leverage to flip him off of me. When he hit the ground, I mimicked him—sitting on his stomach. Instead of hitting him I made sure my knees were holding his arms in place so he couldn't fight back. He struggled until I pushed his head into the floor with my arm—strategically placed so he would stop struggling and slowly choke at the same time.

His face slowly turned from red to a purple-ish color.

"This stops now," I murmured. "You can hate me all you want. But *this*—" I motioned to the others in the room, regarding the way he was treating everyone else. "—This stops *now*." He panted and gasped, but his eyes conveyed his anger still. I got up and stepped back, letting him get up.

He shoved me once before turning and stomping out the door. Over his shoulders, I could see the dark outline of trees and lights in the distance. There was more beyond these walls, I just wasn't allowed access to the fresh air that sat just a few feet away.

As he slammed the door, the incident I had caused crashed down around me. Five pairs of eyes made me feel like a bug on the ground about to be crushed. I had to run; I had to get out from underneath those *eyes*.

"I'm *sorry*," I whispered, before darting towards that sacred hallway. "*So* sorry."

I *had* to stop swallowing the blood that was pooling in my mouth. My stomach was beginning to feel as if it were turning in on itself; I felt like I was moments away from throwing up. I ran to the eerily clean sink in the bathroom and continuously spit until the running water ran clear rather than pink. My jaw was dark purple and ugly. My cheek was swollen. I had a few bruises here and there, but nothing was too bad. I had looked worse in the past

I hadn't looked at Christian. I had no idea how bad his injuries were compared to mine. I wasn't excited to find out, though. I knew it would be a while until he returned, but when he *did*, things weren't going to be pleasant.

After finding a frozen bag of some unidentifiable object in the freezer, I found my way into his room. It was the last place I should be, especially in the event that he did come back tonight; finding me in his room would only piss him off. But the living room was too empty, too lonely…

Sitting in his room was a risk I was willing to take.

I brought a few blankets and a pillow from the living room with me and sat in the corner of the room, next to his closet, making sure not to touch anything. I wrapped myself up burrito style and laid down, positioning the frozen object underneath my jaw in an attempt to stop its aching.

Why did you do that? I asked myself. I had practically attacked Christian in front of four complete strangers and one semi-acquaintance. They would see it as my hatred for him—which honestly, some of it *was* the reason behind my actions. Matelyn might see it as me not wanting her to get into trouble.

More than anything, I had done it to save myself. Because if the little pack killed each other off and I was the only one left because I had cowered in the other room, *guess* who would be blamed for it all?

It sure as hell wouldn't have been Christian.

Everyone in the pack would forgive him for his actions today. They understood that he was stressed out because of *me*. No one would blame him; and if they did, they would justify it regardless. But would anyone justify *my* actions? Did I really *care* if anyone justified my actions?

When would I be let into their little circle? When would I be considered a friend and not an enemy? Did I really *want* to be considered a friend? *Would* I ever be considered a friend, or was I just supposed to sit by quietly while everyone went on with their lives?

There were so many questions left unanswered.

Once again, I thought about the rage that had colored Christian's face. He really didn't consider me a living *thing* at all. I was just something that had ruined a portion of his life. Like a stray animal no one wanted, but no one had the heart to kill either. So instead of doing anything with me, I was just given the bare minimum of basics and ignored.

At least you're getting fed now. I reminded myself. *Well, at least you were up until today.*

If my last meal had been Matelyn's spaghetti, life was alright.

Things would have been so much easier if I just hadn't stumbled. I had been so close to making it through the mess I had gotten myself into.

What had my team done without me? Christian had been there to fish me out of the water once I had died. That much I knew. So had they seen him? Did they know what had really happened to me, or did they think that the river had just swept me away?

Were they looking for me? Would they *find* me?

It's only been two days… I reminded myself. Why did it seem like it had been so much longer?

Even if they were searching for me, there was no way my team would be here soon. Then there was the matter of what I was now. I didn't want to accept the fact that I was something completely different now than I had been three days ago; but the fact of the matter was that even if they *wanted* to rescue me from the prison I was in now, they couldn't take me far. Now, they would consider me a monster.

Hell, even *I* considered myself a monster.

The thought made me curl in on myself even further. *I was a monster now.* There was no getting around it. In a few weeks, I would see the consequences of the mess that had been made out of my life, and there was no way to stop it.

I had no idea how long I had been laying on the ground, wallowing in my thoughts. The sound of the door clicking open in the other room brought me out of my trance. Panic sent my stomach into knots and my mind spiraling out of control.

It was too late to run and hide somewhere—and that wasn't how I did things. Not to mention, even if I tried, there really wasn't anywhere *to* hide. I could hear his footsteps now; he was coming this way. So I did what any child would have done…

I pretended to be asleep.

It worked, too.

I focused on keeping my breathing slow and steady when I heard him enter the room. I heard a heavy sigh slip from his mouth, no doubt in regards to finding me lying in the corner. I was terrified as he moved closer. He kneeled down beside me, though I had no idea how close he really was because I couldn't open my eyes.

"Dammit," he whispered. I felt him touch my jaw and froze—forgetting to breath, forgetting to function completely.

Please don't hit me again, please don't hit me again…

"You're a terrible faker, you know," he murmured. I heard him grunt as he flopped down onto the floor next to me. "And don't act so scared. I'm not going to hit you while you're down."

"But you *will* hit me again? Thanks for the warning." I opened my eyes and sat up slightly so I would be able to glare at him. "You *piss* me off."

"The feeling is mutual." He grumbled something incoherent and grabbed my makeshift icepack, and unwrapped it from the pillowcase I had wrapped it in. It had thawed enough that I could see it had once been corn.

"I'm going to go put the corn back where it belongs. I'll

grab you a real icepack from the big kitchen."

I was weary of his new behavior. Mostly because I had never seen him calm like this, and also because I had no idea how long it would last. When he returned, he handed me the icepack he had promised, wrapped in a dishtowel.

"How come you aren't hurt?" I grumbled. I knew I had gotten in a few decent hits. He should at *least* have a few bruises *somewhere*.

"Don't you know we heal quickly?" he furrowed his eyebrows. "You would be fine already if it weren't for the fact that you haven't phased yet. You got me pretty good, though. I couldn't tell anyone what happened because I couldn't move my face."

I sniggered; the movement made my jaw hurt.

"I think you broke one of my ribs, too," Now *that* made me proud of myself. It had been awhile since I had broken anyone's ribs. "It looks like I got you pretty bad, though."

Once again he touched my face, turning my head so he could see the dark splotches that colored my jaw line.

"Thanks for containing the pain to one side of my face."

"I'm not proud of this," he said with a small shake of his head. He wasn't amused by my sarcasm.

"Sorry…"

"Why *did* you attack me?" he asked, somewhat changing the subjects.

"For *one*, I didn't attack you. I provoked you. Then *you* attacked *me*," I muttered. "I did it because you were fighting with your friends. Your problem isn't with them, it's with me…"

"You did this so I wouldn't get into a fight with Elena?"

"I suppose that's one way of putting it," I shrugged. "Also, I hate you and I really wanted an excuse to hurt you."

He chuckled darkly. I couldn't tell if I had actually amused him, or if he was just making an effort not to punch me again.

"The feeling is mutual," he repeated dryly before getting up.

Oh, if only he knew how aware of that I really was. Tonight I had seen a rare, tolerable side of Christian. It had me wondering whether or not things were making a turn around. Perhaps he had decided I wasn't as poisonous as he had previously believed me to be.

Though when the morning came, he was gone before I had even woken up.

When he returned there was yet another tense conversation out in the den with whom I assumed to be Elena—the girl who had made an attempt to calm him down the day before. Only now, she seemed to be riling him up. I didn't listen in on too much of their argument; only enough of it to find out it was about me.

When things grew quiet out there, he moved back to his room. A look of disgust clouded his features when he saw me sitting on the couch. He was distant. Not a word was spoken to me.

And the hatred continued.

CHAPTER TWELVE

I didn't leave that room again. Matelyn continued to come; continued to try and coax me out of the dormitory-style prison cell I had exiled myself to. She reminded me that I could leave—that I didn't *have* to stay back here.

I continued to remind her that this was where I needed to be.

My change in mood made her weary. I could feel it every time she walked into the room. Call it a wolf's sense. She wasn't as comfortable as she had been—as if she was waiting for me to attack her like I had Christian.

Yet every day, she came back.

"Why do you keep coming back here every day?" I asked her once.

"Because you're back here all alone."

"But you don't like it back here; I can tell," I murmured. "I make you nervous."

"You've always made me nervous. You make everyone nervous, Levie. Christian told us what you were from day one."

"And yet, here you are."

"I'm just waiting for you to prove me wrong. That's all. So far, you've done a good job of it."

I didn't want to prove anyone wrong, though. I wanted to be the leader again. I wanted to scare others with my authority. I longed to hold a bow in my hand again—to shoot something, hit something, *anything*. I wanted my old life back, and I couldn't have it.

I'd never get it back.

The times when that realization made itself clear again put me in a dangerous mood. I had allowed myself to get *way* too comfortable in this place—this hellhole. It was the comfort that confused me. These *animals* had killed some of my friends; people I had grown up with. They had even come close to killing me a couple of times, that is, until Christian finally succeeded in doing so.

With all of their offenses, why did they seem so kind? They didn't seem like the killing machines they had been made out to be. They didn't constantly train for battle; they worked as a whole to keep everyone alive and happy.

There was a window in Christian's room that allowed somewhat of a view of what was outside my prison cell. From looking out that very window, I could see the things that went on every day. Some people would do some sort of farm work, growing what they could for the entire group. Others would take the ingredients grown in the field and turn them into the things that people needed, like bread, pasta, and sauces.

There were the younger kids who took sparring lessons in the grassy area near what appeared to be the communal kitchen of sorts. They were taught how to hold their own, and nothing more. They weren't trained to be psychotic killers, or skilled assassins. They were simply trained to do what they needed to do.

When they were done practicing I watched as the boys

would laugh amongst themselves. They would argue, and play fight, and even flirt with some of the girls as they showed up for their lessons. They didn't have a care in the world. Not one.

A few days of watching this, and I *knew*. We had been lied to and cheated out of a good part of life. I didn't laugh when I was little. There was no play fighting, only real fighting. Instead of arguing and joking, there had been silence and the occasional knowing glance between two comrades. I didn't have a good childhood like these kids surely did. I didn't really have a childhood at all.

What scared me more than anything was the question that haunted my thoughts while I watched the world go on without me:

Was I really a monster now, or was I a monster before I came here?

Which one of us were the real monsters?

Almost everything stayed constant during the weeks that I kept myself locked up. Matelyn kept me company everyday. Once Christian got home, she would sit and visit with him; trying her hardest to include me… with no avail. Christian wouldn't talk to me if his life depended on it. Sometimes Matelyn would sneak back in at night and sleep by the couch with me… sometimes she wouldn't. It just depended on how her day had gone.

On top of it all though, the thing that stayed constant more than anything else, was the cold. The nights I spent on the couch were the worst nights I'd ever experienced. In the dark, I was able to look up at the ceiling and picture what my comrades were doing.

Were they still looking for me? Or had they given up? Had they ever *looked for me at all? Did Arthur know I was gone?*

I had so many questions… so many answers came with them—just, none I could figure out on my own. The more I thought about everyone I had left out there, the more upset I grew. This led to some very cold, very depressing nights.

But somehow, I had made it through.

I made it through dealing with Christian—who seemed to hate me even more now. I made it through all of the freezing, depressing nights. And if I took it a week at a time… I would make it through everything else.

CHAPTER THIRTEEN

Too early! **My** mind told me as the couch was kicked repeatedly. I squeezed my eyes shut tight to block out the sun. It wasn't until my hair was tugged on that I opened them.

"*Ouch*, what do you *want*?" I growled, pulling my hair away from Christian's hand and glaring at him.

"Get up. We've got stuff to do today."

"*We? Since when is there a 'we'? 'We' don't exist… therefore we don't do anything.*"

I shucked the covers off my body and rolled off the edge of the couch onto my feet. There was a pair of cutoff shorts and a t-shirt lying on the coffee table next to a pair of worn out, dusty shoes; both of which were shamelessly stuffed with a pair of underwear in one, and a bra in the other. I was uncomfortably brought to the realization that I had been wearing the same clothes for over a week; a pair of drawstring shorts that had grown too small for Christian and a raggedy, old t-shirt of his—both of which were leaps and bounds away from fitting me. My hair stuck to the back of my neck and seemed to ooze out of my ponytail. All in all, I was an utterly disgusting sight.

"Go take a shower and get dressed, then we'll get going."

I followed his orders without a word, gathering up the clothes and walking into the bathroom as quickly as possible without looking desperate. *What was it that was important enough to require me?* I tried to figure it out while I scrubbed at my greasy hair a few times to make sure it was completely clean.

There was a cynical voice in the back of my head assuming this was some sort of plot to kill me off in front of a large audience. I violently shoved the thought back into the dark place it had originated from and continued to clean myself up. *If this is the way I'm meant to go, then so be it…*

I wrapped my hair up in one of the discolored towels that had been thrown under the sink in the bathroom and dried myself off with another. I pulled on the underwear I had been given, wondering for a moment to whom they actually belonged before realizing that knowing their previous whereabouts would only make things weirder. The shorts fit my waist but were by far the shortest pants I had ever put on in my life—my fingertips passed the edge of the fabric when my arms hung at my sides. The bra I had been given was a size too small and showed through the sheer white shirt that had been donated by someone I didn't even know.

I grumbled as I slid the shoes on and contemplated screaming at Christian to find me something else to wear rather than walking out in what I had on. I was lucky enough to be given the clothes in the first place though, so I figured I would just make do.

My hair continued to stick to me, even after I had let it fall from the towel, but it felt clean and refreshing as I braided it off to the side. My mood had changed so drastically that I started to hum an old song Arthur had enjoyed singing to me while I was growing up. My humming soon turned into quiet singing. I tied the braid off at the end just as Christian began pounding on the door.

"Are you *singing?*"

My stomach dropped instantly. I *never* sang in front of people. And he *heard* me.

"N-no…" He opened the door without asking whether or not I was dressed and pointed an accusing finger at me.

"You're a liar."

"God, Christian. What if I hadn't been dressed?" I shouted.

"What does it matter? I've seen you naked before?"

It suddenly felt like I couldn't breathe—like the walls were closing in on me.

"*What?*"

"Yeah, how do you think you got out of your wet clothes that night?" I stared him down for a painfully awkward amount of time before he grinned and began laughing loudly. "I'm kidding, Levie. Calm down, I had Matelyn and Elena do it."

"Oh, great. So *other* people have seen me naked? That's fantastic."

"Would you rather it have been me?"

I could physically feel my face turn from a neutral expression into a frown as the words left his mouth. Another painfully awkward amount of time passed while we stared each other down.

"I'm good."

"That's what I thought, too."

Without another word he walked out of the bathroom, flicking the lights off as he went and forcing me to chase after him. He passed through the door and went out into the hallway. I took a deep breath; the place I had thought of as a prison for the past three weeks now seemed more like a sanctuary. I closed the door behind me and ran to catch up with him. He was waiting for me in the den, and as I rounded the corner he moved towards the front door.

"You ready to go?"

"Honestly? I'm not sure..."

"All we're doing is harvesting potatoes. It's pretty hard to screw that up. You'll be fine."

As he opened the door a blast of hot air surrounded me like a hug. The sun was bright enough to cause me to see spots until my eyes adjusted and I saw everything I had been missing.

It was obvious that the area hadn't been an open space until the pack migrated here centuries ago. There were a few trees scattered around, with pathways marked off with hunks of wood—which had most likely been taken from the limbs of the trees that had once inhabited the massive area the wolves had taken over. The pathways consisted of dirt, with a few weeds here and there; everything else had been trodden down.

In the distance, I could see more oddly shaped buildings large circles, which on the inside resembled the one I was in now. There were other buildings—much more simple in design—that people were coming in and out of. Two buildings, which were right next to each other, seemed to attract the most attention. The people who came out of these buildings all carried baskets that were either full of food or clothing.

Further off in the distance, I could hear the sound of men shouting at one another before watching as a tree slowly toppled over, sending up a cloud of dirt.

Christian tugged me out the front door, and after closing it behind me, pulled me around to the back of our living quarters so that I could see the other side of the territory.

On the other side were the two very large things Christian wanted to show me.

One of them, more living spaces, only bigger.

The other, fields that seemed to go on for miles. There were fields of corn, and what looked like wheat, along with rice, lettuce, and various fruits. He pointed to the one on the far left.

"That's the potato field we'll be in later. We've got the 11 o'clock shift, so we've got a couple of hours. I figured we could go scrounge up some clothes for you. Some that might actually fit…" he looked me up and down quickly before grimacing and starting off the porch and onto the path that led to the nearby "stores".

Christian seemed to know everyone. They would wave and smile, and he would return the gesture. They even smiled and waved at me, and I did my best to look sincere as I did the same; I wasn't sure if it actually worked, or if I looked as confused as I felt.

"Do they *know*?"

"Of course they know."

"Then why are they *waving* at me?"

"Because they're pretending, Levie. If you show them that you're not a psycho like they used to think you were, then they won't even have to pretend. We aren't all bad, you know?"

He was right, *I guess.* So I kept my mouth shut and followed him to the steps that led up to the door of the clothing "store". As I reached for the door, someone with two small children burst through. One child was in her arms, the other, who was the reason why the door had almost hit me, was already running down the stairs.

"*Emmett*, get back here right now. Mommy doesn't have time for this; we've got to get you to school. *Come on.*" She was so flustered it took a second for her brain to register that

I was holding the door open for her; waiting for her to move from the doorway so I could let it close.

"You need some help with anything?" I asked, holding my arms out expecting to be handed one of the baskets she had in her hand. I froze when instead of being handed a basket, she handed me her baby; dropping the baskets I had expected to be handed, and chasing after little Emmett.

"*Oh, God*," I fumbled with the child, struggling to hold him the way the woman had been. I shifted him to my hip and refrained from thinking of myself as a creep when I put my hand under his butt to support him. He graced me with a baby's equivalent of a grin and fluttered his eyelashes at me.

"He likes you, Levie," Christian laughed. "He's flirting with you."

Ew.

He grabbed the end of my braid, and after flopping his forehead against my shoulder, stuck it in his mouth.

Ewwww.

Emmett's mother chased him for a few feet before picking him up and swinging him around; he squealed and she smiled as she carried him back to where Christian and I were standing with the mystery baby.

"I'm so sorry. Here, I'll take William back now," she held her arms out for the baby—*William*—and smiled at me. "He likes to chew on things."

"It's alright, it's pretty long so I can spare a bit of hair."

She chuckled quietly. She was young, maybe somewhere between eighteen and twenty. Definitely too young to have two kids.

"You're the new girl, right?" *As if she didn't know already.*

"Yeah," I murmured, looking down at my borrowed, beat-up sneakers.

"How come I haven't seen you around before, then? You must have been here for almost a month by now," she looked over at Christian and frowned. "You know when they say to keep a close eye on new bites, they mean you *keep a close eye on them…* not to keep her locked away like a dog with rabies, *Christian.*"

"Don't give me any crap, Amber. I just didn't know how she would react, *okay*?"

Yup, everyone definitely knew what my given situation was, that's nice to know… at least everyone understands that I may have a mental break at any second. I mean, oh god, they're everywhere, so many wolves…

God, give me a break…

"Well, you must be nervous about tomorrow night… if you think about it this way. I mean—it'll all be over really soon, and then it won't be so bad ever again."

"What's tomorrow night?" I threw a sideways glance at Christian, who bit his lip. Amber looked between Christian and I.

"The moon…?" she mumbled, making it sound more like a question. I clenched my teeth to keep from having the full-blown panic attack that Christian, no doubt, had been expecting.

"Oh, right. Well… I'll just be glad to have the first one done with I guess." She nodded in understanding and started to gather up the baskets she had dropped when she ran after Emmett.

"Well, I should be going. I've got to get the kids over to my mom's house and then head over to the kitchen. It was good to see you again, Christian. It's been awhile. Oh, and nice meeting you, Levie." She smiled and then, hoisting William up onto her hip, taking the baskets in one hand, and then grabbing Emmett's hand with the other, she walked away.

"I never told her my name…" I whispered to Christian.

"Well, a lot of people were interested in you when you

first got here; when they'd ask about you, I'd answer their questions. And I'm sure the news spread quickly."

I rolled my eyes and followed him into the little ramshackle building. Inside there were shelves on either side of the room that held totes, one side labeled *men's* with the sizes small through extra-large written on a piece of tape and stuck to the side of each individual box. There was a column for shirts, sweats, jackets, socks, and underwear; and then a separate column for pants, with numbered sizes. The same could be said to describe the woman's side as well, only there was a column for bras added to the mix.

"Hey, Christian! What can I do for you today?" the woman at the counter asked.

"Here to get Levie some clothes that will fit her," he said with a glance in my direction. She followed his gaze and made a face at me.

"Well, I'll say she's in need of them. Just follow me and we'll get you everything you need." I followed the dark-haired, fragile looking woman to the wall. Her hair was French-braided, starting from the top of her head and falling down to the middle of her back—it swished as she walked. "I'm Lissi, by the way."

I smiled at her as convincingly as I could. *She already knew my name, so there was no reason to repeat it, and therefore, no reason to reintroduce myself for conversation's sake.*

When I didn't say anything else, she looked around the room and fidgeted before taking a deep breath and forcing another smile. "Okay, then. What sizes are you in everything?"

I took a deep breath and recited the sizes of the things I could remember.

Medium in shirts—because I liked them to fit a bit looser, but if I was getting any tank tops, they should be smalls.

Sweats should be extra smalls.

Any jacket should be a small, but if I got a sweatshirt, it should be a medium—because I liked to feel warm and secure in them.

I wore a size four in shoes, so whatever size socks would fit my foot were acceptable. Lissi told me she would probably have to find socks and shoes for me in the kid's stuff in the back, and I grumbled internally. *Kids shoes suck.*

At this point, I had been handed a basket full of the clothing she had grabbed for me so far—five shirts, four tank tops, three pairs of sweats, one warm, well fitting jacket, and one sweatshirt. The handle was cutting into my hand with its weight, so I set it down on the floor.

"What about jeans and shorts?" she looked me up and down, and chewed her lip. "You look kind of tiny…"

I looked down at my legs and sighed. "I think the last time I got pants, I got them in a size one." I *hated* my body. How *small* I was… height and otherwise. Not to mention, whenever I mentioned my size, people looked at me either with envy or confusion—neither of which I appreciated.

Lissi gave me a look that was somewhere close to confusion, and then proceeded to dig through the tote labeled *ones.* She picked out four pairs of jeans, and then four pairs of shorts and placed them in another basket.

"What about underwear?"

"Smalls," I grumbled. *Just like my ass…* she pulled out ten pairs of underwear, ranging from comfortable looking, to *ew*, to somewhat scary. I kept my mouth shut, though.

"And last but not least, bra size?"

"Thirty-two C" I spat as quickly as possible. She dug around in the appropriate tote and then threw two bras—one black and one white—into the basket; adding a couple of sports bras for good measure, as she said.

I turned around to make a face at Christian for putting me in this awkward, tortuous situation, but the look of pure discomfort on his face caused me to choke back laughter instead.

"You're not going to be angry with a pair of hiking boots for shoes, right? Because we don't have much more than that..."

"Any shoes are fine with me, as long as they fit better than the ones I have on..." *the giant shoes...*

I followed her into the back room of the "store", where the same setup was present on both walls, except it was all kids clothing. Along the very back wall were shelves lined with shoes.

"Pick whatever two pairs of shoes you want. I suggest a pair of tennis shoes and a pair of boots—they'll be the best combo for you."

I grabbed a pair of sturdy brown boots, similar to the ones I was used to, and a pair of tennis shoes almost identical to the ones I had on, only they were in my size, and not a few sizes too big.

"These ones are good," I said, handing them to Lissi.

"You *sure*? We have to ration the shoes big time, so you'll only get a new pair every other year. After these two pairs, I mean..."

"I'm sure." *I think.*

"Then I think we've got everything you need, you should be good to go." Lissi grinned genuinely this time, rather than her smile being somewhat forced. "Just make sure you bring the baskets back eventually."

"That's it? No fittings, no paperwork, nothing?"

"What do you want me to do, write up a contract for your clothes?"

"Not exactly but I—"

"I'm not very good at sewing either, so if they don't fit, *tough*." Her condescending tone was coupled with another genuine smile. I resisted the urge to snap at her like I normally would have if she were Christian or someone else I knew. Instead I grabbed for the baskets that Lissi had set on the table. Before I could get one, Christian had snatched both of them up.

Oh, come on. This is no time for chivalry; I just want to get out of here. I don't know what to say anymore, things are getting awkward…

"Alright, Lissi. You can stop scaring her now. We've got stuff to do today." He clapped me on the back and I flinched; part of me wanted to take it as a friendly gesture, while the other part of me wanted to turn around and glare—possibly with some unfriendly hissing.

I decided the best option was to do neither.

"See ya tonight, guys. Have fun today, Levie!" she said, tossing me a couple of packages before waving and returning to the back room. I looked at the packages as I followed Christian out the door—one contained a few oversized cotton shirts, while the other had the same amount of cottons boxers.

"What are these for?"

"To wear during the phase so you don't blow out your good clothes."

Oh… I chewed at the inside of my cheek and followed Christian back to the house to ditch my baskets of clothes so we could get to work.

It wasn't very late in the day, yet it was already getting hot outside. It was only ten o'clock or so in the morning, and I knew by the time we had to be out in the fields the temperature would have rocketed even higher.

"I'm going to *die…*" I mumbled, grabbing a shirt and bra that actually fit me; soaking in the significantly cooler air within the room.

"Why?"

"It's hot, I'm *pale…* those things don't go together well."

"You'll be alright. They keep a steady flow of water going

to the fields, you can drink it and shower in it if you want to, and they don't care. Plus there's aloe plants all over the place here; sunburn is inevitable though, so you'll have to suffer through it like all of us do."

I grumbled all through changing into my new clothes—it wouldn't be so bad if I only burned… but along with the roasted skin came *freckles.* They would appear over the span of a few hours; dusting my shoulders and falling across my nose. The worst part was that I *knew* Christian would make fun of me for them…

I let my braid out and unwound the plaits by shaking my hair out and revealing the still damp waves that had formed. I pulled it all up into a sloppy ponytail so it wouldn't stick to my neck and trudged out of the bathroom.

"Where should I put all this?"

"Just throw it on the floor for now, we'll figure out what to do with it all later."

I tossed it down by the corner, blushing and kicking it away when the old, hand-me-down bra somehow ended up on top.

"Here, if you wear this you won't end up with a lobster face." Christian grabbed a dusty, tan ball cap out of a drawer in his dresser and put it on my head; he pulled my ponytail through the back and pulled it down over my eyes while I complained.

"I hate hats."

"Would you rather have lobster face?"

"I don't even know what that *means*!"

"Then rather than sit here and discuss it, let's just go get our work done."

My *God* it was hot. My butt was sweating. My butt had *never* sweat before. We had only been out for a little over two hours, and I could already feel my skin singeing in the sweltering sun. *We've still got fifteen minutes to go until break*, I reminded myself.

I'm going to have lobster face…

Christian was in front of me; picking what he could reach and occasionally glancing backwards and holding short conversations with me while I pulled the stems off the potatoes and putting them in the basket behind me. The band on the hat I was wearing was making my neck sweat and itch. My fingernails were near black with dirt, as was most of the skin on my hands and arms.

The passers were behind us, doing the job Christian and I would be doing after we had our break. As we picked the potatoes, we handed them back, and the passers carry the baskets back when they were full down to the bins, where a few groups were washing the potatoes and putting them into storage bins that would eventually be taken to the kitchen.

It wasn't a glamorous job, but at least we wouldn't be digging anymore. Or hopping over the plants when I needed to switch rows; the passers would switch out with someone when the pickers had to move down the row.

Why am I going over the job process right now? It's too hot… I'm going insane. Dammit.

Somewhere on the far end of the field, whoever was in charge blew the whistle.

"Race you!" I shouted at Christian; jumping up out of the dirt and leaping over the legs of my passer, whom I hadn't spoken more than a few words to during the past couple of hours. It took him a few moments to realize I was serious, but by then I was already far ahead of him—too far for him to catch up.

I was out of breath and quite possibly dying by the time I finally hit the trees—and the *shade*—but I didn't care because someone immediately thrust a cup of water into my hand. I gulped it down greedily and accepted another cup as it was held out for me; this time it was Christian who was offering.

"Thirsty much?"

"Just a little," I finished drinking my second cup and stacked them together. "Where do I put these?" He pointed at crate on the ground next to the nearest tree.

"I'm going to go see if I can get us out of our next shift—they've already got too many people here anyway, and we've got stuff to do."

Like what?

I stacked my cups in the crate and stood in the shade, struggling to see through the hoard of people to figure out where Christian had disappeared. I felt like a child who had stumbled into an adult gathering by accident. I was conscious of the fact that I was shrinking in on myself in an attempt to hide from the curious eyes.

Christian… please come back… ***Christian…***

I whined quietly and decided that sitting down and casually pretending to rest was the best idea. There were quite a few people standing around in groups, or sitting in the grass with their legs pulled up to their stomachs; all of them laughing and talking with each other while they fanned themselves or wiped the sweat from their foreheads.

Tall, short, skinny, heavier, brown hair, black hair, blonde hair, even some red hair mixed in and mingling with each other. Tank tops, t-shirts, tight, loose, tennis shoes, sandals; everybody looked so different from one another. There were no uniforms of any kind; only enough common sense to know that there wasn't any reason to wear jeans in a potato field.

The only uniform thing between the people who surrounded me wasn't something physically identifiable. *At least, not until tomorrow anyway.*

They were all one in the same—each of them a member of the pack… the pack that protected each other at all costs, regardless of risk. They would protect me without question; so eventually, I would have to do the same; no matter why they needed to be protected.

I inadvertently began to sink in on myself again.

I watched as Christian shoved through a group of people; he laughed as a couple of guys clapped him on the back. One of the girls in the group punched his arm and grinned at him. I heard someone mention that it was "nice to see him around again." Someone else mentioned that they would see him later that night. *What's going on tonight?* I remembered Amber saying something along the same lines. *Christian shut the hell up and get over here so I can stop sitting here alone like an idiot.*

Like magic, he left the group and walked back in my direction.

"Calm down, Levie. I'm right here."

"What do you mean *calm down?*"

"I *mean* because I'm technically your alpha I can feel your extreme emotions. Stop panicking, you're starting to freak *me* out." He stood and watched me, giving me an unintentional look of fear, as if he was waiting for me to lose my mind at the fact that he could feel my emotions.

"If it's not one thing, it's another," I grumbled.

CHAPTER FOURTEEN

The worst part about Christian's shower, was that while the water *did* get hot, it didn't *stay* hot. There had been so many showers back home; the water heaters had been massive. So the water had stayed warm for hours at a time.

I remembered falling asleep in the shower the morning we left for the mission.

The mission I hadn't returned from.

I went through the motions of washing my hair and body, before sinking down onto the floor of the shower—totally exhausted from the day's events.

Working with everyone—even people I didn't know—had been nice. It made me sure of the fact that I wasn't going to be held hostage or locked away for the rest of my life. It meant that people expected me to begin pulling my own weight. I didn't have a problem with that.

It was the confusion that came with the day…

It really *had* been over night that Christian changed so

drastically. I wasn't quite sure I understood why. Maybe he was just tired of pretending to hate me? Or maybe he actually *had* hated me, and he finally had gotten over it and decided to be friends with me?

If only I had the courage to bring it up…

What made it so hard was the fact that I didn't *want* to be his friend. I didn't want to enjoy being around the people I had always been taught to dislike. I sure as hell didn't want to be friends with any of them; or be under the control of one of them, for that matter. But the longer I was here, the more I wondered if it would have been so hard for us to all get along. That maybe they weren't brainwashed like we had been; they were really able to do what they pleased.

The longer I was here, the more I wondered whether or not *they* had really been the monsters.

But I resisted these thoughts with all my might because the people back home were still my friends; they were still the people I had grown up with. That *place* was still *my* home. I refused to think that those things were any less than they had been simply because of who I was now.

The warm water was gone; I was now uselessly sitting at the bottom of a cold shower. My hair had begun to dry while it was out of the water's reach—growing frizzy from the humidity; my skin was wrinkly where it had been left in the water.

I shut the water off and got out, wrapping myself up in a towel before I could drip water all over the clean floor. Once I had dried off, I tugged on a pair of jeans and one of the t-shirts I had gotten early that day. I pulled on a pair of socks and tucked my pant legs into them so they wouldn't bother me while I wore my boots. The routine reminded me of what had been; I bit my lip to hold back the tears that, for some reason, threatened to roll down my cheeks.

I took a deep breath and allowed one tear to sneak free, just in time for Christian to knock on the door.

"Hey, what's the matter with you?"

"Nothing," I murmured; my voice cracked.

Shit.

He barged through the door without asking, and frowned when he saw me wipe at the tears that now rolled silently down my cheeks.

"Levie?"

"Just leave me alone, Christian. Don't worry about it."

"Considering I can—"

"Considering you can *feel my emotions*! I know, I know. I get it, alright? I'm sorry my emotions are such a burden for you!" I shouted. I tried to shove by him to get out the door, but he shoved me back and pinned my shoulders against the wall to hold me in place.

"Don't you *dare* do that to me. If I've done something wrong, then *tell me.* If not, knock that shit off, Levie. Because I've been nothing but nice to you all day, and I don't deserve that." He didn't shout, or scream, or say it in even a remotely loud way. His tone was quiet, stern, maybe even a bit exhausted.

The place where his hands pinned my arms to the wall were burning; I wanted to shove him away—or even hit him—so badly, but I couldn't do it. If I thought of a plan that involved any violence, it was like my body wouldn't follow through. I couldn't move my body, partially because he was using quite a bit of force to hold me down, but also because if I moved, I would have hit him, and the alpha side of him wasn't going to allow that to happen. So I opted to use my eyes and my voice instead.

"*I hate you so much.*" I hissed, praying my eyes showed the same thing my voice was saying.

"Don't kid yourself," he came back. "You're lying. You know it. And so do I." He stepped back, and it was like a weight had been lifted from my shoulders.

"Don't you *ever* do that to me again. You may be my *alpha*—" I made a mockery of the word as best I could. "but the next time you control me like that, you *will* regret it."

"Then don't blame your own confusion and problems on *me*."

I dug my nails into my palms as he turned to walk away. Grabbing one of the shoes I had kicked off before my shower, I threw it at him as hard as I could. He didn't so much as flinch when it hit him in the back of the head.

"Oh, that's real *rich* coming from *you*. Considering you *are* the reason behind it all!"

"You want to do this right now?" he turned on me and was in front of me again in seconds. "You *really* want to do this right now?"

"You're all *sweet* and *kind* and *nice* today, and yet I don't understand why you were such an *asshole* before! Which one of your moods is fake, and which one is real, *Christian*?"

"*That's* what you're picking a fight over?"

"I'm just *confused*!" I screeched before I could put enough thought into stopping myself I pushed him—caught him off his guard and sent him into the doorframe. "And you're *not* helping at all!"

"What, so you think us getting into a fight is going to help?" he took a step forward expecting me to flinch, but I held my ground.

"I'll stop being confused because I'll *know* you're an asshole!"

He shook his head and grabbed me by the shirt; I started to struggle to get away from him. I lifted my hand to hit him, but before I could do anything he pulled me against him; crushing me against his chest.

"*What are you doing?*" I screeched, trying to push him away but failing completely.

"Proving you wrong."

"Please let me go," I whined. "I just want to get this over with."

"Not until you realize that I don't want you to be upset. That contrary to popular belief, I do actually want you to be happy here."

"Okay, I get it!" My voice cracked; my mind was going into overdrive. I was emotionally exhausted and I was one more caring phrase away from loosing it.

"I care, Levie. Whether I want to or not."

And there they are—I wiped at my cheeks as best as I could.

You pitiful, weak, little girl…

"I don't want to go to the bonfires," I murmured against his chest. "I don't want to go anywhere with you." It was a pitiful; last ditch effort at pretending to hate him still.

"Oh, you're going. It's your first phase, and you *have* to go. No matter how big of a cry-baby you are." *And he was back to his old self again…*

As soon as we left the dorm, the fire and smoke was visible, even through the trees. There was more than one pyre; once we got closer, I could see that dozens of people surrounded each one.

Christian steered me towards one of the pyres off to the left side of the clearing in the center of the camp. I recognized some of the faces from the day I had gotten into the fight with Christian in the den, but not all of them. As we got within shouting distance, they started yelling at him, telling him it was about time he showed up.

"I was just waiting on Levie," he said laughing and clapping his friends on the back. As if they magically hadn't seen me before, their eyes were all suddenly on me. I wished I could curl into a ball and hide myself from their stares. "Guys, you haven't been formally introduced to her yet—this is Levie."

"You can come sit by me, Levie!" Matelyn shoved the guy who was sitting next to her over in order to make room. Christian put a hand on my lower back and gave me a reassuring nudge in the direction of the log everyone was sitting on. As soon as I sat down, two of the people sitting closest to Matelyn leaned forward so they could see me and speak with me easily.

"Levie, this is Nora and her brother Dustin," Matelyn said, motioning to each of them. I could tell she was concentrating on keeping herself from bubbling over.

"Hi," I murmured attempting to arrange the features on my face into an expression that was at least somewhat happy. "It's nice to—well, I guess I already have met you. Kind of. I'm sorry about that fight, I just didn't—"

"Don't worry about it, honey. We've all wanted to hit Christian at some point in time. I'm a little jealous you got to, though." Dustin said, reaching across Matelyn to pat my knee. "Do you know what the sudden change in his attitude was? I mean, no offense, but he kind of hated you a little bit…"

"I just asked him the same thing, but I don't think he really knows himself. Maybe you could get the answer out of him yourself."

"Nah, he's definitely not the one to figure that out," Nora muttered, grinning enough to show off her pretty smile. "Matt might know though."

"Matt might know what?" a deeper voice asked from behind us. I turned to see a couple; the boy, or Matt for that matter, was a head taller than the girl he was with. His dark hair was only visible thanks to the fire in front of us all, but it gave it an odd copper tone. The girl's blonde hair had the same copper tone to it, causing it to glow gold rather than amber like Matt's.

She jumped over the log I was sitting on, and flopped

down next to me; it was Elena.

"Levie, this is my alpha, Mateus. He goes by Matt unless you're angry or annoyed with him." He nudged her with his knee gently and she rolled her eyes and shoved him away.

"And I'm—"

"Elena. I remember your name." She grinned and threw her arms around me, pulling into one of those unbreakable embraces that seemed to be popular amongst the wolves.

"I'm so glad you're here." She said quickly, giving me another squeeze before letting me go. "You, me, and Matelyn are going to be the three amigos."

I wasn't quite sure of what to say, so I smiled and looked around at the little group that had gravitated closer toward me, and I knew the onslaught of questions was getting closer and closer every moment we sat together. There was Elena on one side of me and Dustin and Nora on the other; Matelyn had gotten up and moved to sit on the other side of the fire with Matt to avoid the smoke. Christian had disappeared the moment I sat down with everyone, and I hadn't seen him since.

"Where's Christian?" I wondered, without really thinking before I opened my mouth. Elena snorted. "What?" I asked.

"I just remember when I used to do that…"

"Do what?"

"Get anxious when Matt wasn't around. It goes away after awhile, though. So don't worry."

"I'm not anxious, he just dragged me out here and then ditched me. And he's been gone for forever."

"You haven't even been here for ten minutes, Levie," Dustin piped in. They were teasing me now.

"I'm *not* anxious."

They all laughed.

I wasn't anywhere near as uncomfortable as I thought I

was going to be, but I pushed at what little discomfort there was in an attempt to get Christian to recognize it and come back from wherever he had gone. It worked like magic, and I was proud of myself for taking control of a situation; for a couple of seconds I had been the alpha. He showed up quickly, with yet another unfamiliar person in tow.

"Sorry, Levie. I was trying to find Jace. He's my alpha. Jace, this is Levie."

Jace kneeled down and patted my arm. "It's nice to meet you, Levie."

"It's nice to meet you, too." I said smiling. Jace stood and made his way over to the other side of the fire to sit with Matelyn and Matt.

"You alright?" Christian leaned over and murmured once everyone was distracted.

"I'm fine, I just didn't know where you were and I wanted you to come back," I smirked and added "Who's the alpha now, *bitch*?" He shoved me and laughed before shaking his head.

"You really are something else, you know that?"

"I do now."

The "feast" that was supposedly consumed before every phase was apparently composed of hot dogs and whatever anyone had brought from home… that happened to be pretty much a whole lot of nothing. We roasted the hot dogs until we couldn't possibly eat another. What made it a feast, more than the food, was the fact that everyone was together. Not necessarily around the same fire, but *together*. In the same mindset, and the same mood. They were all happy. And regardless of the fact that I had set out tonight to be as unhappy about the situation as possible, I was happy too.

I had met everyone that I had been living with for the last

few weeks, and they genuinely liked me—which was confusing, but I focused on ignoring that because all it did was make me upset. They weren't afraid to ask questions, though. They had flooded me with them all night.

"Levie, did you guys ever have feasts like this?"

"Kind of… we had bonfires before big missions and things like that."

"Did you have hot dogs?"

"Sometimes…"

"What other food did you eat?"

"Normal food, I guess."

"How did you get it, because I mean, we have to send people out for days at a time to get stuff and bring it back if we don't grow it here… did you do the same?"

"Everything was brought to us by our elders."

There was a chorus of "lucky" and "it must be nice" after I said that; I laughed at their jealousy.

"So tomorrow night we all have to hang out in the same cell," Elena stated, smiling at me.

"Elena, we'll be there. Don't worry about it." Christian glared at her to get her to stop talking, but in all honesty, it was too late.

I hadn't been thinking about the phase at all, and now I was starting to panic. I wanted to ask questions, but I didn't want to do it in front of everyone. Instead I stayed sitting on my log and slowly fell apart on the inside with fear.

I felt like I was going to throw up, and I prayed that Christian would feel my discomfort and get us out of there as fast as possible.

I nudged him with my elbow; without even turning to look at me, he nodded.

"I think Levie's falling asleep over here, so I'm gonna get her back so she can get some rest. We all need it."

They nodded in agreement and said their goodbyes. Matelyn and Elena gave me hugs; Dustin gave me a kiss on the cheek that, despite my current mood, made me blush.

"I feel like I'm going to throw up," I whispered, embarrassed.

"You gonna make it back, or should we go somewhere closer?"

"I think I'll make it."

Christian picked up his pace and we walked a little faster until we hit the door to the den. Rather than walk down the hall, I flopped onto the couch and buried my head in my hands.

"I thought you were going to throw up?"

"I'm scared," I murmured, not bothering to fight back the tears now.

So many tears these days. When had I turned into such a baby?

"I would tell you it isn't that bad, but I know that the first time is bad for everyone…"

"How bad does it hurt?"

"Bad… it's bad, Levie. But just remember that we've all been through it. I'll be in the same cell with you, and I'll help you through it as best as I can, I promise. I'll be there for you." He walked around the couch and sat next to me. He hesitated before patting my back lightly. "It'll be okay."

CHAPTER FIFTEEN

I hadn't been nearly as uncomfortable around all of the other wolves as I thought I would've been.

Though they still didn't seem to understand how different I truly was from them.

Or at least, how different I truly *had* been.

The thing that confused me the most about the entire night, were my own feelings. I couldn't help but feel as though I was starting to grow attached to the people around me—even though they were my enemies only a handful of weeks before.

Sadly, my night quickly went from being warm and exciting, to cold and lonely the second I laid down on the couch in Christian's dorm.

I was scared about the phase; scared about what it meant for my life, and what would follow it.

I started to think about my team again, and where they might be… what they might be doing. I thought about what it might have been like if the people I had spent most of my life around were more like the wolves. And of course, by the time I finished thinking about all of these things, I was freezing. My body shook without control; as if an invisible force was shaking me for everything I had.

My teeth clicked together so loud, I was sure everyone in the house could hear.

I kept my eyes squeezed shut though; praying for sleep. When it didn't come, I prayed that Matelyn would sneak in and try to sleep by the couch—at least that way I'd have someone to keep me warm. When that didn't happen, I began to cry—silently and relentlessly, tears rolled down my face; almost seeming like they were freezing to my cheeks in the process.

"It'll be about a month."

Christian's words ran through my head on a constant loop.

There's only a few hours left, if I can make it that long, I thought to myself; bringing on another round of tears. I couldn't stand it any more. I *had* to get some sleep—the exhaustion I was feeling was only making me higher strung, which in turn, only made me colder. It was a vicious cycle.

I crawled out from underneath all of the covers, and padded across the carpet, and into Christian's room.

Taking a deep breath before rounding the corner, I tried my hardest to clench my mouth shut to keep my teeth from chattering.

What's the worst he's going to do? Say no? He'll probably hate you again afterwards, so it'll be no different. If he says yes, you get a good night's sleep. Suck it up! I told myself, in hopes that a pep talk would get me through what I was about to do.

It was embarrassing, to say the least.

My eyes had to adjust to the amount of darkness, before I could actually see his sleeping figure underneath all of the blankets on his bed. I tried to nudge his shoulder—with absolutely no affects on his part. I resorted to plan B.

"Christian…"

Nothing.

"Christian…" I whispered a little louder.

Still nothing.

"*Christian.*" I nudged him, and whispered louder. This time, he budged slightly. "*Hey…*"

"Hmmm?" he mumbled into his pillow.

"Never mind." I chickened out and started to walk away; my teeth chattering worse, once again. But he caught me by the sleeve before I could get away.

"Damn you, now you woke me up. If you don't tell me what you want, I'm going to kill you, do you understand?" I sighed.

"I'm cold, and scared, and…"

"And?"

"Can I sleep with you?" he sat up completely, looking at me incredulously with sleepy eyes.

Some part of my mind noted how his eyes looked when he was sleepy. It wasn't a description well put into words.

"You want to *sleep* with *me*?"

"I just want to be warm… and *not* by myself. You can put a pillow in-between you and I. I just-"

"If I let you, will you stop talking?" I nodded.

"Okay," he murmured, rolling over to give me the spot he had already warmed up. "Go ahead."

I didn't hesitate to take his spot, the way I probably would have in any other situation. The second my body hit the warm bed, I stopped shivering; my body relaxed completely.

And if I wasn't conscious of Christian right next to me, I probably would have fallen asleep immediately. I grabbed one of the many pillows behind my head, and went to put it between us.

"Don't worry about the pillow." He murmured. "If you roll over on me, I'll kick you off. And I'm sure you'll do the same, I think we can handle ourselves." He chuckled. I forced myself to laugh a little in an attempt to lighten the awkwardness of the situation.

It didn't work…

I'm not sure how long we actually lay in silence—but it was Christian who broke it.

"You awake, still?"

"Mmhmm."

"What was going through your head tonight?" I rolled to face him, finding that he was already facing me.

"What do you mean?"

"Everything that happened tonight—meeting everyone, the phase…" he paused, making sure I wasn't going to panic again. "What was going through your head?"

"I was upset at myself." I murmured, honestly.

"Why?" he frowned, forming two angry creases above his eyes.

"Because I've always hated you all. And now I'm starting to wonder why."

"It's just how you were raised to think. The same way we were… only, we're a little easier to convince otherwise."

"Clearly…" I mumbled, referring to the way everyone had accepted me.

"What was it like? Growing up the way you did?"

"I grew up in the matter of a few days, Christian. I didn't get to *grow up*—I was born to be who I was. No choices were given to me. That's just how it went."

"It's wrong to force a child into something like that."

"S'not so bad. I turned out okay."

"That's debatable." Christian murmured. Without thinking, I reached over and slapped his arm.

"You're sharing your bed with me, obviously I'm not *that* bad." I grew worried when he didn't respond. *Had I done something I shouldn't have?* "Are you still awake?" I whispered, not wanting to wake him if he *had* fallen asleep.

"Mhmm. I'm just trying to get over that slap." He murmured honestly.

"Oh, come on! I didn't hit you *that* hard!"

"No, it's not that. You're just acting like a human being and not a robot. It's a nice change."

"I have never acted like a robot in my life," I grumbled.

"That's definitely debatable. You were a Christian-hating robot." He said, chuckling a little bit.

"Can you blame me for hating you?"

"Not really, no…"

He didn't ask if I still hated him or not. Instead, he just sat in silence and seemed to contemplate what he was going to say next. Eventually he changed the subject.

"What is the base like?"

"Big," I mumbled, laughing. "No, it's… *different.* We don't really have much schooling. But by the time we're able to walk and talk, we train."

"Train to fight?" I nodded.

"When we're young, it's mostly just finding out what we're best at. So we can be classed accordingly."

"You were best at archery?"

"Mmhmm. They could tell I would be best at archery because of my posture. When I was little, Arthur used to tell me I had the posture of a queen."

"Who's Arthur?" Christian asked.

"My commander. In a sense that you'd understand; he's my 'alpha'. He raised me after my parents passed away…"

"When did they die… if you don't mind me asking?"

"I was only six." He shook his head in disbelief.

"I'm sorry… I shouldn't have asked."

"It's okay… I don't remember them much. So there's not much to miss about them."

We lay in silence once again; I knew he had more questions. And If he wouldn't ask, then it was *my* turn.

"Do you hate me?"

"No," he said harshly, as if it should have been obvious. "I don't hate *you.* I hate the mistake that you are." He seemed to think about what he had said, his eyes growing big at the realization of how harsh his words had sounded.

"Oh, god! I mean… what happened to you was a mistake. I shouldn't have done what I did; I have to deal with the consequences every day."

"Am I really *that* bad?" I asked, chuckling.

"No… but knowing I ruined your life is pretty bad."

I didn't say anything; there was nothing to say. I couldn't comfort him, because what he had said was true. "If you have anymore questions—and I know you do—don't be afraid to ask them. I'm not going to be able to sleep tonight anyway."

He hesitated once again. There had been so much hesitation on his part tonight.

"Is the stereotype true… about the Flickers being…" he trailed off, not wanting to finish his sentence.

"…About the Flickers being… *promiscuous*?" I laughed. It was a terrible—but true—stereotype that we—not including myself—had gained.

"You said it, not me."

"It's true… *kind of*," I admitted. "But it's more like a side-affect. We're raised to somewhat embrace lust—bloodlust more than anything. We're raised to want to kill things, to want to fight. All of that falls under the category of lust. We *lust* for the hunt, the fight… the kill. It's just how things go. And lust for… well… *you know*—it just kind of comes along for the ride."

"Are you…?" I couldn't help but laugh again.

"No, I'm not like that… it's stronger in some, more than others."

"Like Alan?" I froze at the sound of Alan's name.

"Y-you… how do you know Alan?"

He bit his lip, as if he shouldn't have said what he had.

"I had to follow you around the final day of your change—to make sure you didn't die, and come back somewhere else. You wouldn't have understood what was going on. You could've gotten hurt…"

"You were there the entire time?" he nodded.

"You've got quite an arm on you… I saw you slap Alan." I couldn't help but laugh. I felt guilt rise up in me though; the last thing I had said to Alan was that I didn't want him, and never would. While what I had said was true, I hadn't said anything else to him for the rest of the mission…

Which meant those had been my last words to him…

"I feel bad for slapping him… that was the last time I spoke to him before I… *you know*," I sighed and shook my head. "I shouldn't have done that."

"He deserved it!" Christian said a little louder than he had been speaking before.

"You don't even know him! How can you say that?" I whispered harshly. I felt my body begin to shake out of anger; I started to grow cold again.

"The guy was a pig, Levie! He was checking you out like a piece of meat!"

"It was still wrong for me to do that!" I bit my lip in an attempt to keep my teeth from chattering, and drew blood instead. "G-god, you see what y-you d-did?"

I reached up and wiped at the blood, trying to keep it from getting all over his sheets.

"Oh god, I'm sorry... just, give me a second." I watched—still shivering—as he crawled out from underneath the covers, making his way to the other room. I had to hold back a gasp when I realized he was only in his boxers.

Think fully clothed thoughts, Levie. Fully clothed thoughts... how did you miss that one? You're in bed *with him!*

He came back with a damp washcloth. And motioned for me to sit up.

"I don't n-need your help, C-Christian," I said while reaching for the washcloth. My hands were shaking so badly it was hard for me to get a good hold in it. "You're shaking so hard, you can't even get a grasp on the washcloth. Now come on, let me help you."

I turned my head away, like a child.

"*No.*"

I felt his hand touch my face; warm and just slightly calloused. I froze, biting my lip again and causing more blood to pool.

"Let me help..."

I sighed and turned my head to face him. He smiled and started to wipe at the blood with a touch so light, I could barely feel it.

"You've got to stop biting your lip, especially when you're upset like that."

I couldn't talk, since Christian was still wiping at the blood, so I nodded instead.

"There's no reason to be embarrassed, you know?" he murmured, and I froze once again. I knew my cheeks weren't red. I wasn't avoiding his gaze or anything; I couldn't keep from watching him. I hated that he could feel how I felt.

"I think it's fine now." I laid back down, and pulled the covers up to my chin, facing away from Christian's side of the bed.

"Levie I didn't mean-"

"Just go to bed, Christian."

He sighed. I felt him shift his weight as he lay down; I could feel his eyes on my back.

"Sorry," he whispered.

"That's why I hated you so much to begin with, you know. Because I could feel *your* hate. And it started to rub off… I'm sorry for that. You didn't need it then, and you don't need it now—which is why I'm trying to turn over a new leaf." Once again, he waited for me to say something.

Too bad I was too busy trying not to cry.

"You're not making it easy on me, Levie." He murmured. He turned over, to face the wall instead of me; not saying anything more.

It was getting harder and harder not to cry these days. Not just when it came to situations like this one, but in *every* situation. There was always something that was a reminder of what *used* to be my life.

I wasn't sure if I could take it anymore.

Maybe I *did* need someone to talk to…

One side of my mind told me—*Don't be silly, you've got Matelyn! She love's you, you can always talk to her!* This voice was growing harder to hear. It was getting harder and harder to hate him for what he had done.

The other side of my mind was egging me on—*Levie, tell him. You* need *a true friend here.*

I made the mistake of whimpering; Christian rolled back over to face me.

"Levie? Are you okay?" I knew full well that he knew I was upset.

I tried as hard as I possibly could to keep quiet—it didn't work. I started to cry harder; finding the air sucked from my lungs faster than I could replace it.

"Levie? *Levie?*"

"I just want to go *home*!" I wailed, unable to hold it in any longer. "I'm scared and confused. No one here knows me. They're all skeptical; it's not hard to see the fear in their eyes. Even *Matelyn* is careful! I miss my friends, I miss my family – what little family I had left. I don't understand how anything goes here! *More than anything I just want to go back home!*"

By the time I had finished, I was screaming. My entire body seemed cold enough to belong to a dead body. That realization only made me shake harder.

"Levie-"

"Oh, yeah! You wanna know what the *real* kicker is in all of this? Unlike the majority of you—*I'm dead*!" I didn't give him time to respond; instead, I raced out of the room, headed for the only mirror in the house. I could hear Christian quickly following after me.

I stared at myself, expecting there to be some big difference that I hadn't noticed before. But there wasn't much to see. *Maybe a little paler; skin a little softer.* My once greenish-blue eyes, had turned to grey—the irises rimmed in a dark blackish-blue color. That was it.

But I was still *dead.*

"Levie…" Christian had been standing behind me, no doubt trying to deal with my feelings. *My* doubt, *my* fear, *my* anger and sadness. "I'm so sorry…" he whispered. He stroked my hair, before pulling me into a hug.

I tried to pull away, *but he was* so *warm…*

"Christian, why did I have to die?"

"I don't know, Levie. I'm so sorry…" he sighed, never letting go of me. "You need to warm up. And sleep. Those are the most important things right now. If you don't calm down and get some rest, you're going to end up hurt."

"I'm already hurt…" I whispered.

CHAPTER SIXTEEN

CHRISTIAN

Her words were like another stab to the gut. *I'm already hurt.*

I sighed, and scooped her up—she was freezing already, and getting colder by the second.

"No, Christian. I… I can… I can walk."

"No, Levie. You can't."

"You're right…" she was so weak from her outburst that she could barely form coherent sentences.

I laid her down on her side of the bed, crawling in beside her and doing my best to try and get her warm again. It took awhile, but eventually, her skin was warm to the touch rather than icy.

I wrapped my arms around her waist, trying my hardest not to touch any part of her *anatomy* that she wouldn't appreciate me touching. I didn't want to end up with a broken arm when she woke up in the morning.

I was growing fonder of the mystery girl, but I still wasn't her *biggest* fan.

Either way, if I didn't get her warmer, I'd end up with a *really* dead body in the morning, rather than a living, breathing person.

She murmured incoherently about a number of different things; things I didn't understand, even *when* I could make out the words she was saying.

"Christian?" I froze when she said my name. *Shit, I thought she was asleep.* I tried to move my arms from around her waist, but her hands were already there; holding them in place.

"Christian?" she murmured again.

"Hmm?"

"I hate you…" *Ouch. That one hurt a little bit.* I hoped it was her fatigue talking, and not her real feelings.

"No, you don't, Levie."

She sighed. I know…"

Not a few seconds later, she was out.

CHAPTER SEVENTEEN

"Levie." *Was he waking me up early* again? *Why? Not two days in a row, please…* I had always loved sleeping in. Last night I had actually been able to sleep.

"Mmmmmm…" I grumbled, rolling over and covering my head with blankets.

"No, Levie, *seriously*. Come on, *get up*." I sighed, and wrestled with the covers until I had gotten free of the blanket-burrito, and forced my eyes open. The clock on the wall read 6:00 o'clock.

"It's only six," I shouted, burying my head underneath the covers.

"Yeah, six in the *afternoon*! We have stuff we have to do and only a few hours to do it!" I grumbled again and ignored him. He stood there for a few moments before using his knee to scoot the bed across the floor a few inches.

"Fine, I'm up." I rolled out of bed, slowly dangling my

feet over the edge of the bed and feeling for the floor before I tried to stand up. "How much do we have to do?"

He threw a big black shirt at me, and a pair of shorts; I recognized them from the baskets of clothes I had gotten yesterday.

"Unless you don't care if they rip, I wouldn't suggest wearing a bra or underwear." I raised an eyebrow skeptically. When he didn't change his serious look, I rolled my eyes and made my way into the bathroom to change.

When I came out, he threw a duffel bag at me.

"Pack it full of water bottles and your clothes. Put some granola bars or something in there, too."

"What are you going to do, then?"

"Do the same thing." He held up another duffel bag.

I sighed and walked out to the communal kitchen. Everyone else was up and doing the same thing.

"Morning, Levie," Elena grumbled, handing me a cup of coffee.

"Good morning." I took the cup, hesitantly sipping at it to make sure it wasn't too hot, before taking a few gulps and setting it down. "Thanks."

"No problem. You'll need it, anyway."

"You don't have a bra on, do you," Nora asked. "That's a bad idea."

"No… Christian told me not to wear one."

"Kinky," Dustin muttered from across the room as he shoved bottles of water into his bag.

"*Shut up*," Christian and I said at the same time. Christian pelted Dustin with a granola bar causing everyone to chuckle.

"Are all of the granola bars gone already?" I asked timidly, not wanting to take anything that had already been claimed.

"Nah, they're right here." Matt tossed the box onto the table in the center of the kitchen. "The chocolate one's are mine, though." He snagged one out of the box.

"Don't be greedy!" Elena snatched it out of his hand and threw it into her duffel bag. He punched her in the arm playfully.

I just grabbed a couple of handfuls of the granola bars and went to grab a few of the water bottles, leaving the others to bicker over who got what.

"You guys ready?" Christian asked. He threw me a pair of clean pajamas, and motioned for me to throw them into my bag.

"Yeah, I think we're all good," Elena said. "Matelyn! Are you ready?"

Matelyn bounced out of the bathroom.

"Mhmm, I just wanted to put my hair up." She flipped her platinum ponytail around and smiled. Once we were out the door, the others raced ahead—claiming they wanted the good spots.

"What do they mean," I asked Christian. I scanned the fields around me and saw dozens of groups walking in the same direction as we were. The only difference was that Christian and I were taking our time about it.

"There are man made tunnels underneath the base," He murmured, taking the bag from me and throwing it over his shoulder.

"There are cells like prison cells in there. It's where we go when we're phasing, so we don't end up going wild and attacking someone."

"*Attack* someone?"

"We can phase on our own… we're completely in control when we do that. But on a full moon, we're forced to change. It's much more painful and we're not in control of ourselves or our actions."

I crossed my arms over my chest as we walked. Clenching my jaw, I thought about not being able to control my own actions. I ignored the thought of pain as best as I possibly could, though. I was scared enough as it was.

"It's a door opening for you, though. Once you change there's no going back." He grinned and punched my arm lightly.

"I couldn't go back anyway, so I guess I have no choice."

"That's the spirit," He shouted, throwing his arm over my shoulder. "Way to be positive!"

I rolled my eyes.

"Are you ready for this?" he asked, stopping outside of a crypt-like building with open doors. The entrance was well lit, as was the rest of the tunnel that led underground.

"Do I have any other choice? I have to be ready…"

"Are you scared?"

I nodded.

"I don't know how to do this…"

"I'll help you. You'll be okay, I promise." He held his hand out and smiled. I hesitated before taking it.

"Okay."

Christian led me down into the tunnels, which were *much* nicer than I imagined. The amenities weren't worth five stars by any means, but they weren't damp and cold either. There was a line of makeshift woodstoves down each aisle of concrete rooms that kept it warm during the winter and there were lights in every cell. The only thing that made the rooms feel more like *cells*, were the thick iron chains connected to each wall.

"What do we do now?" I asked, letting my eyes roam over the cell where Christian had just put our stuff. The cell doors weren't made of bars, but rather thick metal slabs that slid into place the same way a closet door might.

"We hang out with everyone and wait until the alarms on the clocks tell us it's almost ten o'clock."

I nodded.

"Sounds *exciting...*" He chuckled and grabbed my hand, tugging me down toward the end of the row of cells, where I could hear Elena's laughter echoing through the halls. I glanced at the clocks on the walls as we walked back to where the others were. They all read 8:30.

Only an hour and a half left until your life changes forever...

"Oh, *come on*! That's *my* cell and it has been for *years* now! Switch back with me," Matt shouted as we walked into the cell that everyone was sitting in.

"Not in a million years! It's the biggest one and I've been trying to snatch it from you for years," Nora shouted back.

"It's not like you get *that* big when you change! Why do you need the room?"

"Because I *want* it! So *there*!" She grinned. Matt groaned loudly and plopped down on the floor.

"You're not fair."

"Stop pouting, it's just a cell. You use it for one night a month, and you don't even remember it when you *do* use it," Elena muttered, chewing on one of her pointed nails.

"Are you nervous, Levie," Matelyn asked from her spot in the corner. I went and sat down beside her.

"Yeah, I don't know how to do this."

"You don't really need to know much. Your body does it for you," Dustin murmured. "You just have to be able to let go of the pain so it doesn't last as long."

I nodded and sat quietly by Matelyn while the others carried on conversations of their own. Mostly they were upbeat and full of laughs and chuckles.

They weren't afraid; they had been through this before.

But I couldn't bring myself to join in on their happy conversations. I was far from happy, and I had never been good at pretending. Rather than listen to their peppy conversations, I closed my eyes and focused on the pictures that danced across my eyelids. I used to do this a lot when I wanted to tune out the real world. Sometimes the images I saw were pretty and happy. Sometimes they were upsetting or sad. Either way, they distracted me from what was really going on.

I liked to think of random names and watch the futures of others play out. It was like people watching; only it felt more like a dream. Although this time, nothing appeared. There were no faces, or noises, sights, or smells. Only the ones my imagination could muster up – but no visions. Those had disappeared a month ago.

But a buzzing, ringing noise is what brought me out of my trance.

"Levie!" Christian shook me. "We've gotta go back, it's time."

I opened my eyes and watched while some left the cell to go to their own and as others started to chain themselves up with the chains that were connected to the walls.

When I didn't get up off of the ground quick enough, Christian hoisted me up into his arms and walked at a brisk pace back to our cell.

"You have to sit on the ground so I can help you," he said, setting me on my own two feet and waiting for me to sit down.

As soon as I was sitting, he kneeled beside me and started his work.

His hands moved quickly as he pulled all of the kinks out of the chains beside me and started to untwist them.

"Hold out your arms," he muttered quickly. His movements were jerky and I could see the sheen of sweat beginning to form on his forehead. I did as he asked and tried to ignore the fear that boiled in the pit of my stomach at the sound of the chains clicking shut around my wrists.

"Hold your legs up, now." He repeated the same steps he had with my wrists, wrapping the chain around my ankles and padlocking them shut tight. He tugged on the chains to give them a little bit of slack before crossing to his side of the cell and chaining himself up.

"Christian, I'm scared…" I whispered.

"I know, Levie. I'm here… I'm going to help as much as I possibly can." As soon as he finished his sentence, I started to hear the noises.

The screaming.

People all up and down the halls were *screaming*. People I knew, people I didn't, they were all in pain.

And they had been through this before.

I could feel my body growing hotter with every second that passed; I was sure the sheen on my brow matched Christian's now. The screams that echoed down the hall grew louder. I swore I could pick out Elena's and Matelyn's mixed in with the rest of the screams that filled the room and made it impossible to focus on anything—like in a horror movie.

Christian was on his hands and knees, panting and gritting his teeth.

"Levie…"

"Christian I-"

"Levie… you… you have to sit like this." I mimicked the way he sat on his hands and knees. "It makes it easier."

His entire body was shaking—I realized mine was, too.

I was shaking far worse than I ever had when I was upset or cold; now, the shaking was almost seizure like. My joints felt like they were locking and unlocking over and over again. I could tell Christian was fighting his change off, trying to last so he could coach me through mine.

I was just about to tell him that he shouldn't put himself through the pain, when my own pain hit me like a wrecking ball. It felt like someone had dropped a thousand pound weight on my arm, cracking and twisting it in an unnatural position. Now it was my screams that prevented me from hearing the screams of the others.

"*Christian*," I screeched, yanking on the chains and trying to curl into a ball. "*God, it hurts!*"

I looked down at my arm; it had twisted around completely—forming the upper and lower portions of a wolf's leg. My elbow stuck out a good three inches further than it had before. I panted and gritted my teeth, holding back screams as my other arm twitched and writhed.

"Levie, you can't hold it back! You'll hurt yourself more!" Christian grunted and clenched his fists against the ground. His arms were shaking the way mine were. "Focus on pushing your arm out—like you're *trying* to pop it out of its socket."

I did as he said and my arm immediately did what the other one had. Another screech erupted from my mouth at the same time a guttural snarl came from Christian. I looked over, panicked, and saw that his arm had popped the way both of mine had.

"*Christian! I don't know what to do*!"

"Just keep working through the pain," he roared. "Imagine you're pushing your body inside out!"

The second I imagined my body being inside out, every limb I had began to shake. My muscles locked and unlocked repeatedly. My bones felt like they were growing and ripping through my skin; though, my skin was stretching *with* the bones.

Christian wasn't as far along in the change as I was – he was holding back. *Trying to coach me through it.*

The realistic side of me wanted to tell him to stop, to just let it go—that I would be fine. But the side that was more potent—the side with all of the fear—wouldn't let me open my mouth to say the words.

The shaking in my limbs grew more painful. I focused on pushing my body inside out again and my legs began to crack and pop.

"*Christian! My legs!*"

"It's okay, Levie! Just focus on getting them to pop out of place!"

A couple of agonizing minutes passed before my legs cracked and morphed back into a different position. At the same time, my hips shifted forward and down. I now had four legs instead of two, my balance was off and I struggled to stay standing.

My head spun faster than I could comprehend, before I knew it I was splayed out on the floor. Every time I tried to move, my head spun faster. So much pain… so much confusion. I didn't know what was going on anymore.

How long had it been since the timer had sounded? A minute? An hour? A day? I couldn't tell anymore.

I knew the ground had been cold an hour ago—I had been sitting on it; now it felt like fire, like I was laying on lava rock rather than cold cement.

The room swirled again; nothing stayed in place.

"*Christian…*" I wasn't sure if it had come out as a whisper or as a scream. I wasn't sure if it had even come out at all.

What if he had changed already? I thought in a panic. *Who will help me then!*

"I'm here, Levie. I'm not going anywhere." Was he really as calm as he sounded? Or was it just my imagination? I felt a slight amount of pressure on my hand and looked down to see Christian's fingers barely touching mine.

"I'm scared…" Another wave of shuddering ran it's way through me, causing me to wail with pain again. His fingers never left my hand.

I looked up at him—he was straining against the chains

just to reach out and reassure me…

"It'll be okay," he said through clenched teeth. "I'll be here."

The room started to spin again; at the same time, my body began shaking at a more rapid pace.

Christian started to say more, but my screams drowned it out. I had finally calmed down enough to send my body through the rest of the change. My spine wrenched in opposite directions and everything turned red. The last thing I remembered was seeing my reflection in the small window in the cell door.

Dark red fur and grey eyes starred back at me.

Snarls erupted from Christian as his own back wrenched in separate directions. I watched through red-tinged vision as his body tripled in size and became covered in dark brown hair. His eyes were the same color as they always were.

He lunged at me, snarling. I snarled back.

We snarled and barked and snapped at each other for hours. Each trying to break through the chains that bound us to the wall—far enough away that we couldn't do any real damage to each other.

By the end of our pointless quarrel, I was exhausted.

I laid down in the corner, watching the big brown wolf through slits for eyes until I drifted off and fell asleep.

It was dark when I woke up, and I was *way* too comfortable to still be on the cement floor in the cell.

"Are you awake?" a voice whispered. I knew *exactly* who it was the second I heard it.

"I don't know, are you?" I whispered back sarcastically.

"You made it," Christian breathed. "Congratulations."

"Thanks." We lay quietly for a while; I was unable to fall asleep again, though. My mind was running too fast for me to shut it down. "I can't sleep…"

"Me either," Christian whispered. "What are you thinking about?"

"Wouldn't *you* like to know?"

"I would, actually. You know, that's why I asked."

"It's official now. I'm officially a wolf and not a Flicker… it's crazy to think about."

"Are you upset or glad?"

"It's strange, actually… I'm *happy*. I've never been happy – not like this. I feel like this huge weight has been lifted off of my shoulders.

"I can't really explain it. But I feel like I'll be okay… and I wasn't sure before this happened. A month ago, if someone would have asked me if I thought my life would have been okay, I would have looked at them like they were crazy. Who asks a Flicker that? Flickers don't care… you know?

"But now, whenever someone asks me that… I'll have an answer. *Yes*, my life *will* be good. Because everything has changed in some way or another… and those changes changed *me*."

"What about your team mates?" Christian asked quietly.

"I don't know. I don't know a lot of things…" I murmured. "If they turn out to be better than I'm thinking they really are, then I'm willing to let them back into my life if I can."

"What if they're not?"

"Then I won't have a choice but to cut them out entirely."

"Will you be able to?"

"If it means I get to stay here and be happy, then yes."

A month ago, I had been a Flicker… something born and raised to kill and do nothing more. I had been full of lust rather than happiness.

As a Flicker, the things I was saying now would have never come out of my mouth. I was nothing more than a sheep, following orders and rules like *that* was what life was all about. And it took *dying* for me to realize that it wasn't.

"For someone who's never been this happy, you're sure willing to do anything to keep it."

"Wouldn't you," I asked, rolling over to look at him. He was staring up at the ceiling. I could tell by the expression in his eyes what he was thinking.

"I definitely would… but in all honesty, I'm not sure if I would be able to go as far with it as you would."

"Why not?"

"People who have lived with happiness for their entire lives feel like they'll never loose it. You've just earned your happiness and you're willing to work for it because you're never going to be willing to give it up."

"You pretty much just summed it up…" I whispered, giggling sleepily.

"You really need to sleep," Christian murmured, chuckling.

"I'm not done giving my speech yet!"

"You've got five more minutes." I sighed.

"You wanna know what the best part is?"

"What?"

"The door to my old life is closed… it's almost gone, actually, but there's this new door now. It's here, with every single one of my new friends, and it leads to a better life than I could have ever imagined."

"Are you done now?"

"Yeah… Goodnight, Christian," I whispered, curling up into a ball against his side.

"Goodnight, Levie."

CHAPTER EIGHTEEN

3 days. Make that three days in a row *it* was waking me up before I wanted to be awake.

"You're bouncing on the bed. *Why are you bouncing on the bed?*" I opened my eyes to find him standing over my legs. As soon as I made eye contact—angry eye contact—with him, he started bouncing again.

"We've got things to do today."

"*Nope.*" I pulled the covers up over my head. I bounced a good four inches off the mattress when he flopped down on top of me. "*Oh my god, Christian. Give it a rest!*"

"You're such a bitch in the morning. Just get up." he proceeded to roll *over* my body and off the bed on the other side of me, taking the covers with him.

"God *dammit*, Christian. What is so important that it causes you to be idiotic enough to wake me up?"

"If you don't want a badass job that *isn't* picking crops, then *fine*. Be a loser."

I groaned and rolled out of bed, rubbing my face with my hands in an attempt to wake myself up further.

"What are we doing today, then?"

"Do you miss being in charge of things, Levie?"

"Yes…?" I said, unsure of what he was getting at.

"Then I'm going to put you in charge of something really important."

Too much pressure, too much pressure!

"Um, okay…"

"You shouldn't worry about showering, because you're just going to get all sweaty again anyway, so just go put on clothes that you can move easily in but that won't get in the way."

Christian was so high strung it was starting to scare me. He was practically jumping around at this point, throwing clothes and shoes in my direction and shouting at me to hurry up. I was hardly able to get around him and into the bathroom to change; he seemed to be everywhere at once.

I tugged on a pair of 'spandexy' shorts and a tank top, before walking out of the bathroom feeling severely underdressed.

"I feel like a whore. Is prostitution even allowed here?" I asked sarcastically.

"Considering that the first time anyone has sex, they mate with their partner, I'm going to go ahead and guess *not*. Mating kind of defeats the purpose of prostitution, I would think." He tossed my shoes and socks at me and motioned for me to put them on.

Whoops… awkward.

"Come on, let's go!" He didn't just walk down the hall, he *ran*. Before I had even tied my first shoe I heard the door at the end of the hall being thrown open.

"Good God." I muttered. I tied my last shoe and

sauntered down the hall slowly to annoy Christian further. When I reached the end of the hall he threw a water bottle at me; glaring and annoyed, he stood by the front door, waiting to leave.

"Can we go now?"

"Only if you're ready." I sniggered. He grabbed my arm and yanked me out the door, slamming it shut behind him.

"Now they've all probably gotten to the field before us, and they're going to give us that *look* when we walk up." He grumbled as he jogged around the corner and in the direction of the grassy field near our dorms.

"Who *they*? And what *look*?"

"*Them* and *that* look." I followed his gaze and saw a large group of kids mingling; both girls and boys. It was the group of kids he trained to fight.

My stomach dropped and I felt the strong urge to yank Christian down to the ground and beat the shit out of him. *What are you doing, bringing me out here to help you train? You've got to be kidding me! These kids are going to eat me alive!*

"Calm down, Levie. They'll like you, I promise." He whispered; we were within hearing range and the kids started to comment sarcastically about Christian being late. He waved them all off and told them to get into their groups. I watched as they split up into groups of seven, and stood quietly—waiting.

"Alright, guys. I told you last week we would be getting another alpha, and here she is."

Alpha! What?

He looked at me and nodded encouragingly. "Introduce yourself." He whispered.

"I'm Levie," I gave a little wave. "Apparently I'm here to help."

"Wait, *you're* Levie?" a girl spoke up from one of the groups, flicking her dark hair away from her face she glared at me with disbelief.

"My mom say's you're the *flicker* that Christian accidentally changed, and now he's *stuck* with you."

"Assert yourself, Levie. They've got to learn to respect you before they learn anything from you." Christian breathed quietly.

She's a dweeby teenager, can't I just kill her instead?

"I can't believe they even let you in here. Haven't you *killed* wolves before?"

I took a deep breath before exploding as calmly as I possibly could.

"That's got to be the most idiotic question I've ever heard in my entire life. *Of course* I've killed wolves. I've killed more wolves than I can count on the digits of my body, *and* I have no problem adding a 15 year old with a bad hair day to that number." Most of the kids snickered at my comment… the petite, brunette-haired girl on the other hand, did *not* find it funny.

"Not to mention you've only been through *one* phase, so I don't understand what gives you the right to be called our '*Alpha*'."

"She's your elder, and you should respect her, *Rebecca*." Christian said sternly.

"She doesn't look any older than me!"

"She's older than *me*," he lied. "And she's got leaps and bounds more experience in the field than you could ever dream of having."

I stepped forward and held my arms out, motioning for her to step forward, too.

Hopefully Christian won't get too mad at me for this.

"If you want the chance to prove that you're stronger than me, then take it. Here it is. If you feel like I should respect you, rather than the other way around, take the opportunity to prove me wrong."

She stared at me like I was a punching bag; sizing me up and trying to figure out how long it would take for her to take me down.

"This is what you've been training for, right? To take down a flicker? So here's your chance."

It didn't take much coercing before she charged at me. I stood my ground and let her hit me once—just to make her feel better about herself—next I stepped, putting my leg in between hers, and grabbed her right arm and tugged it towards me. She tripped over my leg and slammed face first into the dead grass.

This time, no one laughed. Rebecca stood up—clearly pissed, but keeping herself contained—she held her hand out to me. I grabbed her hand and she shook it once, quickly, before nodding at me and stepping back.

"You're the alpha," she whispered, and walked back to her place in the group.

"Run your lap!" Christian shouted from behind me, and they all took off; running towards the wall on the other side of the field we were in and following it down until they were out of sight. I turned around to thank him, but got distracted by a man standing up from the rock he had been sitting on for God knew how long.

"Byron! What do you think of her? She's great, isn't she?"

Byron. My stomach dropped. *Oh god, not the pack alpha.*

"Well, she's… something else, that's for sure." Christian chuckled and turned around, motioning for me to come stand by him.

"Have you been here all along, sir?" I asked as confidently as I could.

"Of course I have. Christian came to me weeks ago and suggested you as a trainer for the young girls. I simply told him I would observe when he felt you were ready. Surely he told you."

Half of me felt the urge to drop to the ground and curl into a ball.

The other half of me wanted to take *Christian* down to the ground and beat his head against a rock until he died…

"He must have forgotten to tell me…" I growled, elbowing him in the ribs.

"Anyway, you handled that situation very well."

"Thank you, sir."

"Please, Levie. Call me Byron. The use of the word 'sir' isn't necessary. I'm only being so proper because you are." He laughed and clapped me on the shoulder. "So what do you say we figure this out once and for all. Do you want this job?"

"Yes." *At least I think I do…*

"Alright. If you can outsmart Christian, you can have it. Go stand about, oh, say 40 feet away. He'll sneak up on you, and you can prove you're worthy right here and now."

"*Easy*," I muttered, walking by Christian and bumping him with my arm.

"I could take you down in my *sleep*."

I walked out into the middle of the field and stood, facing away from Byron and Christian.

"I'm *ready*!" I shouted dramatically.

The field went silent; I stood in place, *waiting*, for a good five minutes before I started to get a little worried.

If they're playing a trick on me, and left me in the field I swear to God…

Then I heard him. He ran from the side of the field, like he had cut across and into the trees before running back across towards me. I stood and waited, grinning; when he got close enough to reach out and grab me, I planted my foot in his stomach and pushed him away—giving him the perfect bait.

He took it, grabbing my foot and pulling it so that I ended up on the ground. He stared at me and laughed, like he had won.

"What are you doing? Finish the job, Christian! One more good blow and I'd be out! *Come on*!"

He kneeled beside me and pulled his arm back like he was going to punch me. When he hesitated, I kicked my foot up, hitting him square in the jaw. While he was distracted, I used my leg to knock his out from under him. He landed on his stomach, so I grabbed his arm and flipped him over; sitting on his chest and using my knees on his arms to keep him down, I mimicked his punching stance before reaching forward and slapping his cheek lightly.

On the other side of the small field, Byron was *rolling*.

"Sorry, Christian. But she got you!"

"Yeah yeah, whatever!" I stood up and helped him up; laughing when he punched me in the arm lightly.

"So do I get the job?" I asked. Some of the kids had gotten back in time to see our fight, and were explaining what had happened to the others. The guys found it hilarious that I had taken Christian down.

"I don't see why not," Byron said. "You are pretty much over-qualified, after all."

CHAPTER NINETEEN

"No, no, no, Alexus. Take her down by the neck, not by the shoulder. Wrap your hand around the back side of her neck!" I watched as Alexus struggled to reach far enough to get her hand on the other side of her partner's neck. *Poor little thing can hardly take her down.* I knew playing favorites was kind of unfair, but during my first month as their trainer, I found that I couldn't help but feel for little Alexus. She had turned 13 less than a week ago. She was the youngest and the smallest in the group; she phased much younger than the others had—a trait she had inherited from her father.

The other girls treated her like a baby sister, which was a relief most of the time, because at least they weren't picking on her. But she didn't want siblings, she wanted *friends*—and didn't have many.

"*Girls*!" I shouted, calling them over to where I was. They formed a half circle around me; some of them knelt, others stood hunched over. It was hot, and the day had been a long one already. "Get some water and then come back here. Walk, *please*. Don't over-work yourselves. Your parents will kill me if you get a heat stroke."

"Why aren't they *running*?" Christian screamed while grinning.

"Because it's hot, and I'm not a drill sergeant!" he shook his head and chased after a group of the girls, causing them to screech and run towards the kitchen with everyone else. "*Hey*! If my girls get sick, *you* get to talk with their parents! *Not me*!"

"*Lexi*!" Christian shouted after his baby cousin. "Bring Levie and I back some water!" She gave him a thumbs up before running up the steps to the camp's kitchen.

A couple of the girl's carried back a pallet of water and laid it down in the shade underneath one of the trees, before coming back and sitting in front of me. Once the rest of the girls had hustled back, I knelt down and brought them closer together.

I had a plan.

"You girls wanna embarrass the guys?" They nodded, smiled, and whispered excitedly. "Alright, but you've got to help Alexus out. We're going to get it so that she can take down Robbie." I turned around and pointed at the kid, who at the moment was making a fool out of his partner. Robbie was seventeen and *massive*; easily the strongest and most talented fighter in Christian's group.

"No *way*! I'm not pairing up with him! I'll *die*!" Alexus whimpered.

"Shh, Alexus. I'm going to teach you how to take anyone, and I mean *anyone*, down. You can practice on all of the girls, and when you realize that you can take all of them down, you can move on to Robbie. You'll be fine."

The girls watched her until she nodded, then they looked to me.

"You girls go distract Christian and the rest of the guys while I teach her this. Make sure you keep Robbie from seeing it at all, okay?" The girls took off across the field again, jumping on and attacking the guys—even Christian. I waited until they were all distracted, before smiling at Alexus.

"Alright, first off you've got to keep an eye on your legs while you're fighting, because that's the quickest way for someone to take you down…"

I watched as Alexus's confidence grew with every girl she took down. She struggled a bit because of how short she was. As soon as her opponent made the mistake I had taught her to watch for, they were down on the ground. She beamed with excitement; and though the girls were confused by her newfound skills, they were excited, too. They wanted to see their little sister take down the biggest guy they knew.

"You ready?" I asked when she had taken down the last of the girls. She nodded nervously. I grabbed a half full bottle of water and threw it at Christian's back, getting his attention.

"What the hell was that for?" he shouted, throwing his arms up dramatically.

"I've got a proposition for you!"

"And what's that?"

"Robbie against Alexus."

"You're out of your mind."

"I *guarantee* she can take him down." Robbie gave me the same look Christian did. "No letting her win; no letting her take you down. Just a fair fight."

"What do I get out of it?" He asked while his friends laughed.

"If you win, she'll take you out on a date!" Christian shouted, sending the kids into fits of laughter. He smirked at me.

"*Fine*. It's a date—*if* you win."

"If you loose, you run laps during training for the next week." Robbie looked miserable. But there was no way I would let him back down.

"*Fine*."

He stepped forward into the space between the two groups and waited for Alexus.

"Are you sure I can do this?" She asked in a whisper, looking up at me with doubt.

"Just watch his feet, and you'll do fine." I patted her back a couple of times before pushing her further out into the field. Within a few seconds they were circling each other like seasoned pros. Five minutes in, Robbie made the mistake I had taught Alexus to watch for. As soon as he crossed his feet, one over the other as he walked, she charged him.

Little Alexus used all her might to throw her shoulder into his chest; because his feet were crossed, he tripped over his own feet and collapsed to the ground. Even though she had technically already won the bet, she knelt on his arms to prevent him from standing back up; grinning while she humiliated him further.

Christian and I were both screaming, both for two very different reasons.

"You let her *win*!" He screeched. I laughed so hard my stomach hurt.

"You're just mad big ol' Robbie got taken down by a ninety pound girl!"

"You guys cheated!"

"No she didn't! She took down each and every one of my girls, *and* your *biggest* guy! Deal with it!"

"Yeah, *Christian*!" Rebecca mocked. "I bet Levie could take *you* down." The girls agreed with roaring excitement. He didn't even hesitate to think about his decision; he simply took off at a charge towards me, grinning from ear to ear. If

I hadn't been a hair faster than him, he would've tackled me within a few seconds. Instead we both circled each other, laughing. I laughed so hard I almost missed my opportunity; with tears streaming down my cheeks I watched as he crossed one leg over the other while sidestepping. I charged him, hitting his chest and screaming as he grabbed onto my shirt and took me down with him. Rather than land at all, I kind of *flopped* instead.

Oh shit.

His shirt was soaked through with sweat from too many hours out in the sun. His nose was red, and I was close enough to his face that I could see he had missed a spot shaving that morning; on the left side of his jawline, just a little patch near where the angle of his jaw curved to meet his ear. His eyes, nearly squeezed shut from laughter, were as blue as they always were.

I leaned my head on his chest while I laughed; my laughter growing worse with every comment the kids made about Christian getting beaten by a girl *again.*

"Are you two gonna make out already, or are you gonna get up?" one of the guys shouted above the laughter that was beginning to die down.

And that was my cue to get up…

CHAPTER TWENTY

"Come on, Levie! Please let me play with your hair!"

"You've got scissors in your hand, Elena! That's not *playing*! Just leave it alone! I can finally keep the hair you cut last time back in a ponytail!"

"Those are called *bangs*, Levie. And I'm not going to cut it all off, I'm just going to put some layers in it or something."

"Leave my hair *alone*."

"Can I at least braid it?" she whined. The other girls had already suffered the hair wrath of Elena, and were sitting on the floor, inspecting the ends and making sure their hair didn't look like a travesty. I had to admit, Elena was pretty good with a pair of scissors, but I liked my hair the way it was, and didn't want it changed any time soon.

"If you put the scissors down, then you can braid it." She threw them down on the table and waved them off when they clattered and slid off the edge. She hopped over Matelyn and Nora's blankets and pillows before flopping onto her own bed, where I had been lounging for the past hour and a half.

"Sit up." She commanded as she scooted closer to me.

"But I'm so *comfy*..." she pointed a self-manicured finger at me; her mouth puckering into what I assumed was a stern glare. I sighed and pushed myself away from the pillows.

As soon as I was sitting, she started brushing through my hair. She tugged through the knots lightly, trying not to hurt me. She was doing the opposite, actually; she was effectively putting me to sleep.

"Levie, do you like Christian yet?" Matelyn murmured.

"*Matelyn*," Nora hissed, slapping her leg. "You can't just ask people that kind of stuff."

"I kind of want to know the answer to that, too. Honestly..." Elena said from behind me.

"I don't hate him anymore, if that's what you mean." I muttered.

"That's *not* what she means." Nora stated. "Like... you've got *other* feelings for him..."

"Do you think he's *hot*?" Elena spat; crawling forward so she could see me and gauge my reaction.

"Oh, *come on* you guys! Are you kidding me?"

"I *saw* you in class that day! When you had to take him down in front of everyone! You were on top of him for like, *forever*!" Nora shouted excitedly.

"Levie! You were on top of *him*!" Elena and Matelyn shrieked in unison. I felt the incessant need to curl into a ball and hide in the corner. I wanted to throw a tantrum, and hurl things around the room to prove my point.

"It wasn't like *that*!" I screamed in time for the door to fly open.

"*Can you three shut up?*"

Oh God no...

"*Christian*! You didn't say anything about Levie being *on top of you*!" Elena screamed. I wanted to choke her; bludgeon her to death with the nearest hard object. Instead I threw myself down on Elena's bed and covered my face with the covers. I peeked out from the covers in time to see Christian lean against the doorframe with a grin.

"Which time?" he smirked. Everyone screamed again; Elena started slapping me through the blankets.

"*Oh my god, Levie*!"

"You take that *back*! Tell them the truth, *Christian*!"

"I just did!" he faked a confused shrug. "Now *please* shut up. I'm trying to sleep, and so is everyone else!"

"I hate you!" I yelled, throwing a pillow from Elena's bed at him; it hit the door as he closed it quickly behind him. I hid my face in my hands and breathed deeply, trying to keep from crying. *They're just kidding around. Don't be so embarrassed.* But that's exactly what I was…

"Hey, Levie. We were just being stupid… we know you don't feel like that… Christian knows too, so it's okay." Elena patted my back softly.

Once I was sure I wasn't going to cry, I looked up and nodded.

"Not all alphas end up with the person they changed…" Nora murmured.

"They almost *always* do, Nora." Matelyn countered.

"No they don't, look at Elena."

"I'm not sure mine and Matt's relationship is the best example, you guys." She said tying off my braided hair with a rubber band. "It's not like we haven't come close…"

"Come close to what?" I asked tugging on the end of the braid that almost reached my waist. The other girls giggled quietly, and Elena shot them a dirty look.

"Mating, Levie."

"Oh."

"Seriously, Elena… why *haven't* you two mated? You've said you loved him thousands of times."

"I have *not*."

"*Do* you love him?" Nora asked sarcastically.

"Of course…"

"Then why not mate?"

"Because I hate him, too. I've already told you this!" She was flustered now that the conversation had turned to her rather than me.

"I just don't understand that…" Matelyn murmured, chewing on her upper lip in thought.

"It's like—I don't really know how to explain it. It's like a *cycle*. I hated him in the beginning. Oh *god* did I hate him. It was like every time I saw him I wanted to rip him to shreds. I hated him so much it hurt. But as time went on, I realized that even though I had other friends, he was the only one who knew everything. He knew exactly who I was and how I felt at any given moment; it really makes you get attached to a guy, you know?" She looked at me, eyes growing wide. "You can relate to that, right? I'm not the only one?"

I nodded. *I could relate to every word she had spoken…*

"Most of the time it feels like a giant rock in the pit of my stomach; I'm so confused of how to feel when it comes to Matt that I just pick the easiest to portray."

"That's why you two are always screaming at each other? Because *hate* is the easiest?"

"We've been on a good streak lately! Give me a break! Levie, you've been here for three months now, how many times have you heard or seen Matt and I fighting. Like *real* fighting?"

"I don't think ever…" I muttered. *How many times had Christian and I fought in the last three months? A lot…*

"See! So we've been doing alright!"

"Elena…"

"Hmm?" She asked, fidgeting with a nail polish stain on her comforter.

"Can I ask why he changed you?"

She bit her lip and stared down at the comforter some more. I watched her count an unknown number out on her fingers.

"Wow," she whispered, looking at Matelyn. "Have I really been here for that long?"

"I was nine when you showed up. I'll be nineteen." Matelyn said with a shrug; pointing a finger. "You're *old*."

"Am *not*."

"Well, you *would* be."

"Give me a break, I'd be like twenty-eight."

"That's *old*." Nora repeated with a snigger.

"*Anyway*," She spat. "I was human. Matt went with his dad and quite a few others on a run to get like new clothes for the next year and things like that. They were picking up stuff in the local mall where I lived, and I was there with my friends. Matt came up to us asking where he could find the nearest cooking ware store. He was really formal about it though; which was weird for me. Being the terrible person that I was, I made fun of him for it. When it made my friends laugh, I really tore into him. I said a lot of terrible things, and it literally came back to bite me. I hurt him so badly that he wanted to get revenge, and I don't blame him for it one bit… at least not anymore."

"So he changed you because of that?"

She nodded.

"Do you think you'll ever mate with him?"

"Some day, when I can get my emotions under control." She murmured. "Until then we're stuck in this cycle, I guess."

Three months was a long time. It didn't feel like three months at all. Three months was enough time to grow attached to people, and make new friends. Three months was enough time to watch a baby begin to turn into a toddler; William was starting to babble and talk now, and Amber was so excited. I found out one day, when she had come over, that Nora and Dustin were her cousins; and that she liked to visit them every once in a while—if only for the fact that Nora liked the kids, and Amber wouldn't have to deal with them for a couple of hours.

William recognized me the second they entered the den, and when Amber sat him down on the floor, he scooted and crawled over to the couch I was sharing with Christian. He chose to stay there for most of his visit, playing quietly with both of us.

Emmett was just as loud and disobedient as ever; giggling whenever he did something wrong, and running around like a maniac for half of the visit and then falling asleep in his mother's lap for the rest.

The girls in my class were getting stronger and better every day. They never treated me with hatred because of what I had been. They looked up to me, and because of them, I felt like a person with value again, rather than a mistake. When they went up against the guys, they were fair competition, and even won a few matches. They made me proud.

Life was good.

CHAPTER TWENTY-ONE

"*Ohh,* **look who's** still got *skills.*" Christian screamed obnoxiously, putting his hand directly in front of my face expecting a high five. I slapped it away instead, and grabbed for the pocketknife he had in his other hand.

"Shut up and let me have my turn! I want to see if I can still do this!" I snatched it out of his hand and stood the same distance away from our target tree as the rest of the guys had. To our left, Matelyn was sitting with Dustin, watching from a further distance while they warmed up the giant pot of spaghetti that Matelyn had made earlier that day to take to the bonfire. To our right, were the rest of the guys, along with Elena, Nora, and Jace—who happened to be really good at throwing knives.

"Levie, if you can stick three throws in a row, we'll give you a queen's ride around the bonfires." Jace said, making everyone else laugh.

"That makes me *not* want to do it!"

"Come on! It'll be fun, just do it."

I threw the knives and before I knew it, I was up on Jace's shoulders and everyone in the immediate area was staring the group of chanting men down.

"You guys are *idiots*!" I screeched. "Put me *down*!"

Jace didn't just put me down, he *dropped* me. When I stumbled, he caught me and laughed.

"I know I'm good looking, Smalls. But if you fell for me I think Christian would be pissed."

I shook my head and pushed him away, laughing.

"You *wish*!"

Jace was an interesting character to say the least. Regardless of his superiority over Christian, they got along so well sometimes it almost scared me. They were polar opposites, almost completely. Jace was spontaneous and completely adored himself and the fact that he was in charge—but it wasn't in a way that drove anybody nuts. I had learned recently, that the only thing Jace didn't enjoy about being in charge of other alphas was the fact that he wasn't allowed out on any runs anymore. He stated that it was the price he had to pay for power.

During my first month here, and the three since, I had come to the conclusion that Christian never did anything spontaneous in his entire life. Even when he committed acts of kindness, they had almost certainly been planned out for days, if not for weeks or more. He never really thought about himself much; but thought constantly of the people around him. I knew he wasn't selfless, because those kind of people never really existed, but he sure as hell didn't make it obvious when he did anything for himself. He was a careful planner. The only thing him and Jace *really* had in common, was their love for fighting.

Because of *somewhat* recent events, though, Christian refused any and all missions that came his way.

"I don't think I'm ready yet." He would tell Jace. I didn't feel guilty about much when it came to *that* particular situation, but every time he shot Jace down, I couldn't help but feel somewhat sad.

We had smelled the spaghetti in the house all day, and now that it was almost finished cooking, we were all frothing at the mouth. I had practically starved myself all day just so I could gorge on the one food that Matelyn could make to perfection. And gorge did we *all.*

After eating half my weight in spaghetti, the only thing I wanted to do was go home and put on pants that were significantly looser than the jeans I had on now. Eating, I had learned, was always the final event of the night. There was something so final about eating yourself into a food coma and waddling sleepily back to your bed. It was comforting knowing that your only worry for the next day was choosing a cell to phase in. We always slept late, we always woke up without an alarm and dressed without a care in the world, we always packed food and extra clothes, and we always phased at midnight. Only to pass out afterwards and wake up at twilight, just in time to waddle back to bed again.

There were no surprises; no random missions or attacks that needed our attention. At this point in time, my life was so predictable that most of the time I remained blissfully in place—just allowing life to drag me along like a feather.

The day after tomorrow would be peacefully busy. Everyone would wake up at our normal time. We'd all eat breakfast together and laugh together like we always did. Christian and I would teach our classes, then hand the older kids over for their short classes on self-phasing. Once the older kids were gone, we would have introductory class with the incoming kids. Afterwards, Elena, Matelyn, Nora, and I would go visit Amber and her sons, like we did every Wednesday.

I thought over the plans for that day while Christian and I headed back to our room, with the rest of our group not far behind us. Most of the fires were being extinguished as we walked, so with every step we took it grew darker.

We were only half way to our house when I saw *it* move out of the corner of my eye.

"Shh, *stop walking*." I hissed, throwing my arms out and turning around, motioning for the rest of our group to be quiet as well. I pointed silently across the small, but open field. About twenty yards away, in the damp grass, sat a twitching, nearly unnoticeable mass. I assumed at one point it had been a woman, but as of now the only thing feminine about it was its long, matted hair that hung only a few inches off the ground while the woman crouched and shuddered from pain and thirst.

Vampires like this were the reason behind the "crawler" nickname.

"*Shit*, Levie go warn everyone back at the bonfires. Go tell Jace or Byron, if you see him. We have to warn everyone so they know to be on the lookout and—"

"You're being idiotic right now, Christian. They don't need to be *warned*, we all need it *dead*." I swiped his knife off his belt loop, ripping the fabric in the process and took off running. By the time everyone began their chorus of "Levie, what are you doings", I was already half way to the crawler, and she had *definitely* noticed me.

I flicked Christian's pocket knife open and realized it was only a four inch blade.

Shit, this is going to suck… I knew I was going to end up hurt, simply because I was going to have to get *way* too close for comfort. *Just don't get bit, don't get bit, don't get bit…*

"***Dammit*, Christian! Press** a little harder, why don't you?" I said it with gritting teeth and squeezing my eyes shut tight as he held a rag soaked with alcohol to my arm to try and stop the bleeding.

"I'm just trying to get it stopped, Levie. What do you want me to do, let you bleed all over the place? Lord…"

Everyone had been equally impressed and worried by my "courageous" act. I had taken it down by myself with nothing more than a four-inch pocketknife, and come out with a nice, nasty set of scratches down my arm from the crawler's long, overgrown nails.

Amongst the list of worriers, though, Christian was at the top.

"They're just scratches, you know?" I reminded him as he continued to dab at my arm with the rag.

"I just want to make sure it's nice and clean. It's already starting to heal, but that doesn't mean it won't end up infected." He murmured.

"I don't think you can get it any cleaner," I pushed his hand away from my arm and let my face fall back into the pillows on my side of the bed. "I'm tired, I just want to go to sleep. Please just wrap it up or something so I don't get any blood on the sheets."

He grabbed a roll of cotton gauze and wrapped it gingerly around my arm before tying it off in a knot. His fingers were cold, and they felt good against my arm's over-cleansing induced pain.

"Can you keep your hand there?" I murmured, curling up under the covers. "It makes my arm hurt less." I heard him chuckle before he placed his hand lightly over my arm, patting it ever so slightly.

"You're such a bad ass, Levie."

"Thanks, I try."

CHAPTER TWENTY-TWO

"Rise and shine, lazy asses!" I flopped over to glare at Dustin sleepily, accidentally punching Christian in the face in the process. He grunted and rolled over, hiding his face from the light that Dustin had flicked on.

I looked at the clock on the wall and wanted to scream.

"*Oh screw you, Dustin!* It's only six o'clock! We have an hour left to sleep in!"

"If you don't stop screaming in my ear, I'm kicking you off of our bed. *Shut up*," Christian grumbled reaching over and hitting me with a pillow.

"Shut up, Christian. And what happened to the special treatment, Dustin," I said, throwing the pillow Christian had hit me with across the room in an attempt to hit Dustin with it.

"You've been here for five months, Levie! Your special treatment's *over*." He left the lights on and slammed the door, laughing as he walked away.

I groaned and rolled out of bed. I flicked the lights off as I walked out and slammed the door again.

I was awake… if Christian could go back to sleep, *good for him.*

"You're such a dick…" I spat, walking by Dustin and punching him on my way to the kitchen.

"What's for breakfast?"

"Cereal…" Elena muttered through her mouth full of miscellaneous breakfast food.

I flashed Elena a thumbs up and climbed up onto the counter so I could reach the cupboard with the bowls in it. I pulled a bowl down and jumped off of the counter.

"These are all that we have left," Elena said, handing me the box of fake, sugary cereal. "The guys got up before I did."

Christian walked into the room and punched Dustin the way I had.

Nora made a comment about him lacking a shirt and he grinned.

I rolled my eyes.

After five months, we were like a completely rehearsed sitcom, or a well-oiled machine. It was the same every morning, and yet it wasn't as repetitive or as boring as it should have been by now. It was *our* morning routine. And I didn't mind it one bit.

Every morning Christian plopped down next to me, throwing his arm casually over my shoulder.

Nora came and sat on the other side of me; moving my legs out of the way before sitting down and allowing my legs to rest on her lap. Matelyn would be curled up on the loveseat next to Dustin, using him as a pillow. Elena and Mateus would sit together on the couch on the opposite side of the loveseat.

And this was what we did…

Our internal clocks were set so close together that we were in sync. Getting up and eating breakfast at the same time, then sitting and visiting was part of the morning schedule. I had grown accustomed to it; it had become *normal* for me, rather than being unbearable like it once was.

Sometimes we'd sit and talk, other times we would play card games; laughing at each other when we lost.

Showers came later; getting dressed followed.

Often once our morning routine was finished, we would split off into our little pairs and trios; leaving the house either to our jobs, or to go visit with friends.

Today though, was a different story…

Christian explained that each household took turns keeping patrol around the outer borders of the camp.

Similar to the Flicker's base, the wolves' camp extended past the walls that surrounded it. The walls only protected the center. Surrounding the walls were miles of forests; as was the case for the Flicker's territory.

He drew on a piece of paper, a picture of the area we lived in… the area we protected in comparison to the areas around it. For miles, the forest stretched around the walls of both the bases for the Flickers and the wolves alike.

Our territories sat in a triangular formation, with the Wolves and the Flickers much too close for comfort at the bottom angles of the figurative triangle. There were only two problems…

One was that the rules set up by the elders inhibited us from attacking each other where our borderlines met. We were only allowed to fight outside of our borders… in the no-man's land that made up the rest of the triangle or if one or the other crossed the line completely.

The other problem… was that the no-man's land was infested with Crawlers...

And occasionally, some of them would sneak into the land

in between the bases.

This was why patrols were necessary, but it also created a lot of tension with the two patrolling teams. Unfortunately, it still needed to be done. It wasn't so bad, though. Mostly it was just like going on a walk with the entire group.

The scenery was beautiful, the trees and shrubbery here were even greener than the plants back at the camp. Though, with less open space, it was warmer—more humid here, under the canopy of the trees. The signs that someone, or some*thing,* had been through the forest recently were everywhere though, and I felt the need to point them out.

"There..." I said, pointing to a tree about a yard off of the trail we were on. "You see the torn up cloth?"

"It looks like zombie clothes." Matt sniggered.

"You're an idiot," Elena muttered from beside me. Her face was shiny with sweat and her hair was plastered to her forehead. Mine wasn't any better.

"Well, didn't it look like zombie clothes, Christian?"

"Shut up, Matt," He muttered, wiping the sweat off of his forehead. He sighed and finally gave in like all of the other guys and pulled his shirt off over his head and threw it around his shoulders.

I stared too long and ended up tripping over one of the roots that had grown up through the dirt. I started laughing the second I hit the dusty ground and so did everyone else.

"I... can't believe... you just did that," Dustin howled. Matelyn doubled over, putting her hands on her knees and laughed.

"Why... *how* did you manage to do that," Christian asked, helping me up.

"Your shirtless state distracted me," I said in between fits of laughter. He grinned and flexed.

"Yeah, I know. That happens a lot."

"Whatever," I said, shoving him away from me. He

caught my arm and yanked me into him; he made it a point to get as much sweat on me as possible. "You're disgusting!"

I struggled to get away from him and ended up on my ass in the dirt, yet again.

"I hate you so much."

"Jace will be *super* impressed with your patrol skills, Levie." Christian stated while he scratched at the rash on his leg through the sweats he had on. "Are you seriously going to make me wear these to bed?"

"I'm *not* sleeping on the couch, and I'm *really* not going to let your poison oak rub off on me, so either you sleep with sweats on, or you sleep on the couch. And it's not like that was a big deal, we basically went on a giant walk for four hours."

"This is *my* bed." He grumbled.

"*Our* bed." I grumbled back, kneeling on the edge of my side.

"Nope, pretty sure it's still *my* bed…"

"*Fine then*," I frowned and started to stand. "I guess the couch in the other room is *mine* now."

"No, come on Levie, I was kidding!" he yanked my arm back to keep me from leaving. I lost the grumpy façade I was trying to keep up when I lost my balance and fell on Christian. We giggled for a few moments, until I sat up.

I was sure I looked like a dear in headlights; it was just that *feeling*—the feeling you get when for some reason your mind believes that something is about to happen that your body isn't ready for, it's like a horrific mixture of fear and excitement that usually causes your stomach to drop to your toes and induces body-wide panic in mere seconds.

"What's the matter with you?" I swallowed my panic and grimaced.

"Do you want the truth or a lie?"

"That's a stupid question, Levie."

His face had been so close to mine that I had completely jumped to conclusions. *Friends don't just kiss their other friends Levie*, I reminded myself. *Not in the real world.*

"I thought you were going to kiss me…" I muttered. He raised an eyebrow and smirked at me.

"Did you *want* me to kiss you?"

"*No*! *Oh god, that's so not what I meant*!" I shouted, feeling the skin on my face burn from embarrassment. "It's just, you know when your mind jumps to conclusions without you consciously doing it, *I don't know*! God, I'm sorry, it's just I—"

"No, no, I understand. You're wildly in love with me and were hoping I was going to declare my love for you. Sorry to break it to you, Levie. But I love myself far too much to ever love another."

"Please shut up."

"It's okay, you don't have to deny it."

"*Please*, I'm *begging* you."

"Oh, what's that? You're begging me to kiss you?"

"*Christian*—" he leaned in like he was actually going to kiss me and I shoved him away, causing him to loose his serious façade and start laughing. "If you kiss me, I'll *kill* you."

"You couldn't kill me even if you wanted to!"

"You wanna test that?"

"*Absolutely*."

It was then that I realized my mind was a complete and utter traitor. A traitor that, in completely uncalled for moments, enjoyed causing me to panic; a traitor that, when panic was necessary, failed to help me out at all. Because when Christian all but tackled me, the only thing I could do was stay frozen in place.

Part of my brain understood that he was just being an asshole; he had gotten too caught up in our banter, and taken it *way* too far. But most of my mind didn't understand at all why he was kissing me.

He's kissing me.

I wasn't even sure if I was kissing him back. It was like my thoughts were so centered on my own confusion I couldn't even figure out how to move my arms again; I couldn't remember what muscles were needed to slap the shit out of someone.

But his lips were so *soft*, and his hand—equally as soft—was on my shoulder, holding me in place. Like he had forgotten the whole thing was a joke.

He is still kidding, isn't he?

It had only been seconds, yet my mind had bounced around so fast that I had run out of thoughts to distract me from the situation at hand.

The noise my hand created when it came into contact with Christian's cheek echoed off the walls in his room.

"I can't believe you just did that," I spat. I stumbled off the bed and ran, hitting the front door before Christian could say my name. I threw that door open, ran down the hall and across the den, and threw the main door open as well before taking off across the grass and running in no particular direction.

I ran until my lungs were burning and my eyes watered from the wind and the confusion. I knew it wasn't that cold outside—it was only the beginning of September—yet I was freezing and shaking, just like I had when I first got here.

I was at the edge of the fields now, where rather than the potatoes that had been grown before, the rows were full of corn. The stalks were almost my height at this point in the season; it was the perfect place to hide from everything around me.

I chose a row at random and ran down in between the stalks until I was out of breath again. I was in underwear and a baggy t-shirt, but I sat down in the dirt regardless. I pulled my legs up to my chest and took a deep breath before simply allowing myself to fall over onto my side in the dirt.

I couldn't wrap my head around what had just happened. I knew he was trying to be funny, and I'm sure at this point he knew it hadn't been funny at all. I also knew Christian well enough at this point to know he definitely felt like an ass after what had happened. I had every right in the world to be angry—but I wasn't.

It was human nature to not *think* in the occasional situation; and I knew at least for Christian, one of those situations had just occurred. I wasn't angry; I had gotten all of my anger out when I slapped him. Now I was just *confused.*

My stomach churned more and more with every thought that crossed my mind, but there were two thoughts that refused to go away.

The first was surprisingly the lesser of the two; it had been all fun and games—all joking—until he kissed me, and that kiss was far from joking…

The second thought was the one that confused me the most…

A part of me wished I hadn't stopped him.

Friends don't kiss friends, Levie, I reminded myself with a sigh.

I watched as a june bug began its trek up the stalk that was nearest to my face. The green plant was covered in dew from the cold night air, and the bug couldn't get enough traction to climb very far. Its wings were too wet to fly to the top.

"I know how you feel," I whispered allowing it to crawl onto my finger; I lifted it up to the ear of corn at the top. "Sometimes you just need someone to pick you up out of the dirt." I laid back down; this time on my back, so I could look up at the sky. The moon illuminated the clouds enough that, even though the sky was dark, I could see them moving.

Once I managed to calm myself down, I fell asleep under the clouds.

I woke up and rubbed my face, feeling the dirt on my hands. I knew I was back at home, though; I'd recognize Christian's bed anywhere, especially considering I had spent a part of the night on the ground outside.

The sheets were too cold though, and I knew he hadn't slept here the night before. I slid out from underneath the covers and saw the dirt I had left behind on his white sheets. I was a wreck.

I peeked around the corner of the hall and saw him, curled up on the couch as best he could. I chuckled and padded across the floor; kneeling at the side of the couch I shoved him lightly to wake him.

"Hmm?" He grumbled, keeping his eyes closed.

"When did you come find me last night?"

"I was two rows over from you the entire time waiting for you to fall asleep so I could carry you back home." I smiled; when he finally opened his eyes, he smiled too. "I'm sorry, Levie. I didn't mean for things to get out of hand, sometimes I just forget that I can't mess with you like I do the guys."

I refrained from asking him when he had ever kissed one of the guys, knowing it would only make things even more awkward than they already were.

"I'm not one of the guys?"

"Not quite," he murmured.

"You're a dick," I reminded him, punching him in the shoulder before hugging him.

"So we're alright?"

"I *guess*."

CHAPTER TWENTY-THREE

"Levie," a voice whispered somewhere near my ear. I opened my eyes slowly; I knew it wasn't Christian, and I was curious. It was still dark outside, far too early for me to be awake. I grumbled quietly.

"Hmm?" I rolled over, and came face to face with Matt. He peered at me through the darkness, smiling slightly and rubbing at his eyes.

"You wanna go hunting with me?"

"*Hunting*," I whispered, "Hunting for *what*?"

"Food," he replied, kneeling on the ground. "We've got to go early if we want to catch anything. You don't have to go… but I figured you'd like getting to shoot again."

"*Deal*." I slid out of bed and did my best to ignore the look Matt made when he realized I was only in a pair of underwear and a tank top. *Give me a break; I can't sleep in pants, Jesus.*

I put on a pair of my sweat pants and tugged on a

sweatshirt over the shirt I had on. I shoved my feet into my boots and pulled my hair up into a ponytail while he led the way out of the house; grabbing a duffel bag on his way.

The sky was dark outside; there were no signs of dawn whatsoever. The grass was slippery from the drizzle of rain that had been falling all night, and that continued to fall as we made our way across the grass and into the empty fields. The corn had only been harvested a few days before, and yet there was already talk of the next crop. Everyone was hoping for more vegetables, but it would always come down to what could survive the winter ahead.

We made it to the edge of the property line, and Matt dropped the duffel bag on the ground; when he unzipped it and handed me a black bow and a handful of arrows, I could have screeched with excitement.

"Anything you shoot that's edible, we take back. If it's too big to fit into this duffel bag, then you'll have to carry it."

"Sounds good to me."

We walked side by side for what seemed like a long time, keeping our steps as light as possible. The rain had soaked the ground enough to keep anything that had once been dry from cracking under our feet. I could hear plenty of animals around us; the only problem was that I couldn't *see* them. But I didn't want to be the first to speak… so I kept quiet. We walked until the sun was just barely beginning to peak through the leaves above us.

"Can you climb?" He whispered, pointing to the trees above us. I nodded. "Because this is our spot for the morning." He walked to a tree a few feet away and pointed at the lack of bark on its trunk.

"What's that?"

"Rub marks from a buck. They get pretty big in this area, so if we shoot one, it'll feed our group for a week or so as long as we eat it with other things." He led the way to a tree directly across from the one we had looked at and motioned for me to climb it first.

"Give me a boost up." Matt laced his fingers together and kneeled so I could step onto his hands. He lifted me up easily; high enough that I could climb onto the lowest branch and start to climb up higher. He followed me up by simply jumping and catching the nearest branch. I watched the muscles in his arm ripple as he pulled himself up.

"Show off!" I whispered as he sat next to me on one of the main branches. He chuckled.

"And now, we wait."

"What do we do to pass the time?" I asked, grinning.

"Play the question game."

"How does that work, then?"

"I ask you questions and you answer them."

"Sounds simple enough."

"How good of a shot are you?"

"*Great.*" I fidgeted around on the branch and made sure I had my balance before nocking an arrow. "Throw a piece of bark into that tree."

"There's no way…" he muttered. He broke off a decent sized piece from the branch beside us and lobbed it into the tree that had the rub marks on its trunk. Once I heard the flapping of wings I pulled the string back until it was brushing my lips and aimed down the arrow. As soon as a bird broke free of the leaves, I released the arrow, letting it soar through the space between us and pierce the bird before it disappeared into the brush on the forest floor.

"Can we eat that?"

"No, you just shot a crow."

"Oh, *come on*! You can eat crow!"

"Are you going to cook it? Because no one else knows how."

"Sure. I'll shoot some more and cook enough for

everyone to eat."

He squirmed at the thought of eating crow but ultimately kept quiet.

"You've got to get that, because if I jump down you'll just have to get down and help me up again."

Matt rolled his eyes and dropped down from the branch; he hit the ground wrong and his legs collapsed out from under him, causing him to fall face first into the wet leaves and dirt. I sniggered at him when he stumbled up from the ground, and laughed even harder when he attempted to throw a handful of the leaves at me and failed miserably, causing them to fall back into his face.

Matt jogged off into the brush a few yards away and pulled the arrow out of the ground, leaving the bird impaled on the arrow while he carried it back. He held it up as high as he could and I used my feet to grab onto it while he jumped up onto the branch and climbed up again.

"Right through the neck. Good job, Levie."

"Thanks." I smiled. I pulled the bird slowly off the arrow and threw it in the duffel bag that was hanging from a branch nearby.

"It wasn't that far away, though."

"Are you *challenging* me or something, Matt? You realize it was *moving*, right?"

"Alright, alright. You've clearly got an awesome shot. I was just giving you a hard time."

We sat in silence for a while swinging our legs and watching for signs of animals.

"Are we still playing the question game?" I asked finally.

"Do you still want to?"

"I don't mind. It's kind of boring just sitting here in silence."

"Alright," he bounced his leg a few times, attempting to

think of a question to ask. "How long have you been sleeping with Christian?"

"Oh… what kind of sleeping are we talking about here?" *Awkward.*

"The normal kind, the normal kind!" He sputtered, causing me to laugh.

"Uh, well… I've been here six months total, right?"

"I think that's right…"

"Then it's been close to five months." The look on his face was one of disbelief.

"I had no idea he had… *liked* you for that long. I mean I knew you were on friendly terms, but damn."

"It was supposed to be for a few days or so until he was able to get permission for me to move into the empty room in our building but I don't really know what happened to that plan." To be honest, I wasn't even sure he had even attempted to follow through with that plan…

"Why don't you just move now? You can probably get permission to move on your own at this point, since you've been here for so long."

"I don't mind, really. It's not that big of a deal where I sleep." He nodded and left it at that. *He has Elena*, I reminded myself. *He understands.*

The truth was I had never even brought up moving out to Christian, because I didn't *want* to leave. I had grown accustomed to him being an aspect of every part of my day. He was constant; from the moment I woke to the moment I fell asleep, he was there—either in person, or in thought. He was my best friend, and the thought of not being near him as often as possible had my chest tightening.

What would I do without him?

"So do I get to ask about you and Elena, since you're asking me about Christian and I?"

Matt chuckled and shrugged, "If there's anything she

hasn't already told you, then go for it."

"Well, I mean… I know her side of the story, but I don't know *yours.*"

"Ask away."

"I guess mainly I just don't understand why you two aren't together…"

"Keep this between you and me," he whispered, as if the animals in the forest around us would hear and understand. "But there's really only one thing holding us back; she's scared. She won't even admit it to me, either, but I still know." He pointed to his head and held my gaze. "It's hard for her to keep her emotions straight, and the more Christian tells me about you the more I realize that she really can't help it. Not that you have it anywhere near as bad as she does, I don't think."

"What do you mean?" I humored him, even though I knew *exactly* what he was talking about.

"Well I mean… when we get into arguments, she hates me—it always ends up like that. It goes away so fast though it scares me sometimes. She'll run off and hide for a while, or she'll try to hurt me, but she always ends up changing her mind. Like she runs out of hate. But when she decides she loves me, I can feel how strong it is—that's why it's so hard for me; I feel the same way, the only problem is that she's afraid she'll run out of love just like she runs out of hate. At least, I think that's what she's afraid of…"

I resisted the urge to hug Matt and picked at the bark instead.

"You really do love her, don't you?"

"I have for a long, long time."

By the time the sun had fully risen, we had shot enough crows to last us nearly two weeks in the way of dinner, as well as two deer. I stayed in the tree for a good twenty minutes while Matt ran back and dragged a pajama-clad Christian with him back into the woods to help carry the deer back. Leaving me to carry the bag of birds, regardless of the fact that I could've carried the deer without too much hassle.

I walked behind the two of them on the way back, watching the way Christian stumbled over his too long sweat pants and contemplating everything Matt had told me.

There were *far* too many similarities between Elena and Matt's relationship, and mine and Christian's; too many for me to ignore it, anyway. It had been a month since he had kissed me without thinking, and if I thought about it enough, I could still remember the way it felt—and that made me uncomfortable… It had been awkward and upsetting, even hurtful in some ways. So why did I *blush* when I thought about it? Why couldn't I bring myself to sleep anywhere but by his side?

Normal friends *enjoyed* each other's company—they didn't *crave* it.

I wasn't sure Christian and I were normal friends, and that scared me. So much had changed in my mind that morning, and yet, the day went on the same as every day for the past six months—*normally*.

CHAPTER TWENTY-FOUR

Three weeks ago I had made the mistake of mentioning that I knew the exact number of days I had been a werewolf. Ever since, the guys had been reminding me with each day that passed. Today was 215 days—*seven months*. It seemed like a much longer length of time than it actually was. It seemed even longer still, considering everything that had changed from my very first night here until now.

Quite a few of the girls in my class had phased on their own, so starting next spring they would be training on four legs, rather than two. They would have a new teacher, and I would have a *mostly* new class of girls I had never met before. When the training season had ended, I told Christian that next year I wanted to train the kids all together—because the honest truth of it all was that they needed to be able to take seriously the fact that they may very well end up fighting someone of the opposite sex; there would be no going easy out in those woods when things became real.

Christian agreed, and surprisingly, so did Byron. Jace even saw how enthusiastic I was about the plans that he joined in; suggesting that we should start administering a "test" of sorts, to make sure the kids were really ready to move on from fighting—thus cutting back on the number of wolves that would be lost in future battles, because we'd know for sure we weren't sending amateurs out into the field. Christian and I, with Byron's permission, decided to have Jace come to a few of the classes out of the week to help out starting next year; Byron even agreed to make appearances often as well. The boys and girls alike would be so much stronger than ever before.

I had grown much closer with everyone—Matt especially, which had been unexpected. Matt and I would often go on walks in the mornings; long before anyone was awake—when the sun showed no signs of rising and the grass was slippery from the dew. He'd sneak into mine and Christian's room in the morning and wake me up in various ways, ranging from a wet willy, to simply shaking me. I'd layer up and follow him out the door, and as soon as we were out of sight of the house, he'd rant about whatever was on his mind.

Of course, more often than not, it was Elena that had him upset. I wasn't quite sure why *I* was the one he ranted to. I figured when he wanted answers he went to Christian, and when he just wanted to get things off his chest he came to me; mostly because I had absolutely *no* idea what to say in return—but someone had to just listen every once in a while, right?

Then there was mine and Christian's... *relationship*; regardless of how one-sided it may be. I had gone from hating him so *strongly* that first night to... to be honest; I had no idea *what* I was feeling now. What I did know though, was that when I opened my eyes in the morning and he was already awake and smiling, I couldn't help but smile back.

"Seven months," he whispered, poking my nose as hard as he could. I swatted his hand away sleepily, rolling my eyes.

"It's not like it's a big milestone or anything, that was last month."

"We can still celebrate, though."

"By doing what?" He grinned and tugged the covers loose from my grip and flung them over our heads.

"Sleeping in!"

"But we're already awake." I giggled as I watched him struggle to get comfortable again.

"But *they* don't know that." He said, pointing in the general direction of the den. I rolled my eyes but silently thanked the part of Christian's mind that came up with this idea.

"Whatever you say." I murmured.

"You sure have changed a lot," he blurted out after a few seconds of silence. "It'd be hard to convince someone that you were ever a flicker, if they didn't know already, I think…"

"Sometimes I forget…"

"Really?"

I nodded, "We've all got down such a routine, you know? It feels like I've been going through the same routine for years now, rather than months."

"We have a routine?"

"Well, yeah, I mean… every morning we wake up and go out to the den and eat breakfast with everyone and talk, then we go do our thing for the day, training, helping in the fields, visiting your aunt or Amber or both of them sometimes—" he started chuckling, cutting me off. "I guess it's not much of a routine for you, but it is for me. And I *like* it thank you very much."

"Considering the turn around you've made while you've been here, by all means, *keep* your routine." He held his hands up in defense causing the blankets to move and cover his face. I giggled quietly while he slapped at the blanket in an attempt to keep it away.

"How do you think you've changed the most?" he asked after he had turned the blanket into a tent once more.

He watched as my forehead wrinkled in thought. There were so many things about me that had changed for the better; it was hard to pick just one thing that I thought had changed the *most.* My personal preferences, my outlook on friendship and loyalty, my thought process—*everything* was different.

"I have a heart now," I murmured. "That's what has changed the most."

"What do you mean?"

"I mean I *care* now. I actually care about people, *and* I care *for* people. There's no more cold-hearted, half-lifeless Levie. I have a sense of humor, and a personality, and thoughts, and feeling, and *a lot* of things I didn't have before."

"You went from being a robot, to being *human.*"

"Well, not exactly human. But yeah." He chuckled and touched my arm gently.

"I hope you don't take this the wrong way, Levie. But I really like the person you've become." He smiled again before closing his eyes. His gentle touch became a grasp as he pulled me closer and into a hug. "Now we're going to sleep in."

CHAPTER TWENTY-FIVE

Today would be another long day. With the news Jace had been given about the whereabouts of the vampires in the area, it was sure to be serious, rather than the playful mission we had last gone through.

"Ready to go yet?" Christian asked, ruffling my hair while I attempted to finish off my braid. I let out an exaggerated sigh, glaring at him as I pulled the braid out so I could brush my hair and start over again.

"You're such an ass."

I had woken up this morning with frozen limbs and an unwilling mind that refused to make my muscles move. I laid underneath the covers, willing myself to just suck it up and roll out of bed. *All it would take was a few quick steps to get to the sweats in the dresser*, I told myself. I would get warm soon enough. No matter how much I willed my arms to throw off the blankets, no matter how much I willed my legs to swing and touch the floor, I couldn't move. It had taken me at least a half an hour to convince myself that getting out of bed was worth it. To be honest though, now that I was up, it wasn't worth it at all.

The floor was cold. The air was cold. *I* was cold.

Even after a pair of sweats over a pair of leggings, and enough layers covering the top half of my body to make it difficult to braid my hair, I was still cold. I wasn't usually a complainer when it came to the temperature, but in my own defense, when I had run missions in the freezing weather before, I was capable of generating my own body heat. Now, not so much…

"Do you think three pairs of socks are enough to keep my feet warm and dry, or do you think four would be better?"

"I think you're over-exaggerating, and it's really not as cold as you seem to think it is."

"Four it is…" I muttered, digging around in the dresser drawers to find another pair. "You must be forgetting that my body heat is *non-existent.*"

"Exactly! So you should only be able to get so cold, right?"

I took a deep breath while I tugged on my fourth pair of socks before meeting his gaze. "Go drink some coffee, *think* about what you just said, and *then* come back and let me know what you think. Okay?"

"No time for coffee, it's time to go!" I hadn't noticed the bag in his hand until he held it out for me to take—full of arrows. The bow Matt had told me to keep was in his other hand. "Everyone else is waiting outside already. They claim they're getting used to the cold." He winked, and I heaved another sigh; grabbing the bag and the bow, I followed him out into the weather.

I had been cold inside the house, but walking outside was enough to make me curse. Everything seemed to be varying shades of grey; especially the clouds above that had been spitting out clear-grey rain since early this morning. Elena saw the face I made at the rain and mirrored it.

"At least it isn't snowing," she seemed to say more to herself than to anyone else.

We trudged through the rain and met Jace at the gates before starting what would, without a doubt, be the wettest and most miserable mission so far.

The grass, leafs, the ferns—everything that had once made up the thick green forest was now withered and brown, and for the most part, plastered in a thick, sopping layer over the ground. Every freezing breath I took burned my nose and made it run, but I could still smell the strange combination of metal and dust that the rain always carried with it.

I was walking in between Christian and Nora; watching Jace as he walked in front of me with both of his boots untied, and praying that he would trip just to give us some comic relief from the continuous silence—other than the rain and the squelch of boots, of course.

If someone didn't say something soon, I was going to run headfirst into the nearest tree. We had been walking for nearly three hours when Christian finally *did* say something, though, and I immediately wished that he hadn't been forced to open his mouth.

"Guys, be quiet," he hissed. I watched as he stared off into the distance until he rapidly turned to stare at me, eyes wide and frightening.

"*Get down, Levie*," he spat. He put his hands on my shoulders and forced me down into the dead, knee-high shrubs. "*Stay down.* I don't care what happens, just *stay*."

They all carefully pulled knives out of their pockets and stood quietly, waiting. A few moments passed and I was finally able to hear the threat coming our way.

The sound of boots crunching against dry leaves was audible, as was the all too familiar sound of laughter...

tinkling and light; it matched with a face in my memory of a small girl whom used to share a tent with me…

I started to get up and Matt flashed me a glare. *Stay down*, he mouthed. I bit my lip and held back tears.

Don't hurt them… please don't hurt them!

"Look guys, it's a pack of *mutts*." I heard Alan shout cruelly. "What are *you* here for, *dogs*?"

"We're only doing the same thing you are; we don't want any trouble," Christian said in a calm tone. I watched as he put his knife back into his pocket and held his hands out in a peaceful gesture.

"You always want trouble." That had been Keegan; his jeering voice wasn't hard to pick out.

"We *never* want trouble! You guys and the rest of the dumb asses on your base are the ones who always start *shit*," Elena spat. The other group laughed.

"Wait, what was that?" I watched as Alan looked around at the rest of the team. "Does anyone know what the little blonde *bitch* said? I don't speak *dog*."

"Don't talk to her like that," Matt growled stepping over the invisible line that separated the Flicker's territory from ours.

Everything happened so fast… the team drew their weapons on Matt and the pack drew their own weapons to defend Matt.

Before anyone could stop me, I was standing up and stumbling my way through the brush to stand in front of Matt and the others.

"*Levie*," Bridget screamed. She started to run across the line, but Scotty grabbed her.

"Bridget you can't…"

"*Bridget!*" Christian grabbed my arm as I started to run. I ripped my arm out of his grip and spun around to glare at him. "Don't touch me! That's *my* team!" I ran across and sank down to my knees, enveloping Bridget into a hug.

"L-Levie…" she wrapped her skinny arms around my neck and sobbed into my hair. "No… you can't be…"

Her words made me feel like my chest was collapsing in on itself.

"I know, Bridget… I'm so sorry for leaving you… I couldn't help it." She stepped away from me to wipe her eyes, allowing me to stand up.

"So, you're *dead* now," Alan muttered from behind me.

That had hurt, *bad*; hit home.

"I'm not… I'm not really dead, Alan."

"Oh, no?" He stepped closer to me and grabbed my hand; forcing it against his chest. "Do you feel that, Levie? That's a heart; a living, *beating* heart. Now check *your* heart! There's nothing there, Levie! You make up part of the living dead now! That makes you an abomination, a freak of nature, something to *fear*."

His words repeated themselves over and over again in my head; *abomination, freak, something to fear…*

"Why are you being so… so mean?"

"I'm being honest, Levie. You're not *you* anymore."

"How could you say that? You don't even know who I am anymore!"

"That's my point, Levie."

"Alan, *shut up*! Stop being a dick," Luther shouted. "There's no reason to antagonize her. She's still *our* Levie."

"No she's not, Luther. Can't you tell? She's one of *them* now."

"You know what, Alan? It's the Flickers who are the monsters, not the wolves. The only person in the entire team who proves that is *you*. You have *no* right to tell me that I'm an abomination."

"Can you really say that? Can you *honestly* say that without feeling any guilt at all?"

"Absolutely," I spat, taking a step towards him.

"Wow, they really *have* brainwashed you, haven't they?"

"Say *one* more thing to her, I *dare* you." Christian was suddenly behind me; one hand at the small of my back, the other at Alan's throat. My old team lifted their weapons hesitantly.

"Levie… if you don't make him back down…"

"We'll have to take him out." Scotty finished Luther's sentence.

"Christian…" I whispered, tugging at his free arm. "Christian, let him go. He's not worth it."

"No he isn't, but *you* are."

"She's not worth much now…" Alan spat.

"*That's it.*" Christian threw Alan to the ground and stepped on his arm with full force. Alan let out a gutteral scream and rolled into the fetal position. "Let's go guys. We're done here."

"Wait!" I turned and jogged back to Bridget and gave her another hug. "I love you, Bridget. And I'm still the same person I was, okay? I'm not going to change. Just make sure you don't get brainwashed by the others. They're not nice people… Just keep that in mind." She nodded and tears started to roll down her cheeks again.

Before I could hear her voice again, I stepped back over the border line and walked with the rest of the pack in the opposite direction… away from my old team.

"I can't believe you did that. You could've gotten yourself killed, Christian."

"I didn't like hearing him talk to you like that…"

"I'm not worth you getting yourself killed, though," I murmured.

"Others would beg to differ."

CHAPTER TWENTY-SIX

It took a lot to get out of bed the next day. I had lost almost every ounce of confidence; I just didn't want to leave the house… or my bed, for that matter.

"Levie, come on… I know yesterday was rough, but you can't let it get you down."

"He told me I was a monster…" I whispered through the sheets that were covering my head. I knew I had already slept in past the "alarm" and that I had probably missed breakfast, but I didn't care.

"I wish you would've let me kill him…"

"You would have regretted it," I murmured, peeking over the edge of the sheets.

"Only because I'm a nice guy…" He smiled wryly and poked my exposed nose. "You're not a monster, Levie. You know that right?"

"Says one werewolf to another," I mumbled. He chuckled and bunched up the blankets that covered me and threw them out of the way.

He cuddled up beside me and faced me; throwing the white covers back over our heads. The light shining through the white covers gave everything underneath a gold-ish hue.

"We're not monsters… we're all just a little misunderstood," He murmured, his face only inches away from mine.

"Now if only that were the truth."

"You know it's the truth, Levie. You're just not willing to admit it because of the state you're in."

"And what state would *that* be?" His expression fell; no longer silly, but serious.

"What happened yesterday hurt you… and I want you to know that not a single word Alan said is true."

"So I'm *not* a dead werewolf?"

"You know what I mean…" I nodded. "You're much more important than them."

"Why do you keep saying that," I murmured. "Why do you think I'm so important? I'm just me… nothing *too* special."

"If you could see yourself through my eyes, you'd understand," He whispered, wrapping his arms around my waist and pulling me into a hug. The movement forced my hands against his bare stomach, where I could feel a long, thin, puckered line. I ran my fingers over the small ridges; the scar wasn't smooth like most scars were, instead it was rough in places and indented in others.

I had seen it plenty of times. For some reason, though, I had always felt the need to touch the scar I had left behind on him. For a long time, I thought maybe it would remind me of my past—possibly remind me that maybe there *was* some good in what I had done. But now, the only thing it made me realize was that I was less of a monster now than I had ever been.

"You know, you're right…"

"Hmmm?"

"I'm not a monster. At least, not anymore."

"Now you understand…" he said, sounding relieved. After three months of confusion and misunderstood moments, the familiar panic I had felt what seemed like so long ago was making another appearance. Being under the covers together meant he was already close, and there were only a few short inches between us when he started to move in. Rather than open my mouth and start asking questions like I had the last time, the only thing to find its way out was a shaky breath. Even after three months, I could still remember what his lips had been like, and as he kissed me again I knew they hadn't changed.

There was no joking this time; when Christian's mouth was suddenly on mine I kissed him back with only an ounce of hesitation. My chest was so tight that my breath came out in little gasps. When he deepened the kiss, I followed his lead, running my hands up his arms until they found the perfect place to rest on his shoulders.

My stomach, my arms, legs, chest… everything ached—and not because I wanted him to take things any further, but because it was physically painful to realize how badly I had wanted this.

Oh, God what is going on?

When Christian pulled away my heart was racing; my hands shook while they remained on his shoulders. "I've wanted to do that for a long time," he breathed. I knew exactly how he felt.

"*Wow…*" I whispered, unsure of what else to say.

"I knew since the beginning this is where you belonged. You were too *good* for them."

As if by magic, I stopped breathing altogether. Like someone had punched me in the gut, causing me to heave my last breath. My body no longer ached—it hurt; my thoughts raced. *No… no, no, no… please…*

"What do you mean?" My question hardly came out as a whisper, but he must have taken it as emotional excitement, because he answered immediately.

"The night of the mission, when I saw you, I knew there was something different about you. I could tell you didn't belong with the others. When we ended up breaking out in the fight—"

"You decided you'd just change me!" I said loudly, sitting up and throwing the covers away from Christian and I, officially ruining the moment we had shared seconds ago. "When you realized you were going to actually have to hurt me, you decided you'd change me and *save* me from myself, is that it?"

"Levie, I—"

"You took *my* life into your own hands without *any* consideration as to how I would handle becoming a werewolf! You didn't even think about the fact that you'd be wrenching me away from everything I had ever *known*, Christian! Not to mention—not to mention the fact that if I had followed the rules, I would have been *killed*!" I stuttered, seething with anger.

"But things are so much better now, aren't they? Can you honestly say your old life was better?" he shouted.

"That's not the point! The point is that you don't see anything wrong with the fact that you *manipulated* my *entire* life, Christian!"

I stood up and darted for the door, once again running away from my problems. He had anticipated my move though, and was at the doorway long before I was.

"Levie, *please*." He grabbed my shoulder and held on tight until I shook myself free again.

"Just leave me *alone*!" I screamed, tears causing my voice

to crack. I went to yank the door open but he grabbed my arm again.

"Levie I'm *sorry*!"

I twisted his arm around the way I had the very first time he had ever grabbed me, stopping just before the point of popping it out of place. "I've done this before, and I'll do it again…" I whispered, willing my voice to hold at least a little bit of the anger I felt.

When I opened the door and walked as calmly as I possibly could down the hall, he didn't follow me. When I was half way to the den, I heard him growl before a loud, splintering sound echoed down the wall. I didn't have to turn around to know the doorframe was no longer in perfect condition.

Matt, Dustin, and Nora were already awake, and their stares were on me the second I walked into the open room.

"Sorry," Matt whispered as I walked past him. "Elena's in her room."

I nodded, knowing she was definitely who I needed to talk to right now. I opened her door just as she was walking to the bathroom. As soon as she saw my face, she dropped the clothes she had been carrying and darted over to me, wrapping her arms around me tightly.

"What happened, Levie?"

"I—I don't really know what happened…"

Elena made a face somewhere in-between sympathy and confusion as she dragged me to her room and sat me down on her bed. Sitting next to me, she put a hand on my shoulder and smiled encouragingly. "Just start from the beginning."

So I took a deep breath and tried to explain the situation that I couldn't quite comprehend myself. I told her about the feelings I'd discovered; and how I had practically told Matt I depended on Christian. I told her about him telling me how important I was to him. Then I began to ramble.

Suddenly stories and moments from months ago were spilling out. I told her about how nice he had been after our fight; even though that had been months ago, it was the first time he had been kind, and it was etched into my dearest memories. I told her about our race after working in the fields. I told her how he held my hand during my first phase. I confessed about the first time he had kissed me, and how confused I had been because I couldn't tell if he had been kidding or not.

And Elena's eyes grew wide when I finally got to what had happened less than an hour before. I told her about him kissing me then, and realizing how much I had wanted him to do it.

Finally, I told her his reason behind changing me. And rather than her being confused, I knew she understood.

"Levie, can we talk please?"

"Oh, God. Please don't let him in here." I whispered, hastily wiping the tears from my cheeks. Elena nodded and darted to the door just in time to slam it shut on Christian while he was attempting to open it.

"Christian! Go *away*!"

"Elena, come on! This doesn't have anything to do with you, let me in!"

"*No*? Well, it has to do with my *best* friend. And you know what she says? She says *not to let you in*!"

"*Elena*, so help me God! If you don't let me in—"

"What? Are you going to hit me?" She shouted, throwing the door open and getting in his face. "You're not my alpha, Christian!"

I remembered almost the same words coming from Matt the last time Elena had taken it upon herself to get in Christian's face. That particular combination of words seemed to set Christian off in a way that nothing else could, and being as angry as I was at the time, I wished more than anything I could say those words and have them be true.

Even though I was in a completely different room—and couldn't even *see* the confrontation going on—I could hear Christian breathing slowly, calming himself down. After a few moments of near-silence I heard Elena attempt to close the door, but something prevented her from doing so; I assumed he had stuck his foot in the door, but he was so angry it wouldn't have surprised me if he had wedged his entire body in the way.

"I want to hear it from her."

"What! you think I'm *lying*?"

"I know you're not lying. But after everything we've been through, I deserve to at least hear it from her."

"You don't deserve anything…"

"Yes, he does." I murmured; having slid off of her tall bed and quietly crept around the corner. Elena turned to look at me and bit her lip before allowing the door to swing open so Christian could see me.

He raised an angry brow and waited for me to say what needed to be said.

"She's telling the truth."

"You don't want to talk? About *any* of this?"

"*No.*"

"So it's all over, then? Because if you cared, you'd want to work this out."

"That's not what I said!"

"Then let's talk about this!"

"There's nothing to talk about! This is your *fault*!" I screamed, throwing my hands up in surrender.

"Then none of it matters? Nothing that's happened recently means enough for you to want to fix this?"

I wanted time to hate him. I wanted time to be selfish and

wallow in the fact that I had finally managed to find a flaw in the man who had seemed so perfect despite what he had done to me; back when I thought what he had done was an accident.

"As of right now, none of it matters enough."

His eyes closed immediately and he began to breathe the way he had a few minutes before. When he finally opened his eyes he looked at me and uttered a single word before leaving the room.

"Fine."

One syllable. Four letters. One word to completely symbolize the massive canyon I had just slapped between us.

My chest wasn't tight like it had been before. Now it was hollow. Empty. Like someone had hit me hard enough to knock the air out of my lungs. I could feel the numb ache in my knees and feet, and rather than allow my legs to buckle I slowly made my way back to Elena's room.

I sat on her bed and stared at my stomach, watching as my heart beat so hard that my stomach kept time with it. My throat prickled when I inhaled, and when I exhaled my breath was shaky. The lump in my throat seemed to grow bigger with every moment that passed.

Finally, though, tears welled in my eyes and spilled over.

CHAPTER TWENTY-SEVEN

"Levie, calm down. Today is supposed to be fun," Dustin murmured as we walked towards the field with Nora and Elena trailing behind us. I had awakened long before Christian did, and hurried off of the couch and out of the room as fast as possible. Because the left over tension from the night before was one awkward morning experience I *didn't* want to have.

"I'm not good with meeting new people," I whispered harshly. Today was just *not* turning out to be my day.

"Yeah, we all know from experience that you're not good with people, Levie. You'll know over half of the people who will be here, so don't worry!"

Looking at the group ahead of me and adding them to the small group that walked behind me, there were close to twenty people. When I got closer I was able to recognize a few of the people there.

The girls from the kitchen were sitting on the ground,

huddled around baby William who waddled back and forth between the four girls and smiled at them.

I could see Jace talking amongst a group of guys I didn't know.

Then there was Christian…talking to two girls who, again, I didn't know.

Jealousy bubbled up inside me and I struggled to shove it back down while our little group walked closer. *You're pissed at him right now, Levie. Come on*!

Elena linked arms with me and steered me over towards the group of guys, where Jace stood. Not counting Jace, there were five other men standing in a semi circle; all of them with unfamiliar faces.

"Hey, Elena." The man with the darkest hair smiled; crinkles formed around his light brown eyes. "It's been a while since I've seen you around. Where have you been?"

"With this one," she said, pointing towards me. I mentally shrunk down to the size of an ant. "Levie, this is Jeremiah." Jeremiah kneeled and kissed my hand with a smirk.

"Pleasure to meet you, Levie."

"And they say chivalry is dead." I sniggered.

"Derek is the sissy boy over there with the blonde comb-over," Elena muttered with a grin.

"It's *not* a comb-over," he shouted. The guy who had been standing beside him proceeded to try and mess up his precious hair. "Don't touch *it*," Derek warned, running through the group and away from the guy who was chasing him.

"The creepy guy who just tried to touch his hair is Connor. And the twins are Aidan and Prestan." The twins greeted me simultaneously and I resisted the urge to laugh. "The taller one is Prestan. The shorter one is Aiden. That's pretty much all I can tell you to help you distinguish between them."

"You ready to play, Levie," Prestan asked.

"What are we here for again, exactly," I asked, turning to Elena for an answer.

"We're playing mud ball," she murmured. "You'll pick it up pretty fast, it's not that hard."

I hadn't noticed until Elena said the word *mud*, that Jeremiah, Matt, and Dustin were tugging on two long hoses, pulling them into the field and spraying the already muddy ground with more water—regardless of the fact that it had been raining for days.

Within a few minutes of watching them, the ground was a soupy mess of thick mud.

"What am I supposed to do?"

"Block the other team from getting the ball…"

"…and run if you have the ball," the twins told me at the same time.

"Come on, let's pick teams," Matt shouted. "I'm first captain!"

"I'll be second," Jace said, walking to stand by Matt.

"I've got Nora and Jeremiah."

"I've got Christian and Levie." I grimaced and walked to stand by Jace; staying as far away from Christian as possible without making it *too* obvious.

"Connor and Aidan."

"Maliah and Dustin." One of the girls who Christian had been talking to came to stand beside me. She smiled at me in greeting, but otherwise said nothing.

Back and forth, back and forth; the two teams picked until the only two people left out were Amber and baby William.

Jace and Matt picked their "starting" team and made the rest of us sit down and wait until we were needed. With every point scored, we'd switch out and give the other group a chance to cool off.

Needless to say, I did a lot of sitting down for a while… mostly because I didn't get the concept of the game and I usually just ended up in the way.

They had to have played five or six rounds until Jace finally called me in.

"Okay, Levie. This is just like a mix between ultimate Frisbee and football. Have you ever played either of those?"

"Do I *look* like I've played either of those?"

"Okay, okay… if you get the ball, *run* in *that* direction. If you get the ball knocked out of your hands or you drop it, *get it back*. And if someone grabs it at the same time you do, wrestle it from them. Get the gist of things?"

"Pretty much, yeah."

"Good, I want you to run ahead of me; I'm going to throw you the ball."

Before I knew it, everything was a blur of motion.

"*Run, Levie*!"

"Katelynne, *get her*!"

I turned around in time to catch the ball Jace had thrown at me, and then ran straight into the other girl Christian had been talking to earlier. *Katelynne.*

This was going to be fun…

The second I collided with her, we went down to the ground. She managed to get her clawed fingers around the ball and from there it was all over with.

I could hear my name being cheered—Instructions being shouted, but I couldn't understand them. All I could do was laugh while I tried to wrestle the ball away from the tall blonde sitting in the mud in front of me. Her high pitched, screaming laughter made me laugh even more.

She stood up and tried to yank it out of my hands; I held on tight while she jerked me forward through the mud. I wrapped my legs around hers and when she took another step back she crashed down into the mud again; sending a wave of mud in all directions when she landed.

The impact caused her to let go of the ball.

"*Levie*! *Run*! *Go*!"

I stood up and leaped over Katelynne's dirty figure; focusing on placing my feet so they didn't slide through the mud and cause me to fall.

A dozen yards or so in the distance, I could see the two poles that had been stuck into the ground to represent the goal zone. A dozen yards was no big deal, it was the dozen people in between that were going to cause problems.

I wasn't exactly sure when my mind decided to make me run *through* the group of people, but when it did there was no stopping me.

People on my team ran ahead and knocked others out of the way; keeping them from getting to me and getting the ball. Before I knew it I had run through the poles and collapsed. I hadn't been on the ground longer than a few seconds before a pair of arms pulled me up again and onto a strong shoulder.

Christian had found the nerve to treat me like he normally would have… it was too bad I hadn't found the nerve to do the same.

The people on my team crowded around Christian and I and cheered; screaming and howling so loudly that I was sure the entire camp could hear. The only one I could hear saying *anything* was Christian.

"Sorry about earlier, Levie," he seemed to whisper. I wasn't sure how I had heard him amongst everyone else, but I had. I nodded and did my best to keep from grimacing, knowing that anything I said would drown in the noise that everyone else was making; not to mention I didn't really know what to say anyway.

We stayed behind longer than some of the others had.

The girls from the kitchen left first; heading back home to shower before returning to work again. Amber had to give William a bath; he had become *very* interested in the mud after our game.

Maliah and Katelynne (the girls Christian had been talking with earlier), left soon after the other girls did. I found out after they had gone that they were Christian's cousins… needless to say, I felt pretty stupid for my jealousy.

The rest of the guys and our little group of friends left one by one until Christian, Jace, and I were the only ones left.

"How many are in your house, Christian?"

"Seven."

"Counting you and Levie?" Christian nodded. "Levie, you can't phase on your own yet, can you?"

"No…"

"You have headset experience right," he asked in a whisper after looking around to make sure we were alone.

For the most part, it was common knowledge that I was a Flicker; but it wasn't exactly a celebrated thing. Most of the wolves trusted me, but they preferred to look the other way on *that* subject.

"Mhmm."

"Good. We'll need as many of you in wolf form as we can get. Levie can be on the headset and talking with me."

"What's going on?"

"We've got a run to make, Levie," Christian murmured.

"For what," I asked, turning to Jace for an answer.

"We've got vampires coming in too close to our boundaries, we've got to get them out and try to capture one, if possible."

"What about the Flickers? They're going to be doing the

same thing… we're going to end up in trouble."

"Don't we always," Jace muttered. "And I'm not going to lie… Levie, you have to go. I'm hoping you'll discourage any big fighting going on, if you catch my drift."

My stomach immediately dropped.

If only Jace knew they wouldn't stop just because of me…

They wouldn't stop for *anything.*

"Levie? You understand what I'm saying, right?"

"You want me to… you want me to distract them so they don't start a fight?"

He nodded.

"You can do that, can't you?"

I hesitated. It suddenly felt like I couldn't breathe.

"Levie?"

"She doesn't have to do it if she doesn't want to, we can make it out okay without her."

Too much pressure! My mind screamed.

I nodded.

"I can do it."

CHAPTER TWENTY-EIGHT

"Watch the table," Christian chuckled as he sat down at the dining room table and watched as I used a steak knife to carve pieces of wood into spikes. "Levie, what are you doing?"

"What does it look like I'm doing?"

"It looks like you picked pieces of bark out of the flowerbeds and now you're carving them into mini stakes."

"Bingo."

"Why are you making mini stakes?"

"Why do Flickers carry silver daggers?" I asked sarcastically. He rolled his eyes upward.

"I'm going to tie them onto my arrows. Normal arrows aren't gonna do any good against crawlers."

He watched me intently for awhile longer; waiting to speak again until after I had strung the new wooden stakes alongside the regular arrows.

"Are you sure you're ready for this, Levie?"

"What difference does it make," I muttered, placing my newly upgraded arrows into my quiver.

"Jace asked me to do something, I have to do it."

"Jace isn't your Alpha."

"No?" I watched the stubborn set of Christian's jaw grow even more defined. I shook my head with frustration. "He's one of them and if one of my alphas wants me to go and help and the other one is actually *going*, I guess I don't have much of a choice." I left the bag of arrows in the kitchen and walked to the bedroom to put on the necessary amount of clothing needed for a cold night out in the forest; Christian followed me.

"He's an alpha, not a dictator. You can tell him you're not up for it."

"It sounds more like *you're* the one who's not up for me going. Are you scared I'll screw things up?"

I eyed him, waiting for him to leave so I could get dressed. When he didn't move, I turned around and focused on my breathing and keeping myself from shaking while I took off the shirt I was wearing and replaced it with a long-sleeved, thermal one.

I took another deep breath; tugging my sweats off and pulling on a pair of leggings similar in material to the shirt and putting the sweats back on over them.

"Did you enjoy *that* show," I asked, forcing the sarcasm out to make him think I was back to normal.

Even though I sure as hell wasn't back to normal…

Not even close.

When he didn't answer, I turned around and caught him staring at me.

"Christian?" He remained quiet. "What's the matter?"

"I don't want what happened to you the other day to

happen again. I don't like seeing you like that... so *hurt.* That's why I don't want you to go," he admitted.

"Christian, I have to get over it all. You can't stop me from getting hurt."

"That doesn't mean I won't try."

"I wish you wouldn't." I whispered. He shook his head; giving up on our argument and disappearing into the closet. He popped his head back out and smiled at me; all traces of frustration gone.

"I've got a surprise for you. I'm hoping this is something you'll like and not something you'll get mad at me for."

"Why would I be mad?"

"I'm still not a hundred percent sure of everything you get mad at... so I guess I can't answer that question."

"What is it, Christian?"

"Well, I actually had my aunt fix the jacket and I've just been hiding the shoes..." He walked out of the closet and handed me a pair of boots and a jacket. When I finally recognized them, I gasped quietly; it had been *so* long.

"These are my-my old..." I let my sentence trail off as I unfolded the jacket and held it out so I could see it clearly.

The dark grey jacket smelled new, rather than like the river it had last been in. It bared freshly stitched scars in the same areas I had scars from the rocks and branches that had caught and ripped at me that night...

"Your aunt stitched up the jacket," I whispered. He nodded.

"I've had it for a while... I wasn't sure if I should give it back to you or not. I wasn't sure how you'd take it, but since you don't have much else to wear tonight, I figured now would be as good a time as ever."

The boots weren't pristine; they never had been, but they were cleaner than they had been that night.

"And then there was this. I wasn't sure what it was, but I kept it just in case…" Christian handed me a leather strap that was all too familiar; from it hung an aluminum pendant that contained a short list of information that seemed foreign to me now.

Levie Russ

Comrade 9, Team 4

368-1059

Leader—Arrows

I sighed and set the bracelet down on the table beside the bed; sitting down and pulling my boots onto my feet.

"I love these things… they're so much more comfortable than the shoes I've been wearing," I murmured as I laced them up. "I might have to ditch every other pair and just wear these."

They were the same dark grey-ish color as the jacket and reached barely above my ankle. They were laced with thick, leather strings similar to the bracelet.

The Flickers enjoyed uniformity.

"Thank you," I whispered.

"It's nice to see you happy about them, rather than upset."

"Why would I be upset over a jacket," I muttered and slipped the jacket on over my shirt. The worn out fleece wasn't very soft anymore, but it was still warm and comfortable.

"Well… after the other night-"

"Don't. Say it," I spat, zipping my jacket up with a harsh tug. "You'll jinx me and it'll happen again."

He held up his hands defensively.

"Well, as long as you know what I meant."

I nodded. "Not like I can forget it." I tapped a finger to my temple.

An invisible cloud of tension had started to accumulate in his room and followed us into the other room; it hung over us now and refused to allow a conversation to last longer than a few minutes.

Glances were being exchanged that shouldn't be given.

Things that shouldn't be thought about were turning the wheels in both of our heads.

I could hear the doors opening and closing in the other rooms around the house; Jace was here, gathering us all together and preparing us for what we needed to do.

Neither Christian nor I budged.

"Where are Christian and Levie?" I heard Jace ask in the other room.

"*Levie*," Christian whispered. "What the hell is wrong with you?" He moved to place a hand on my shoulder and I ducked away.

"We're right here, Jace." I managed to whisper down the hall before turning on Christian and darting into the other room.

We weren't even out of seeing distance of the base and I was already sweating through the long-sleeved shirt I had on underneath my jacket. Even though it was dusk and the temperature was dropping, I had a long time before I'd be able to say I was comfortable in the clothes I had on now.

With a jacket on and a sheath of arrows over my shoulder; taking everything off to cool down would take too long. Not to mention it'd be cold by the time I got finished taking everything off.

So I tugged the collar of the jacket away from my neck, blew down the front of my shirt in an attempt to cool myself off, and pushed forward with the others.

"Getting bored yet, Levie," Jace's voice hummed in my ear. It was sensitive enough that it would pick up my voice without having a microphone near my mouth. The piece, I recognized, was an old version of the earpieces the flickers wore. They were usually replaced every couple of months; now I knew why. When the wolves got ahold of someone with an earpiece in, they took them – if the flickers didn't change their systems often, the wolves could listen in.

"Getting there," I murmured. His laugh tickled my ear.

"What, don't you like your wolf friends?"

"I do, just not when they're actually wolves." The group ahead of me snuffed out what sounded like a group chuckle. "I think they're laughing at me, I can't tell."

They made the same noise as they had before; now I was sure they were laughing.

"They can't bother you when they can't talk." Jace chuckled.

"That's what bothers me the most," I muttered. "I can't tell what they're thinking. I can't ask and expect a response either."

"Don't worry about them then; just talk with me."

"Okay," I murmured, watching as the tails of the others swished in synchronization as they walked. It made me giggle quietly to myself.

"How old are you, Levie?"

"Nineteen."

We talked for a while; about the base, about being an alpha, about shooting arrows… all while I simply followed behind the others.

"How're things going so far?"

"Pretty well, I think. It hasn't been that long though."

"You've been out there for almost two hours, Honey."

I took the time to look at my surroundings. We were in the middle of the trees, on an invisible path that seemed to be leading to nowhere. It was *dark*. I held my hand up in front of my face and could barely see it.

"*Damn*, it's dark out here. You had me distracted, Jace, I wasn't paying attention."

"Good. You've been distracting me just as much. It'll all be finished soon."

"Weren't we supposed to be getting the crawlers out of here, though? I haven't seen one yet."

"That means someone else has already gotten to them," He whispered harshly though the earpiece. "Be on the lookout for others." I could hear him swearing to himself quietly on the other end of the line.

"Jace said to be on the lookout for others," I murmured to the dark wolf in front of me. Christian turned around and snuffed an agreement.

Before I thought about my actions, I ran my fingers through the fur on his back. He made a noise that sounded like a sigh; when I moved my hand away he turned around and nosed my arm as we walked, whimpering slightly.

"Shut up," I muttered, running my fingers through his fur again. "Don't be such a dog. You have something you need to do; you don't need me petting you and distracting you."

He slowed until he was walking by my side and nudged me, making me stumble a few paces to the right. I stepped on a thicker branch with just enough force to snap it loudly.

We froze.

In the distance, the sound of running feet could be heard.

"*Shit*, Jace! They're coming," I hissed.

"*Who*?"

"Crawlers either wouldn't be running, or they'd be making a lot more noise. It has to be a team of Flickers."

I pulled my bow and an arrow out of the quiver on my back, knocked it, and held it in front of my body—ready to aim and shoot if I needed to. Christian nudged me again and whined.

"I'm not hiding, Christian." I swatted him away and watched as the wolves—my friends—gathered in front of me and formed a barricade. When the leaves started to rustle ahead of us, they began to growl.

"I told you it wasn't another crawler!" The familiar voice made my stomach drop.

No… not again…

"It's just a bunch of mutts." A large group had formed around Alan, the kid who had just spoken aimed a throwing knife and stopped short at the sight of me.

"Put it down. I guarantee I can hit you with an arrow before you hit one of *them* with that knife." He dropped it immediately.

"Levie? Levie *Russ*?" I sighed and put my bow and arrow away. "They're telling us that you're dead. I don't understand…"

I didn't know the kid at all. I didn't remember ever seeing him in my life, as was the case for the majority of the Flickers there.

They're on an initiation mission…

Yet they still knew who *I* was…

Bridget and Scotty finally broke through the trees. She started to make a run for me, but Alan grabbed her by the belt and swung her back.

The younger leaders began to focus on an invisible voice, pushing their fingers into their ears to get a better grasp on what their commanders were saying.

"But sir, Levie's here! She's *alive*!"

"Sir, we can't kill them…"

"Levie's here."

"Levie, this is *it.* We can't do this anymore," Alan spat over the arguing.

"I know…" I whispered. "This isn't going to work."

"We're enemies now," Luther muttered taking a step forward to help Alan contain Bridget who was flailing now in an effort to break loose.

"*No*," she wailed.

"We can't keep ignoring our orders because of our feelings."

We all stood in silence as the younger ones argued with the commanders on the other side of their earpieces.

Panic began to set in from their words.

"Reinforcements aren't necessary. We've got it all under control. Levie's here!"

Stop saying my name! I hissed in my head. *You're only hurting yourselves more!*

"Jace, they're bringing in reinforcements because they won't shoot at us," I whispered.

"Get ready to run," He murmured.

"Arthur! Get them to stop the reinforcements! Levie's out here," Alan shouted into his earpiece. My stomach dropped even further…

Arthur…

The wolves backed up further, growling as they moved. For a moment, it was quiet enough that I could make out the sound of helicopter blades in the distance.

They're really coming for us…

"*Levie!* Arthur can't stop them; they're already on their way! You have to *run! Get out of here!*"

"Run in opposite directions—you guys go that way," Keegan shouted, pointing behind the group of Flickers. "Run towards our base, then loop around. We'll do the same."

With that said, I was running; some unconscious decision told me to run and I had taken off ahead of the wolves before they had even started to run. They had an extra pair of legs though and they soon caught up to me.

One constant thought bounced around in my head as I ran.

There won't be a next time, I thought. *Next time they won't have a choice but to kill me. To kill all of us…*

I was focused on that thought so much that when my foot found a rock in the dark, I couldn't stop myself from falling. I fell forward, and even though I did my best to throw my arms out and keep myself from really hurting myself, pain vibrated through my head the second I hit the ground. I couldn't see the rock I had hit my head on, but I knew it had to have been decent in size to cause the kind of pain I was feeling now.

"I fell," I mumbled to Jace as coherently as I could; doing my best to stand up. I touched my forehead timidly, only confirming what I already knew. "I'm bleeding." I started to tumble over but a pair of arms caught me.

"Whoa, I got you," Christian held me up and tried to steady me. "Hold on, Levie. Give me a second." He steadied me with one arm while he undid the backpack I had been carrying and pulled out a pair of sweats.

"Can you stay up by yourself for two seconds?"

I did my best to nod. My head was pounding; with every stumbled-step or movement I made, it throbbed. Regardless of the fact that Jace wasn't saying anything, there was a noise that caused my ears to ring long after I had hit my head. I glanced around trying to focus on the dark trees around me enough to figure out our location.

I hadn't realized where we were until now…

Everything grew silent, until all I could hear was the

current of the river; ripping through the logs and hurtling over rocks that sat in the middle of the wide water way.

I stared at the rolling waves of the all too familiar river and found myself unable to breathe.

The others trotted ahead of me; some of them toeing the water before stepping in and waiting for me so they could cross. Christian turned and glanced at me, recognition coloring his eyes when he saw my expression.

The throbbing continued in my head while my vision started to spin. I was suddenly so tired that I leaned on Christian to the point where he was practically holding me.

"No. *No…* I *can't* do this." I imagined that my lungs were full of water, like the night it had happened; I started to shake, to sob.

"Levie, I know how you're feeling right now, but if you don't cross that river they're going to catch up to you," Jace murmured soothingly into my ear. It didn't help me at all.

"*I can't,*" I screamed.

I imagined how cold the water had been; how hard it had been to swim back up to get air.

"Levie, it's going to be okay. I promise." He held me tightly while I thrashed around in hysterics. I couldn't get control of myself, all I could think about was the water.

"Christian…" I whimpered; he had changed back so he could help *me*. He squeezed me tighter. I looked over his shoulder while he held me, watching, as the other wolves grew more and more weary. He carefully tugged the earpiece out of my ear and put it into his own.

"Levie, you've got to cross one way or the other."

In the distance, we could all see birds scattering from their spots in the trees as the flicker's reinforcements made their way to us.

He stripped the bag of arrows and the backpack off of my back and threw them over his shoulder.

The pounding in my head had picked up a continuous rhythm that matched the sound of the river rushing by us. My eyes stung from the blood that hadn't stopped streaming from my head; my vision was still unfocused and swimming.

Oh, God. Get me out of here; please get me out of here.

The water was roaring in my ears and I felt more lightheaded than ever.

Christian finished securing the bag of arrows on his back just in time to watch me hit the ground, as the world went silent and dark around me.

CHAPTER TWENTY-NINE

I woke up on the couch; the same place I had slept for the past three nights. Regardless, I felt out of place. My clothes, as well as most of the couch, had been soaked through. I realized that I was wrapped in a handful of towels underneath the comforters that were tucked around me. The towels I guessed at one point were in the same predicament as the couch and my clothes, but had since dried and soured. They smelled so bad I struggled on the couch until I was able to throw them as far across the room as possible.

The tale tell signs of the concussion I had experienced earlier were long gone; the concussion had no doubt healed sometime while I was out cold. Though it was another terrible experience under my belt, I was grateful for the concussion—simply because I knew Christian had to have carried me through the water, and I had no recollection of it whatsoever.

This night had gone so terribly wrong; with the screaming

and the realizations, and the running and panicking. It had gone so terribly wrong, and yet with every moment that passed with me remaining on the couch, the worse and worse it became.

I had begged since the day I became a wolf to know why it had happened to *me.* For months Christian had pleaded for my disregard; saying that I wouldn't like what he told me. *Damn, was he right.* I hadn't hated him so strongly since those first couple of days. Yet, here I was sitting on the couch, soaking wet and completely out of hatred towards him.

I tried to focus on the feeling that was barely a blip on my radar at this point; I wanted to hate him for what he did, so badly. But it was just like Elena had explained months ago… I was trapped in the middle of that vicious cycle; the same one she was in.

When I hated him, the feeling was so strong that it fueled nearly every decision I made. When he was my friend, he was my best friend, and I couldn't go a day without being around him. But the *other* feeling was one I hadn't ever felt before. It confused me, and scared me, and excited me all at the same time.

I felt it when he smiled at me; sometimes only the corners of his lips would curl, and his eyes would light up ever so slightly—other times he would grin so wide his eyes almost looked like they were shut, every smile in between was contagious. The smiles we shared, which I would admit were rare on my part, usually led to laughter so strong it hurt.

I could feel it when we made contact of any kind; sometimes to the point were I couldn't focus at all. When he grabbed me—whether to yank me out of the way of something, or to lead me forward—his touch left behind a shock similar to the pain felt when you touched something too cold. Only it didn't hurt at all. And dear God, when he hugged me it took all of my strength to keep from digging my nails into his back and holding him so tightly he would never leave.

Almost three months ago—*wow, it had really been that long*—when he kissed me for the first time, I had shut down from the overwhelming feeling that took over all logical thought going on inside my head. I had done a damn good job of hiding it, I thought. But regardless of my efforts, I couldn't hide from myself the fact that three months ago, when he kissed me, I fell in love with him.

And I was completely terrified because of it. More than anything, I was afraid he wouldn't feel as strongly—that if I told him and he didn't feel the same, I would loose his true friendship forever. Somewhere in the back of my mind, though, was a part of my brain that had been daydreaming for months about the possibility of his feelings reciprocating my own.

It was this part of my brain that often woke me up in the middle of the night; in a cold sweat, gasping quietly to myself, and focusing so *intently* on not waking up the man I had been dreaming of only moments before. It was this part of my brain, though, that motivated me to throw aside the covers and walk quietly into his room.

When I rounded the corner, I found him sitting in the dark with his head in his hands.

"I need to talk to you," I whispered shakily. "It's important." It was a wonder he hadn't heard me while I was walking in, because I could've sworn I was shaking so badly you could hear my teeth chatter. When I spoke, though, his head shot up in surprise.

His face was flushed, his eyes were tired, and his hair disheveled from the countless times his fingers had ran through the knots in worry. He stood almost immediately, and in three or four quick strides he was across the room with his arms around my waist.

"Thank God," he breathed, pulling me as close to him as I could possibly get. His shirt was still cold and damp from carrying me through the river; he hadn't changed, or even bothered to dry off. Which meant he had spent the night worrying, while I was unconscious on the couch. I made it a point to dig my nails into his back and hold him as tightly as I could, for my mind's sake.

I buried my face in his chest and took a deep, but shaky breath; making it a point to try and remember the way he smelled, because I had no idea if I would ever be this close to him again.

"I'm so sorry," he whispered. I could feel his face in my hair; his breath tickled. "I'm so, *so* sorry."

"I… I can't stay mad at you. I can't do it, even if I *should*."

He held me tightly—silently—while my stomach knotted itself up. I was so nervous and scared that I felt like I was going to be sick. I had come face to face with ravenous vampires, and even *died* before, and yet I had never been so afraid in my entire life. Tears started to well up in my eyes, and quiet sobs bubbled up, giving me away.

"Are you okay?" He asked, trying to push me away from him so he could see my face. I held on to him tight, keeping my face buried in his chest.

"No, Christian. For once I'm *not* okay." I took a deep breath. This was it—there was no going back now. If he didn't feel the same way, not only would I be mortified for putting myself out on the line the way I was about to, but I would most likely be losing my best friend as well… for good this time.

"I don't understand my own feelings anymore. I've never *felt* this way before, and I'm confused and scared and nervous and just about everything *but* 'okay'!"

I was so flustered that I couldn't prevent myself from shaking like I had all those months ago, but I couldn't keep my mouth shut either. "I realize that the world doesn't revolve around my feelings, and that just because I tell you this doesn't mean you're going to feel the same way. But I feel like if I don't figure this all out I'm going to go *insane*."

"Levie, whatever you need to say—"

"I'm in love with you." The phrase left my lips in a quiet gust of air, so quickly that I wasn't sure he understood me at all. His hands had rested on my arms after he had given up trying to push me away, but now they fell away and I was forced to look up and see *why*.

The look on his face was somewhere in between scared and shocked. His hands fell half way to his sides where they seemed to become frozen and contorted into a half fist, half claw shape.

My stomach didn't just drop; it knotted up into tight ribbons as if my body were presenting me with the gift of a crushed heart, complete with my stomach tied up in a bow.

No… please, no. It had taken all of my courage to get those five little words out. The room suddenly felt as if the temperature had dropped below zero. I was shaking so violently that I thought for sure I would collapse. *Let him catch me again—like he always does.*

"Levie…"

"I told you it was okay," I whimpered, resisting the urge to run out on him the way I had when he first kissed me.

"I said you didn't have to feel the same way. That's not how this sort of thing works."

How ironic? The girl who was raised without love would die because of it.

"I just can't believe you said it," he whispered, placing a shaking hand on either side of my face. "*First*, I mean. I just can't believe you said it first."

I had pretended to hate him for so long and then faked my friendship for even longer—shoving down the feelings I had for him day after day. Hearing his words out loud brought with them every other feeling I had held back.

He smiled and leaned in, letting his lips linger only a few

centimeters away from mine. "I love you too, Levie."

I couldn't breathe; my lungs refused to suck in any air. Christian closed the tiny gap between us and pressed his lips to mine. My body grew warm—warmest where my heart was or would have been if I were still alive. His hands found their way under my shirt, running across my waist and grabbing greedily at my hips.

He pushed me back gently until my legs hit the side of the bed; not breaking the kiss we were in while he moved. He pushed me down lightly and stopped kissing me.

"Are you sure, Levie," he whispered. "You know what doing *this* will mean…"

"What? That I'm bonded to you for the rest of my life?" I smiled wryly and grabbed the leg of his pants, pulling him down to my level so I could kiss him again.

"You're *mine*," I murmured sheepishly. The phrase sounded ridiculous coming out of my mouth, but Christian chuckled and kissed the tip of my nose. I sucked in a shaky breath and pushed him away so that I could look him in the eyes.

"I love you," I whispered.

"I love you, too."

I laid back and sighed as he kissed down the length of my neck. I ran my hands down his chest; somehow he had managed to get his shirt off without me noticing. His lips lingered at my collarbone; my breathing hitched and I turned my head to the side, catching sight of the bedside table and what laid on it.

Next to the lamp, my leather bracelet sat in a tangled heap. Though, I could see some of the information on the tag. When my mind cleared, I reached over and knocked it down to the floor.

That's my old life; I'm ready to start my new one, I thought.

I tangled my fingers through his hair and pulled his lips

back up to mine.

Nails raking across smooth skin—I could feel the marks now. Not bleeding, but raised from the pressure. My nails hadn't been that sharp. I ran my fingers over the raised lines on his back as I lay with him.

There were deeper scratch marks near his shoulder blades where I had tried to get a grip on something… anything… I ended up digging my nails into the pillows behind me. I buried my head in the crook of his neck—I didn't know what else to do… his hands roamed over my waist again. I felt one hand leave my waist and tug my chin up so I was looking him in the eye. He kissed me deeply—making my body temperature feel like it was rising.

The heat that had built up in my chest while he lovingly kissed me over and over again hadn't left. It never would…

I blushed at the memory of what had happened …what already seemed like a lifetime ago.

He saw the red in my face and stroked my cheek gently; smiling.

I grinned and ducked my head into the crook of his neck.

He was *mine*. He always would be now, the warmth where my heart would have been proved that.

He trailed his fingers down my back; warmth traced the patterns his fingers made, following his touch.

I pushed myself closer to him, molding myself to his curved body and laying my head on his chest. He kissed my forehead and trailed his fingers down my side and continued down my leg, making me shudder lightly.

"Are you tired," he whispered.

"Mmhmm… I'm afraid to fall asleep, though," I murmured against his chest.

"Why?"

"This is too perfect to be real." He chuckled and kissed my forehead again.

"You can go to sleep, Honey. I'll be here in the morning when you wake up, I promise."

I sighed and lay quietly beside him for a moment, taking in everything that had happened.

This had been different from anything I'd ever experienced. It wasn't full of lust, like I had grown up being taught, though there was plenty of lust there. Christian was loving and gentle. He shook just as much as I did; out of fear. Though, he would never admit it. Never harsh or rough; his touch was lighter than a feather. He cradled me like I was fragile, something to be handled with care.

I thought about the things I had said… the thought of some of the things that had come out of my mouth made me blush again.

"What are you thinking about," Christian breathed.

"Everything…" I whispered back. "Did I do everything right?" I asked quietly, fearing the answer.

"*What?*"

"Did I… you know… *do* everything right?"

He stared at me incredulously; the corners of his mouth twitched as he tried to keep himself from laughing.

"Are you serious, Levie?"

"Never mind," I muttered, ducking my head and hiding my face. "I don't want to know."

He growled quietly and wrapped his arms around me, pulling me over him so that I was straddling his stomach. He wrapped me in the blankets and traced patterns across my thigh while he spoke.

"I wish you could realize how perfect you are, Levie."

I snickered.

"Well, I'm no you, but I guess I do alright." His eyes shimmered with confusion; his eyebrows twitched together in the middle.

"What do you mean?"

"I know *exactly* how I am… for some reason you've deemed that perfect-"

"You *are* perfect."

"I'm not complaining," I pecked him on the forehead. "But *you*… You're perfect to everyone but yourself—you just don't see it." He shook his head slowly.

"Silly little thing, you…" He tapped my nose lightly.

"You never answered my question…"

"I like the way it sounds when you say my name…" I watched his face grow softer-looking; the slight difference came from the pink that colored his cheeks.

He was *blushing*.

I had the overwhelming urge to coo at him like I would a baby, but I swallowed it down and smiled at him instead.

"*Christian*," I whispered; he grinned as I leaned down to kiss him.

He pulled me down further and cradled me against his chest.

"I'm still not sure how I did it," he murmured into my hair. "But I'm glad I got you."

"You probably didn't have to try as hard as you did to get me." I chuckled.

"Try a little, try a lot… I don't care. It's definitely worth it either way."

"This is a lot better than just being friends." Now it was his turn to laugh.

He tucked my head underneath his chin as he laughed, wrapping his arms around me tightly. He trailed his fingers down my arm until he came to the scars that he had left there what seemed like years ago.

He traced the scars for a moment, before he began to hum. It wasn't a tune I knew; it wasn't from a song, it was simply soft noise. I felt my eyelids instantly droop.

I finally realized how exhausted I was. It really *had* been a long day, but the exhaustion I was feeling wasn't bad… it felt nice.

Christian deserved the credit for those feelings; I had always enjoyed sleeping *near* him, but sleeping this close to him—literally in his arms—was *perfection.*

His touch became softer, his humming more quiet.

I sighed contently and let my eyes fall shut.

"Sweet dreams," he murmured.

"Always," I whispered back and with that, I feel asleep.

CHAPTER THIRTY

I was terrified to move. I could see the light that flooded the room through my eyelids, but I kept my eyes shut tight. I was afraid that the second I moved, the fantasy would be over. I'd wake up from this impossibly perfect dream.

The slow rise and fall of Christian's chest almost put me back to sleep, but all too soon his breathing faltered and he stirred.

"Good Morning."
"Shh, go back to sleep," I murmured against his chest.

"Why?" He chuckled, running a hand through my tangled hair.

"I don't want this to end."

"It's never going to end, Levie."

I braced myself and opened my eyes to look up at him. Nothing disappeared, everything stayed perfectly the same.

"I thought it might be a dream," I said, propping myself

up on my elbows and grinning at him. "Since it's not, we should probably get up."

"*No…*" he groaned. He wrapped his arms around my waist and held me tightly to his side. Giggling, I managed to peek out from underneath his arms and see the time on the clock by our bed.

"It's almost 9:30, Christian! If we don't get up soon, the others will think something's wrong. They'll come in here and get us…"

"They're going to find out about us sometime, Levie."

"I *know*, but I don't want them to find out because they walked in on us."

"It depends… what will we be doing when they walk in?" He grinned and rolled until he was laying over me.

"Christian… *they're going to walk in on us*," I gasped, trying to keep a grip on what I was trying to say before.

"For someone who used to be a Flicker, you're *extremely* modest." He chuckled and rolled away, moving to sit on the edge of the bed.

"If you come out there with me, I'll make us pancakes," I said, hugging him from behind.

"You're making it hard to agree with anything, with the way you're hugging me right now," he growled. I wouldn't admit it, but it had already started to get to me too. I pushed myself away from him and rummaged around the room trying to find the sweats I had been wearing last night. I flopped down and gathered up the covers; holding them in front of me when I caught Christian looking.

"Christian, where'd my pants go?" He smiled and crossed the room, picking them up from where they sat in the corner.

"I don't really know how they ended up way over here in the corner."

"I'm guessing you just like to throw things." I smirked. He made no move to bring them back to me.

"You're going to have to come and get them," he said, wrapping them around his neck like a scarf. I laughed and let go of the blankets without thinking about it.

"You sure you want to put them back on? We could always lock the doors…" His eyes glistened as he stared at me from across the room

I blushed and crossed my arms over my chest while I crossed the room. When I reached to snag them out of Christian's hand, he grabbed my arm and pulled me up against his chest.

"There's something I haven't told you yet this morning."

"Hmm," I murmured into his chest.

"I love you," he whispered.

"I love you, too."

We stood there in the middle of the room for what seemed like a long time; taking in everything that had happened overnight together, before we finally broke apart and finished getting dressed.

We walked hand in hand to the door that led to the living room and took a deep breath before opening it.

"Why don't we just run out there and announce it," he murmured quietly.

"They'll figure it out on their own… if they don't figure it out in a couple of days, we can tell them then," I hissed back; effectively ending the conversation since we had reached the living room.

I was sure we looked like we always did… we just *felt* different.

The others were in the living room, sitting together on various pieces of furniture like they always were. They smiled as we walked in.

Could they sense the difference in Christian and I?

"I can't believe you woke her up, Christian. After last

night both of you really needed your sleep." I bit my tongue to keep from laughing at Elena's words.

"Neither of us could really sleep," Christian murmured, slyly glancing my way and winking. I glared at him and made my way to the kitchen.

"Do you guys want pancakes?" A chorus of no's followed.

"We already ate," Nora muttered. "I wish we had waited for pancakes, though."

"She means *thanks anyway*," Dustin said sarcastically.

I shrugged and went on about my business, attempting to get out the necessary things to make pancakes and hide my shaky hands.

"There will probably be leftovers, since I'm terrible with portion control. You guys can eat the leftovers when you get hungry."

The noise in the room grew quieter and turned into a hum of noise rather than individual voices.

I washed my hands and poured some flour into the mixing bowl I had gotten out. The noise got ever quieter and suddenly I was in my own little world.

It was a sleepy little world with fuzzy images of people and soft lights.

I turned to grab the eggs I needed off of the counter and ran into Christian. For a moment, my sleepy little world grew more intense and then disappeared all together as the eggs that Christian had been holding cracked as they hit the floor.

"I'm thinking you might need some help in here." He chuckled under his breath.

"I'm fine." I glared at him as I grabbed a kitchen towel and started to mop up the eggs remnants. His hands ever so lightly touched my waist as I stood up and I jumped back with a squeal.

"Christian, *no*! Not right now!" The others had grown silent and were intently watching us. I mentally slapped myself for letting Christian set foot in the kitchen.

I should have known better…

"What are you talking about, Levie?" He was laughing to the point where tears welled in his eyes. He held his hands up in mock-surrender as he slowly stalked me around the kitchen table.

"Come on! Christian, *seriously*? Don't do this!" He just continued to laugh. When my back hit the back of the couch, he took a large step forward, bringing us within arms reach of each other.

By the time I got the idea to jump over the couch, he had already leaped at me. We crashed onto the couch; him laughing louder than I was screaming. He looked up and grinned at everyone else, before he started to lean in.

"*No*," I screamed, throwing one hand up to push his face away, while I covered my mouth with the other. I could tell by the way that Christian was laughing and by the burning in my cheeks, that my face was bright red.

Christian leaned forward again, this time putting his knee on my leg. "*Ouch*! Christian, you're going to crush me!"

"That's not what you said last night," he shouted, wearing the biggest grin I had ever seen. My eyes grew wide and I momentarily forgot why I had been covering my mouth.

"*Christian*," I screamed, jolting up underneath him. He took my momentary confusion as his opportunity, crushing his lips to mine. It took less than a second for me to lose what little control I had over the situation.

It was a *long* kiss; or, at least it seemed long. When he finally pulled away, he kissed my cheek and smiled.

"You did that on purpose," I murmured. He nodded and Elena screamed.

"*Oh my god*! *When did this happen*?"

"Uhm," I bit my lip. "Last night…?"

She screamed and flailed and kicked the chair so hard it

bumped the table beside it causing the lamp to tip over. Dustin caught it and rolled his eyes.

"Calm down, Elena. They had sex… so what?"

"So what? *So what? Dustin*! They mated! Their *mates*! My little socially challenged Levie mated!"

"Thanks, Elena…"

"You're welcome," she spoke so quickly I could barely understand her. She squealed again and started running around the room, pulling people up off of the furniture. "Come on! We have to leave!"

"*Why*? We don't usually leave for another half hour," Matt grumbled as she pulled him up off of one of the recliners.

"*Because*! We have to give them a day *alone*," she said, clenching her small hands into fists around his shirt collar. She could be so dramatic at times.

I watched as she filed everyone out the door; they were lucky they had all been dressed. I knew Elena well enough to know she would have thrown them out in their underwear without thinking twice.

Elena was the last to leave. She winked and waved excitedly before mouthing the words *we'll talk later* before slamming the door shut behind her.

I took in the silence for a while, before turning around to face Christian.

"Congratulations, your little plan worked."

"Yes, yes it did." He smiled and started to make his way closer to me.

"Oh, no. Nice try." I took a few steps back. "You're not getting anywhere near me."

"What are *you* going to do to stop me," he said with an energetic smile; his eyes alive. It was hardly fair after that; I never had a grip on anything after seeing his eyes that way. Before I could comprehend what was happening, I was pinned against the wall.

"You're a cheater," I mumbled softly.

"How so?"

I gently touched the skin next to his eye and smiled. "Your eyes. You distract me with your eyes. You always have."

"What do you mean?"

"Your eyes are pretty." I grinned. "Pretty boy."

"I'm not pretty." He frowned stubbornly. "I'm sexy."

"You can be as sexy as you want to be… but your *eyes* are pretty. Therefore, I'm calling you pretty boy."

"I hate you."

"That's not what you said last night," I quoted him with a poorly contained smile.

He stared at me for a moment—I stared back. It couldn't have been more than a minute before he grabbed me around the waist and threw me over his shoulder, making a beeline towards our room.

"*No*! What are you *doing*," I screamed, fully expecting him to dump me on our bed. I was momentarily confused when he turned towards the bathroom, though; my confusion was cleared up quickly.

He set me back on my feet in the shower; wrapping his arms around my waist to hold me in place when I tried to escape. I screeched again when he turned the water on.

"*What are you doing*," I screamed into his neck as I tried to block my face from the freezing water. "If you're going to force me to be in here, at least turn the water up! Jesus!"

"You'll warm up soon enough." He grinned and kissed my forehead, letting his hands snake under my soaking shirt.

CHAPTER THIRTY-ONE

ADELAIDE

I watched silently from the window as the lights in the houses across the base slowly dimmed out.

"Sometimes these *children* amaze me," I mused, turning to face my brother. "Don't they amaze you, Byron?"

"If you mean by their abilities to keep going all day without much sleep, then *yes*, they amaze me."

I felt the familiar urge to slap my brother, but clenched my fist instead; ignoring the awkward feeling that came from my nails being pushed into my palm. They were long; my nails never broke like the other girl's. I didn't run anywhere in wolf form, so they stayed clean and pretty all the time.

"No, I mean by their ability to *trust*."

"What do you mean *now*?"

He sat forward in his seat and sighed, the way he always did when I spoke. No matter what I said, he hated the sound of my voice… everything I said was unimportant. My brother was always bored, but I spoke anyway.

"The girl with the red hair. They trust her with almost everything they've got."

"Her name is Levie." The familiar urge came back.

"I couldn't care less *what* her name is," I growled, my lips tugging into a snarl. "Everyone knows what she is… and yet they trust her."

"She's more than proved she's loyal to us." He rose from his seat and stared me down. "You've heard the reports Jace brings us. She's protected her pack from her own *team* more than once and *you* know it."

"Are you *defending* the girl, Byron?" His nose twitched the way it always did when he was mad.

"Perhaps I am. It depends where you take this conversation."

"Then you *will* be defending her."

"Adelaide…"

"Can you honestly say she doesn't make you nervous?"

"The thought never crossed my mind."

"You're full of shit, brother."

His eyes flashed with shock at my words; I rarely swore. Usually I was able to accurately express my feelings without the unnecessary words, but this circumstance was beginning to slowly spiral out of control. We would be angry with each other by the end of the night. Regardless, my words were going to be heard, and taken into consideration.

"You mean to tell me that when she first came here, you were never concerned for our group's safety?"

"Of course I was!"

"What makes now any different, then?"

He opened his mouth to speak and then closed it again—his eyes shrinking to small slits as he continued to stare me down.

"What are you getting at, sister," he hissed.

"Just because she has been here for a while, doesn't mean the threat is any less imminent."

"You believe that the Flickers are going to attack us for *her*? She's proven not only to *us*, but to *them* that she is loyal to us. They won't waste their time. If they *were going to*, they would have already done it."

"They're scheming though, Byron. What makes you so sure they aren't just planning to attack us and simply use her as their excuse?"

"Because they don't *care*! You *know* they never cared about any of us! They're replaceable! *Everyone* there is *replaceable*! As long as Evangeline and her siblings have someone to fight their wars for them, they don't give a damn about anyone else!"

The thought of Evangeline and the rest of her siblings had me cringing. I knew my appearance and attitude; I had never once denied my malicious behavior, but Evangeline put me to shame.

"There's no reason to bring *them* into this discussion. This is merely on the matter at hand."

"There *is* no matter at hand, Adelaide. The only matter at hand is your *jealousy*." He said firmly. "And it's nice to know there are still some things in this world that you fear. What ever happened to my little sister that was scared of the world around her?"

"*She grew up*," I hissed.

"Funny," he whispered. "I don't think she *has*. I think she's still hiding behind her bitterness the way she always has."

"I'm not *bitter*!"

There was nothing to be bitter over anymore. It had all happened decades ago… I had let it *go*, decades ago…

"You don't even care, do you?" he said after a long silence.

"I don't care about anyone."

I struggled to keep my stoic appearance, but I could feel it beginning to falter. My brother felt the need to point out my many flaws when we fought, and there were plenty of them to bring to light.

The second I had stepped onto the "base" that had been nothing more than a small camp at the time, my face had twisted into a permanent snarl and remained that way even when my brother and I were asked to lead—and now, I couldn't change it. No matter how badly I wanted to change… who would believe in me then? Who would honestly believe I had changed?

I probably wouldn't even believe it myself.

My wall of pride had been built tall and strong and I wouldn't give in now.

"You're *pitiful*."

"You. Will. Stop. This. *Now*," I screamed. My shrill voice echoed off the stone walls of our sitting room.

"And you *will* listen to me."

It was a special skill, being able to affect another alpha with an alpha's command. It was a skill I had acquired over the years and years of living with my brother.

"Y-yes, sister."

"This has nothing to do with my bitterness or my fear of the elders. This has nothing to do with me being *immature*. This has to do with the safety of the pack—my safety. *Your* safety."

"Just get on with it," he whispered in a tired tone.

He really *was* tired of dealing with me. He knew what was going to come out of my mouth next and he knew there was no way of stopping me now. His eyes grew sad as he continued to stare at me, waiting for my reply.

"I-"

I faltered and almost changed my mind. *No, I won't be weak this time.* I collected myself mentally before continuing.

"I want her *gone*."

I took a deep breath and continued further.

"After tomorrow night's change, you will have someone fetch her and take her to the gates. She can take with her what she can carry."

"You're not giving her any warning?"

"I don't want her getting any ideas into her head."

My brother stared at me for a long time. He sat back down in his seat and continued to stare at me; his eyes growing more and more sad.

When he said nothing, I went back to my seat near the window. I stared out at the darkness, watching the world come to life with the wind. Summer would be over soon and the nights were growing colder. The world seemed so much more beautiful to me when it was cloudy outside. Maybe it was because of my mind, though. My thoughts were often dark and cloudy.

I could feel the familiar stretching in my bones and muscles as the sun began to cast an early morning glow across the world. It was the night of the change and our changes were already beginning.

The changes would be greater for some today, though.

Well… only greater for one.

I felt my muscles stretch and spasm slightly again, so I stood up and walked quickly across the marble floor to the doorway that led to mine and my brother's bedrooms. I needed sleep.

"Who will you send to get her," I spoke finally, after hours of sitting in silence.

"I will go myself."

"Suit yourself, brother."

"And I will make sure she knows who made this decision."

"Again, *suit yourself*." I went to leave the room and his quiet voice stopped me.

"Sister, you *will* regret this. If you are still a person at all, you will regret this someday."

I left him then, my feet sticking slightly to the floor as I padded quietly to my room. My room was dark—the curtains were pulled across my windows and they blocked out the dim, early morning light.

It was as dark as night in my room and the dark fabrics of all the furniture made it feel even more lonely. I walked to the vanity and flicked on the dim lights that barely lit half of my large room. I tugged at my dark hair and tied it up so it hung in a loose bun on the top of my head. I sighed at the reflection of myself in the mirror. My old, tired eyes looked dim—like they couldn't take much more of life.

My brother had been right. Where was the girl I used to be?

I slapped at the light switch angrily, turning away from the mirror. I kicked my jeans off, into the corner somewhere, and replaced them with a pair of silk shorts. My white, button down was replaced with a camisole.

Regardless of how comfortable I was, though, I couldn't find it in me to sleep.

My mind continued to drift to the girl with the fiery hair, whom I had just, most likely, doomed to death.

What was she doing now?

More than likely sleeping or possibly being awakened from the stretching in her body—that had often woken me up in the early days, too.

She slept with her alpha. They were close… she and Christian.

Had they mated?

Were they simply friends?

What about the others that lived in the same house as them? Was she friends with them as well? How many people would be affected when she left tomorrow?

Many, a small voice whispered from the back of my head. *She has many friends. People like her.*

I suddenly felt as though the roof had caved in on me.

The proverbial wall that was built around me—the one that was made up of my life of deceit and cruelty—began to falter. The wall was reinforced with my pride though.

The silence of my room suddenly grew deafening and I realized the one thing my brother had been trying to tell me all night…

My wall of deceit and pride wasn't protecting me from anything. I was stuck behind it and Levie's demise would be the final brick in the wall.

Now, I was trapped…

"What have I done?" I whispered to myself.

CHAPTER THIRTY-TWO

My eyes slowly opened to Christian's and my dark room. I rolled over and moved the sheets that covered my eyes, moaning at the sunlight that filtered through the windows across the room. The muscles in my back twitched lightly as I rolled over and cuddled up to Christian's side.

He started to stir and I giggled quietly.

"Oops, sorry. I didn't mean to wake you up…" I breathed. "Go back to sleep."

"I can't go back to sleep with you cuddling me like this," he whispered back.

I tried to scoot away from him but his arms worked their way around my waist and pulled me back. I squealed softly and laughed, burying my head in the crook of his neck.

"Sorry I woke you up."

"It's fine… it's that time anyway. We've got another long

day ahead of us."

We had woken up later than we normally did for full moon nights, so we had to rush to get together everything we needed.

It was nice to be able to naturally sleep in late on days like these; it was something our bodies just *did* without any decision on our parts. It made it more difficult to plan around… since we never knew how long we would sleep in.

Of course today would be one of those difficult days.

I stumbled around the room sleepily, grabbing articles of clothing and throwing them into the duffle bag Christian and I always took down into the tunnels. With a shrug, I gave up trying to gather extra clothes. Chances were good Christian would wake up before me and carry me out anyway.

"You ready," Christian mumbled from where he stood near the doorway.

Everyone else had already left, the house was in a state of disarray; food and clothing were scattered around the room.

"As ready as I'll ever be." I looped my arms through his and he hoisted the duffel bag over his opposite arm.

As we stepped outside, we realized just how late it actually was. It was twilight; the clouds were equally beautiful and menacing. There were a few bright pink clouds that stood out amongst the dark grey ones. If it wasn't raining by the time we hit the cells, it would definitely be raining later tonight.

We walked around the corner of the house, and saw Byron sitting on one of the rocks nearby.

"Byron," Christian murmured, his eyebrows pulling down in surprise. "What are you doing here?"

"It's my sister, I've simply had enough of her."

"And you choose to sit outside of my house?" Christian chuckled and helped our alpha up off the dusty rock he had been sitting on.

"She's done something terrible this time. I can't see any way around her orders, either. There's no way to get her to comply."

"What has she done?"

"No, no. It's not for me to say, yet." His eyes flicked to my face quickly, and grew sadder. "No, not yet."

With that, he walked away at a brisk pace. He was across the large center of the base before Christian and I moved an inch.

"I wonder what that was about..." Christian murmured, holding his arm out and allowing me to loop my own arm through his again. I looked across the grass center, following the trail that Byron had taken. A few yards away from our tunnel entrance, there was an entirely separate tunnel for the alphas.

Byron had already gone inside, but his sister stood at the door. I cringed when I realized she was staring back at *me.* Not staring, really... but *glaring.*

She shook her head at me and sighed, before turning around and following her brother in to their private tunnels.

The door closed slowly behind them.

"Come on, Levie. What's the matter?"

"Nothing," I muttered. "Let's go."

"You've been really quiet today, Levie. What's the matter," Matelyn murmured.

"You're *always* quiet," I retorted. She smiled slightly.

"Touché."

She didn't press any further, even though I wished she had. I wasn't one to blurt out my problems—so my lips remained pressed into a tight line.

Something was going to go wrong. I knew it. I could feel

it in the air.

It was cloudy, dark, and charged with the electricity that came before a storm.

The muscles in my back and legs began their twitching again, as if to agree with my thoughts.

The cells were unusually cold tonight; usually they were a natural temperature that was neither hot, nor cold. Tonight, I sat in the corner with Matelyn and Elena and shivered.

The worst part about the shivering, though, was that only part of it was from the cold. I hadn't shivered like this in months. It had seemed like forever since I'd let myself get upset to the point of shaking uncontrollably, but tonight, those feelings were rushing back.

I tried to close my eyes and bring a vision to my mind, but nothing would come. The dancing lights had grown dimmer and dimmer over the months that I had been a wolf. Most of the time, I couldn't see them at all. I only got visions through my dreams these days and they had grown so vague that I could never figure out what they meant. I was losing my past and I was okay with it. I simply wished I still had the visions as a means of escaping the real world. At least using them to give me an advantage when things went wrong…

The clocks spat out an obnoxious, ringing noise. The one I had become familiar with.

Matelyn and Elena hoisted themselves up off the concrete floors, smiling as they walked quickly back to their own cells. Dustin, Matt, and Nora followed them.

The doors clanged as Christian shut them; as if on queue, my body jerked and I groaned, reaching for the chains on the wall.

"Let me help. You do your arms; I'll do your legs."

We worked on our restraints silently for a few minutes, once Christian finished my legs; he kissed my forehead softly before moving across the room to chain himself up.

I had gotten *very* good at keeping my mouth shut when I phased. Mostly, I only whimpered. I didn't scream any more.

I closed my eyes and focused on the pain, trying to imagine what it would look like as my bones snapped and refused in different positions. It was a gory idea, but it kept me from overreacting and prolonging the experience; so I didn't complain.

Christian grunted from across the room and my stomach twisted at the sound. It took all my strength not to open my eyes and make sure he was okay. When I saw what really happened to us, I would panic.

It started in my arms; they twisted and writhed until finally, they snapped into place. I hissed quietly when they snapped and started to pant. Out of habit, I attempted to curl up into a ball—yanking on the chains with all my might. All they did was dig into my wrists.

I could feel the warmth that ran down my arms and knew if I were to open my eyes, they would be crimson.

"Levie," Christian grunted. "Stop pulling the chains, you're slicing them into your arms!"

"They'll h-heal."

I focused on imagining my body being turned inside out and whimpered as my legs cracked violently. Once my legs snapped, I was sprawled out on the floor. I still hadn't mastered the coordination to keep myself up during the change.

Instead, I chose to lie on the floor pathetically until I completed the phase and could stand up.

I felt the familiar slight pressure on my hand and knew Christian was there for me. Though, this time, my chest grew warm. I relaxed more than I ever had during a phase.

My hips shifted forward and my back arched as it twisted. The world spun around me when I opened my eyes to look at

Christian's hand touching mine and with that, my spine wrenched in opposite directions.

I finally allowed myself to scream, though, within minutes it turned into a howl.

It was interesting to wake up in the cells rather than wake up in bed like I normally did. Christian was curled up against my side, sound asleep. I chuckled and quietly removed myself from under his arms. I twisted the padlocks on my arms and legs until they unlocked; kicking the chains to the corner once they were off so no one would trip on them.

The tunnels were relatively quiet now. The screaming and growling had been replaced by the sound of scuffling feet, whispers, and the occasional laughter.

I padded quietly across the cement floors, to the shelf where we kept our duffel bag of clothes. I slipped into my fresh clothes before waking Christian up.

"Hey," I whispered, kneeling down and shaking him softly. "If I could carry you back to the house I would, but I can't. So you've got to wake up."

He groaned before rolling over and smiling sleepily at me.

"You beat me to it this time."

"Beat you to what?"

"You phased before I did *and* you woke up before me."

"So," I asked. He smiled at me. I found myself smiling. Almost immediately; his smile was contagious.

"I feel like you're one of my kids, all grown up or something."

"Generally people don't have sex with their children."

My face grew hot the moment I said the word sex and Christian laughed.

"Did you just say the *S* word," he whispered sarcastically.

"Yes, it's a major improvement, I know. Now will you put some clothes on?"

"You ruin all of my fun," he muttered, kissing the tip of my nose before standing up to get dressed and pulling me up with him.

"You like lying around, stark naked, on the concrete?"

"Only when I'm with you."

"You need serious help, you know that?"

"Not as much help as you do, apparently," he tugged on the exposed seam of my shirt—I had put it on inside out. "You can't even get dressed correctly without help."

I rolled my eyes. "Oh, well."

"I think you should fix it…." he said, walking forward slowly and causing me to walk backwards until my back hit the cold cement wall.

"Christian," I whispered. "Not *here*."

Before I even had time to blink, he had me pinned against the wall; his hands trailing lightly over my waist underneath my shirt.

"What? I'm just trying to help you fix your shirt, Levie." I was slowly starting to lose my composure; the longer he had me pressed up against the wall, the harder it got to remember my surroundings and where I was.

"The cement isn't going to be very comfortable, Christian." I struggled to stay silent as he bent to kiss my collarbone. "If you could just wait until we make it back home…"

"I don't think I want to wait, Levie," he murmured against my skin before nipping lightly at my neck. I gasped and jumped, digging my nails into his shoulders. He pulled away enough so that he could slip my shirt over my head and grinned. His eyes smoldered and grew almost grey in color—like the ocean during a storm.

He pushed me back against the wall and kissed me with enough passion to knock my head against the cold bricks.

I found myself wondering how fast my heart would be

beating right now, if I were still technically alive. Though, the thought didn't stay in my mind for very long.

With Christian kissing me the way he was, my thoughts were jumbled. The cold wall behind me was beginning to feel much hotter than it really was. The combination of Christian's lack of clothing, my own half nakedness, and the fact that he was pressed as close to me as he possibly could made me forget the world around me completely.

I ran my hands down Christian's stomach, causing him to shudder. His lips immediately went to my neck again.

His hands had just found their way to the top of my pants when I realized the door behind us was open. *Wide* open.

I shrieked—a noise I never thought I was capable of making until now—and pushed Christian's mouth away from my neck. I continued to cling to him though, because without a shirt on, I was completely exposed from the waist up.

"*Shit*, Byron. Sorry… I, uh, we-" I spun and faced the wall, cheeks glowing bright red, as Christian bent down and picked up my shirt. He handed it to me frantically before diving for the duffel bag that contained his clothes.

On top of my embarrassment, the feeling of fear washed over me again. Something was still wrong.

"I hope I haven't interrupted anything *too* important," Byron murmured uncomfortably. I understood what his emphasis meant.

"We've already mated, Sir. Don't worry." He nodded, his face growing sad.

"That is… *unfortunate*."

"Why?" Christian asked harshly, slinging the duffel bag over his shoulder and wrapping an arm around my waist possessively.

"I'm sorry, Christian." He looked Christian in the eye solemnly before turning to look at me. "But there is something we need to discuss. You should come with me."

I was shaking before I had even made it out of the cells.

I was crying before we made it back to our house. Luckily, no one was around to see me lose it. They were all outside somewhere, visiting with others. Having *fun.*

"I'm so sorry," Byron whispered again once we had made it to our room. "Adelaide has made this decision completely without my hand in the ordeal and yet, I feel as if I need to apologize to you. Mainly because I don't have the strength needed to stop her from doing this."

"What happened, Byron? Anything you need our help with, we're always willing."

"Nothing is wrong, child. Nothing that *you* can help with that is."

I clung to Christian like a lifeline, knowing that my world was about to be turned upside down and yet not knowing *why.*

"Just say it," I whispered, my voice catching on a quiet sob.

"You've guessed, then?" He looked at me with sad eyes.

"You've been looking at me all day. Something is wrong with *me.* It's not hard to guess."

The world around me seemed to grow silent then. Byron took a deep breath, and held out his hand for me to take. I took it gently, but heard nothing of the secluded world outside the walls of mine and Christian's room. For such a young man, it was hard to see Byron's face filled with so much grief. He was a good-looking man, with dark features, but his sadness aged him.

I barely heard his voice as he spoke.

"My *sister* has decided that Levie has become a danger to us here. Since she was a Flicker, Adelaide has come up with the idea that they'll use her as a means to justify attacking us."

"That's the most ridiculous thing I've ever *heard!*"

Christian started to stand and I yanked him back down with enough force to surprise him.

"She wants her gone."

Four words…

Four simple words sent the world around me in to complete chaos. Christian stood before I could catch him and bring him down again. He began throwing things around the room, screaming profanities that I suddenly couldn't hear or understand. Byron remained sitting, holding his face in his hands in shame. All I could do was sit completely still and watch.

I had no concept of time. I had no idea how long I sat in silence. At the same time, I was afraid to let myself go back to the real world. The out of body experience I was having was keeping me from completely breaking down.

It could have been minutes, hours, or even days that I sat there. I would have never known.

I watched as Christian went through the stages of anger. Quite a few things were thrown around. I knew he was screaming. Even when tears rolled down his cheeks, I stayed silent.

Eventually he found his way to the corner of the room. He sank down and pulled his knees up to his chest as tears continued to roll down his face. At least he wasn't throwing things around the room anymore.

Byron went to him then. He kneeled on the ground beside Christian and put an understanding hand on his shoulder. They sat like that for a while.

I remained silent and still. Even when Christian stood up, grabbed an extra duffel bag from under our bed, and began to fill one with clothes of his own and the other with mine.

That was when I finally snapped out of it.

"Christian," I whispered so quietly that I wasn't sure if he had heard me. "I'm the one who has to leave, why are you packing. You're staying here."

"If you think I'm staying here and letting *you* leave without me, you're crazy, Levie."

"But, Christian-"

"*No,* Levie."

I followed him as he went from room to room, collecting a hiking backpack, and filling it with sleeping bags and a tent big enough to fit five people. He threw in at least a dozen packets of matches and small bottles of lighter fluid. Inside of our duffel bags, he packed a few pillows off of our bed.

He started to zip up the giant backpack, but in a last minute decision he ripped the comforter off the bed and shoved it into the backpack. It was so full it seemed like it would rip.

Even though most of my clothes had been packed, there was still a lot of space in my bag. He used the space by filling it up with my bow and arrows.

I hadn't realized I was crying until Christian wiped the tears off of my cheeks.

"It's going to be alright. We'll make it alright." He hugged me to him as he zipped up his own bag and I caught a glimpse of the knives he had packed.

I had never known Christian's preferred weapon was a knife. For some reason it made me sad knowing that the only reason I knew this was because of a situation I had gotten him into.

"Why is she doing this," I asked, turning to look a Byron, who still sat in the corner of the room.

"I wish I knew," he whispered.

"Where are we going," Christian asked. He grabbed my hand and pushed something into my palm. I could feel the leather and metal of my bracelet—the one I had pushed of the table… *had it only been a couple days ago*?

"She wants to meet you at the gates."

With that, Christian grabbed the backpack and tugged it on to his back, throwing the duffel bag over his shoulder and taking my hand in a tight grip. I slung my duffel bag over my shoulder and bit my cheek in an attempt to keep from crying again.

"You'll tell them all why, r-right? You'll tell everyone why this happened," I asked, suddenly feeling the need to hug Byron.

"I'll make sure of it," he said, hugging me back.

With our load of bags, we drew the attention of everyone outside as we walked to the gates at the front of the base we lived on. Gates I hadn't even realized existed until today.

They were big, ominous gates and by the time we reached them, there was a decent sized group of people following us, curious about the ordeal that was about to take place.

Adelaide was a clear figure as we approached the gates; she stood out vividly, even though her clothes were similar to everyone else's.

It was simply the way she held herself. Part of me feared her and part of me wanted to attack her for ruining the life I had *finally* made here.

I will not give her the benefit of seeing me cry, I told myself.

"Christian, this is not your concern. There is no need to carry her things. She'll have to carry them herself."

"These are *our* things."

"Don't be silly, child," she spat. "She is not your responsibility. We need you *here*."

"Too bad. I will *not* allow my *mate* to leave without me." I watched her eyes first grow big, then sad. Even though she tried to cover up her reaction, I could tell her ego was to blame for the majority of this situation.

"Well, then. I'm sorry to hear that."

"Get on with it, *Adelaide*."

Her eyes were clearly the passageway to her thoughts and feelings because when Christian swore her name, her eyes grew dark and hateful.

"Levie, you're being expelled from this pack because you are considered an unintentional danger to us all. Under the circumstances, you will be asked to leave-" she looked Christian up and down with a sneer. "-with your *belongings* and be out of my land within three days. In three days time, groups of our best fighters will leave and search our land for any signs of you. If you are found, you *will* be killed.

Do you understand? This means you have three days to get out of our territory. If you're not gone by them, we will hunt you down… and we will kill you."

The fact that she felt the need to clarify insulted me and made me hate her even more.

"*Do you understand?*"

"*Yes,*" I spat.

"Good." She turned to the gate and unlocked the huge padlock that kept it closed. Off to our right, I could see our friends—Matelyn, Elena, Matt, Dustin, and Nora… Jace was there too. They were all confused and upset. Matt was struggling as Elena fought to get to us; as if she thought fighting for me would make me welcome again.

I looked around the place I had grown to love; the place I had grown to call my *home.*

The grass, all of the beautiful trees, the gravel pathways, and all of the oddly shaped buildings that made this place seem like a dream.

Christian grabbed my hand, giving it a squeeze as we walked, duffel bags in hand, through the big iron gates at the front of the camp. As the gates clanged shut, Adelaide's cold words echoed in my mind.

You have three days to get out of our territory. If you're not gone by then, we will hunt you down… and we will kill you.

"Don't look back…" Christian whispered.

TURN THE PAGE FOR A SNEAK PEEK OF THE NEXT NOVEL IN THE FLICKERS SERIES:

RISE OF THE ELDERS

CHAPTER ONE

"C-Christian," I stuttered. "I'm f-freezing." I fidgeted around in my sleeping bag some more; trying to move until I couldn't feel my feet—and the boots that were laced up on them. I had lost track of how many pairs of socks I had tugged onto my feet hours ago. Other than that, I knew I had on three pairs of sweats, and four shirts underneath a sweatshirt.

I was wearing the majority of my clothes as pajamas… to avoid freezing to death in the middle of the night.

"I'm sorry, Levie. I don't know what I can do," Christian cried quietly to me from across the small tent. His voice was tired and shaky.

We had walked for hours and hours on end. Neither of us was brave enough to sit down and rest. Neither of us was persistent enough to get the other to take a break with the bags.

So instead, we just continued to walk.

We hadn't thought to catch any food, either.

As I thought that, I became painfully aware of the empty feeling in my stomach. I was cold, tired, hungry, and scared—and sleep refused to come and give me relief.

I had tried so hard all day to hold in the emotions that had been running high since we walked through the open gates. And as silent tears began to roll down my cold cheeks, I knew I had lost the battle. It was only a matter of a few seconds before the silent tears turned into wracking sobs.

"*Levie*," Christian moaned. "I'm so sorry."

"I-I just wish I could sleep. At least that way I wouldn't have to think about it." I whimpered, curling up in to a ball within my sleeping bag. I fidgeted around again, finding it hard to move with the boots on my feet. Agitated, I started to whine again. The lack of sleep was getting harder and harder to deal with, and had brought me down to the anger management level of a five year old.

I heard the sound of Christian shuffling around in his sleeping bad, causing the tent to crackle from his body movement. It crackled more, and I realized he had gotten up.

"What are you doing?" I asked. "You're going to freeze, Christian. No."

"Well, I'm tired of sitting across the tent and listening to you cry. It hurts me just as much as it hurts you, and you know it." I could barely see him with the light that filtered down through the trees and in to our tent from the moon. I watched as he dropped a heap of something to the ground after unzipping something—I assumed it was his sleeping bag.

He laid it out completely flat before telling me to stay still, and picking me up—sleeping bag and all. I shuddered when the cotton and flannel material slid from around my shoulders and exposed me to the frigid air, taking the temperature of my sleeping bag down in the process. He set me down on top of his open sleeping bag, and folded it over.

"Christian, what are you doing?"

"Warming you up," he murmured. He zipped up his sleeping bag, and within mere seconds I was beginning to warm up.

"But what about you?"

"Unzip your sleeping bag, and pull it on top of you," he waited for me to fidget around with the obstacle of zippers and get it unzipped. I managed to pull it out from underneath me, and spread it out on top of me. I could have sworn he smiled slightly at the amount of effort it took, but in the lack of light I wasn't sure. "Now scoot over."

The second Christian's warm body slid into our new makeshift sleeping bag I felt the day's stress begin to melt away. Though, I knew the stress would only come back in the morning, I was grateful for the numbing effect Christian had on it for the night.

I stretched out to the best of my abilities in the confined space, and laid my head on Christian's chest.

"Just like home," he whispered in my hair. He let out a breathy chuckle that tickled the back of my neck before kissing my head and tightening his arms around my waist.

"Not quite," I whispered back. Christian patted my back lovingly for a moment, before laughing. "What is it?"

"You're really sweaty now. At least you're not cold anymore, though."

"No, now I'm just going to die from the heat instead." I ducked in to the sleeping bag to work at untying my boots and get my layers of socks off. My hand skimmed Christian's leg as I reached for the laces, and he stiffened at the contact. I smiled wryly in the dark

Even out here in the freezing woods, I could still get a reaction out of him.

I untied my boots and yanked them off, tossing them to the side of the tent before kicking my socks off and throwing them out as well.

The work it had taken just to get my boots and socks off had made me even hotter. In a last ditch effort to get comfortable, I started stripping out of the clothes I had put on to keep me warm. I threw layer by layer into the growing pile in the corner of the tent until I was down to my underwear and the tank top I had thrown on in the first place.

I scooted back down into the sleeping bag once the struggles with my clothes were over, pushing myself closer to Christian and laying my head on his chest again.

He traced an invisible pattern on my leg, and kissed my cheek softly.

"We'll be alright," he whispered.

The morning came too soon; even though the sun was high in the sky, it still seemed too early.

It was sweltering inside all of the layers the sleeping bags provided, and I felt like I was going to drown in all of my sweat. I peeled myself out of the sleeping bags, waking Christian up in the process.

"Sorry, I didn't mean to wake you up," I murmured. I flopped down into the pile of clothes I had created in the corner last night and sighed heavily. The moment I had opened my eyes this morning, my stomach started back up with its growling, and now it wouldn't stop. "I think it's safe to say I'm actually beginning to starve."

"Don't say that," Christian hissed as he got up and started throwing his own clothes around the tent, looking for something to wear. As the clothes hit the sides of the tent, they caused the same crackling noise that Christian had made last night. With every crackle the tent made, a different noise echoed it outside somewhere.

"Shh, *Christian*," I whispered, crawling across the tent quickly and grabbing his arm. I pulled him down to the ground with me, and held on to him tightly. "Be quiet, there's something outside. *Listen*."

I kicked the side of the tent with my bare foot; stiffening afterwards and remaining completely still. Behind me, Christian froze as well.

Near the tent, not very far away, a hissing noise could be heard. I knew what it was before I even looked, but I peeked out the thin screen window nonetheless.

Standing on two rotted feet, about a couple yards from the tent, was a crawler so far gone it wasn't even smart enough to know there was food inside the tent. I had seen plenty of crawlers throughout my lifetime—and to this day, I still wasn't sure exactly why we called them crawlers. Since not many of them ever ended up crawling…

But everyone knew that if you *did* catch one crawling, you kept your distance.

They were strong when they had blood in their systems—they could even be called beautiful. They appeared human when they weren't starving. When they *were* starving, they resembled zombies, and possessed an inhuman strength that came along with their un-relievable hunger.

And judging by the looks of the one in front of our tent, it would put up quite the fight if it wasn't caught off guard and killed.

I sank back down to the hard floor and scooted quietly back to Christian's side.

"It's a crawler."

"What do we do?"

"*We* don't do anything. *I* kill it before it has a chance to realize there's a hot meal inside this tent," I went to reach for my bow and arrows, and Christian yanked me back sharply.

"Absolutely not," he hissed. "No way you're going out there alone."

"I've done it a hundred times before, Christian. I'll be fine," I yanked my arm out of his grip and grabbed my bow and arrows.

"You're not the same person you were, Levie. It's been months since you've killed anything!"

"Some things just don't disappear with time, Christian," I said zipping open the tent's door quickly. "No matter how hard you try."

Before Christian had time to grab at me again, I stepped out of the tent and knocked my arrow. Bringing it up to eye level and letting out a heavy sigh, I whistled to catch the crawler's attention.

It turned and hissed at me excitedly, and for a moment I felt bad for what I was about to do.

This *thing* standing in front of me had once been a person—a living, breathing person; possibly a human, with friends and a family. It had once had a happy life, until one day whoever it was had ended up in the worst place at the worst possible time.

Now, here it was; standing in front of me, taking step by step towards its final end in life. I let go of my arrow with another sigh, sending it soaring through the short distance and through the crawler's chest where its heart would be taking its final beats.

It collapsed to the ground in a rotten heap of flesh, and I watched—unblinking—as its body changed back into the way it would have looked as a human.

The crawler's matted hair went from a murky greyish-brown to a pale blonde; it somehow had come unknotted when *she* hit the ground, revealing what had used to be pretty, shoulder length waves.

Her skin morphed slowly back into the pale creamy color

it had once been. Her open eyes, still hungry in expression, faded from a dark, murky red to a light blue. And suddenly, the only thing ugly about this girl were the clothes she wore—bloody and torn.

I sank down to the ground next to her body and allowed a single tear to run down my cheek before methodically yanking the arrow out of her chest and cleaning it off on her ragged, old shirt.

"Are you okay?" Christian asked quietly from behind me somewhere.

"I'm fine," I whispered, keeping my eyes on the young girl in front of me. "She's just so young. She's so tall, I expected her to have been older."

"Levie…"

"Hmm?" I spit on the arrow to get it cleaner than it already was. Using a different spot on the girl's shirt to clean with.

"You're alright?"

"I will be." I looked into the dead girl's eyes again. She couldn't have been any older than twelve. Her cheeks weren't slim from aging yet—her face was young, innocent.

When had she been changed? Crawlers didn't age…

How old would she have been if she had remained a human?

What did her parents think?

Were they human, or a vampire like their daughter?

Did they know where she was?

Did they *care*?

I silenced the questions running ragged through my mind, and picked up the newly innocent little girl.

"Do you want help?" Christian asked quietly, for all I knew he hadn't moved an inch while I was in my own little world.

"No. I want to do this on my own." For once, Christian didn't argue. He allowed me to carry the girl a few yards outside of out small camp. She was still in sight from our tent, but not close enough to become a danger. I walked silently back to the tent and grabbed one of the many packs of matches Christian had packed before we left.

I walked back over to where her body lay, and smiled sadly at the little girl laying in the grass. I stuck the pack of matches in the waistband of my underwear, and made a wide oval around the girl with the rocks I could find nearby. Out of habit, I allowed my face to grow cold and expressionless, I nodded at her body sharply the way I would have back when I was a Flicker. I managed to hold back my tears until I had dropped the flaming match onto her body; they sprung out and rolled down my cheeks as her body went quickly up in flames.

I half expected Christian to come running and comfort me. But instead, when I turned around, I realized he had chosen to leave me alone in my troubles. He had gone back inside the tent.

I would explain to him later why the fire was necessary—how it would keep the other crawlers away for days because they would know one of their own had died here—Christian would be curious. Though, the real problem would be someone else seeing the smoke from the flames… but we would worry about that later.

Later in life when I look back on this day, I would realize that something had changed in me when I let the arrow fly through the air and pierce this girl's chest. The second she hit the ground I knew for sure, no matter how hard I tried to keep it from the world around me—

There was a killer buried deep inside me, somewhere that I couldn't reach and drag her out. She was patient, though, my killer. She would wait quietly while chaos ensued… knowing full well I would need her eventually.

The day I killed the girl in the woods would remain in my memory as the day I recognized the killer inside of me…

And I chose to let her alone.

ABOUT THE AUTHOR

Rachel Fletcher is the self-published, YA author behind The Flickers, as well as the mastermind behind current Wattpad favorites such as Ghostly and Speak of the Devil. Getting her start by writing fanfiction, Rachel discovered her passion for writing somewhat early in life. During the early stages of her writing career, she had attempted many times to write her own original fiction novel. Failing each time, and loosing interest in the plot, or hitting a streak of writer's block. It wasn't until the summer before her sophomore year of high school that she finally got the winning idea for an original story. On July 19, 2011, Rachel dived underwater into her friend, Kimberly's pool and opened her eyes to look at the water around her. The eerie silence within the water, combined with the panic of trying to reach the surface before running out of air sparked an idea in her mind, and The Flickers was born. 355 days, 35,000+ combined views, and 600 combined reviews later, The Flickers was a success and is was growing more successful every day. With plans to turn The Flickers in to a self-published trilogy; as well as a promising horizon in sight for her newest novels, Ghostly and Speak of the Devil, she hopes to one day make it big with her novels. But for now chooses to share them with her fans through the internet. Rachel is currently 17 years old, and attending her final year in high school. With no plans of college, she intends to focus on her writing career. Rachel lives in Northern California.

Made in the USA
San Bernardino, CA
11 July 2014